魔鬼╳特訓

倍斯特出版事業有限公司
Best Publishing Ltd.

U0066421

新托福
閱讀120

韋爾◎著

兩大新穎的學習法
分別滿足「一本抵四本」、「掌握出題核心」
和「跨單項學習」的學習者

音檔 QRCODE
DOWNLOAD

「跨單項」的整合學習：
一次就打通聽、讀和寫三道大腦脈絡 （長期紮根的初、中階自學者）
藉由整合學習規劃，包含閱讀、聽力、單字、寫作，四項試題的學習，四倍化學習
時間，快速考取110以上高分。

「訊息分類和歸納」的能力：
掌握ETS出題設計和規劃 （短期欲考到理想學校門檻的學習者）
理解出題設計並從中掌握高分關鍵，提升大腦處理資訊能力，一次就獲取聽、讀都
29以上高分。

PREFACE

　　最近從公司口中得知早先出版的《新托福 100+閱讀》已經完售，就想到當初書籍的規劃中所側重的重點是希望書籍能適用於大多數無法即刻使用新托福歷屆試題，也就是 TPO 來刷題的考生來做設計的，並期許考生能在規劃的初、中和高階單元中漸進累積能自學並單獨具備撰寫新托福閱讀試題的能力。其中還包含了幾項特點❶將歷屆試題中的其中兩個試題：詞彙題和指代題，單獨抽出的合併試題規劃，降低試題難度，迅速累積考生信心❷大幅加長文章閱讀內容（養成固定能耐心看完一定字數的文章且不分心），並從中累積近百個同、反義字❸強化跨段落訊息掌握❹部分單元包含配對題等，強化考生訊息「分類」和「歸納」能力❺包含摘要題型，強化「讀」和「寫」的關聯性，也能助於轉學考考生考取佳績❻填空題提升考生字詞使用等。

　　而《魔鬼特訓 新托福閱讀 120》則包含更有效的整合

學習規劃。如同在其他書籍中提過的刷無數歷屆試題僅僅是在提升對試題的熟悉度和考生當下的應試水平，並不會讓考生考取理想成績。因為要考取理想成績是需要更多整合學習能力的提升才能達到的，完全和寫試題不太相關。關於這點，我想我們必須去思索的一點是，為什麼 ETS 要設計包含了 10 個題型的新托福閱讀測驗呢？而當中又包含了「資訊歸納題」和「內容總結題」這兩類題型。很明顯，出題設計者所期望的是考生必須要具備「訊息分類和歸納」的能力，這也和聽與讀兩個單項的學習是有關聯的。只有掌握與具備一定程度「訊息分類和歸納」能力的考生才能考好新托福聽力和閱讀測驗，因為該考生一定能在聽或閱讀一段訊息

後，大腦中迅速將這些訊息處理分類，快速進行答題。具備這樣能力的考生也會無懼聽力和閱讀測驗內容為何。龐大和包羅萬象的考試內容進行搭配只是用於檢測考生語言水平而非考生對於該主題的掌握度。所以，要考取高分的考生要掌握的是提升整合能力，並運用各個單項之間的關聯性，而非單一準備某個訓練。

何謂單一準備某個訓練呢？如果 A 考生，規劃了每周下午某個時段拿來刷閱讀試題，其實就是屬於單一準備的範疇。考生需要的是跨單項的學習，效率式提升自己程度。所以這本書會有以下的整合式學習規劃。整合式學習規劃包含：❶資訊歸納題❷填空題❸字彙實力檢測❹影子跟讀設計❺摘要題規劃❻新托福試題。在「❶資訊歸納題」中，除了閱讀一段文章後寫閱讀試題並檢視對錯之外，還多了另一道程序，也就是考生也需要僅觀看這個題型的題目，聽這段閱讀文章的內容，並從選項 A-H 去選取符合題目特點的選項。這個規劃就包含了聽力和閱讀同步演練，而考生還能做的延伸學習是可以在播放音檔前拿一張空白紙在旁，在播放音檔的同時，紀錄聽到的特點或關鍵訊息，一併演練 note-taking 的能力，這對於答新托福聽力測驗來說是很重要的。所以光是這個部分考生就演練了**「讀」＋「聽」＋「記筆記」**至少三樣能力的運用，而非僅僅是拿出 TPO 開始寫閱讀試題後然後對答案看錯在哪裡。相信考生能藉由這六個整合能力的規劃迅速累積實力，在考前刷部分 TPO 試題後就能馬上考取理想成績。對許多初、中階考生來說，**《新托福 100+閱讀》**和**《魔鬼特訓 新托福閱讀 120》**側重不同的學習規劃，相信這些整合題型的設計，可以快速達到學習成效並馬到成功。最後祝所有考生都考取理想成績。

韋爾　敬上

INSTRUCTIONS  使 用 說 明

📅 **資訊歸納題**

Directions

Complete the table below to summarize the information about four characters in *Far from the Madding Crowd* as discussed in the passage. Match the appropriate statements to the listed animals. **You may use the letter more than once.**

Boldwood	• •
Bathsheba	•
Oak	•
Troy	•

Answer Choices

A. exhibits affections in a state of frenzy

B. whose feelings are swayed by unfamiliar experiences

C. whose flaws are conspicuous for not knowing how to hide

24

D. possesses praiseworthy characteristics to be one's suitable life partner

E. depicts one's benevolence genuinely

F. can be the distraction when it comes to a relationship

G. negligence of a potential danger that can do quite a harm

H. recognition of the meaning of true love after enough life experience

Part 1
資訊歸納題

Part 2
Part 3
Part 4
Part 5
Part 6

Answers
Boldwood: A, E
Bathsheba: B, H
Oak: C, D
Troy: F, G

25

「聽＋讀」整合練習
一次打通關鍵脈絡，瞬間提高實力

・改革了單一的學習規劃（也就是僅撰寫閱讀試題），考生除了撰寫閱讀試題外，對照資訊歸納題試題頁面播放音檔，檢視自己是否能仰賴聽訊息也能答對資訊歸納題，聽和讀的分類歸納能力要同步運用才能迅速提高大腦對於兩個單項「聽＋讀」的學習能力。

"It would have been cruel in Miss Havisham, horribly cruel, to practice on the **1.**_____ of a poor boy, and to torture me through all these years with a vain hope and idle **2.**_____, if she had reflected on the **3.**_____ of what she did."

In *Great Expectations*, Miss Havisham's **4.**_____ wealth does not give her the joy that she is in **5.**_____ need of. Miss Havisham's use of the little girl, Estella, to torture the boy that she hires, on the other hand, fulfills her **6.**_____ and the sense of **7.**_____. As a saying goes, pain and conflict only bring more pain and conflict. Not letting go of the past rigorously hurts or **8.**_____ Miss Havisham's body and soul.

Miss Havisham's _____ can be traced back to an incident happening about twenty years ago. Pip's **9.**_____ with both Magwitch and Compeyson paves the way for a further development. Magwitch, a poor and unlucky guy, under the **10.**_____ of fortune, meets with self-pretentious, handsome, **11.**_____ Compeyson. The chance encounter leads Magwitch to learn the truth about Compeyson and his partner, Arthur. The **12.**_____ from a rich lady, which is believed to be Miss Havisham, earns them a great deal of fortune. However, Compeyson's **13.**_____ spending habits cannot keep up with the money he earns from doing the dirty things.

Doing bad things, and not getting caught for a while seems **14.**_____, but committing a list of crimes and not getting

captured will be deemed unlikely. Pretty soon, both are taken to court for a trial. They both are charged with putting stolen notes in **15.**_____. Compeyson demands that they go **16.**_____ ways, and Compeyson smart thinking does work. Magwitch can only get Mr. Jaggers as a lawyer for the defense.

The "birth" issue and one's education also weigh **17.**_____ on criminals in court, making Compeyson's sentence the half of Magwitch's. Magwitch has been **18.**_____ judged at the court and eventually gets 14 years in prison. They are in the same prison ship, but Magwitch cannot get closer to Compeyson. Fleeing the prison ship leads to the encounter of Pip, the main character, and Compeyson. This time Magwitch has enough time to **19.**_____ Compeyson's face to get revenge.

Magwitch and Compeyson will try every way to bring each other down. Compeyson can report there is a **20.**_____ that flees from the prison ship. Magwitch and Pip's flee then encounters The Hamburg, the steamer, sailing swiftly towards them. People on the steamer demand the **21.**_____ to capture the person wrapping with a cloak on Pip's ship. As Magwitch goes behind the person who tries to seize him, he has the time to tear off another person with a **22.**_____ on the steamer to verify whether his identity is Compeyson. Compeyson is in shock and then waddles. Thereafter, they have a struggle, falling into the river. Other guys trying to seize Magwitch eventually cause the **23.**_____ of the Pip's ship. Magwitch is found seriously **24.**_____, and with no traces of Compeyson. Pip has no **25.**_____ to doubt Magwitch's account of what just happened because it is the same as that of the officer who steers the ship.

Part 1

Part 2
聽力填空題

Part 3

Part 4

Part 5

Part 6

聽力強化練習
藉由填空題演練
提升聽細節性資訊的能力

· 額外的學習規劃，納入聽力填空題提升考生拼字、聽細節性資訊和聽力專注力等能力。（若難度太高請播放兩次音檔並完成試題）聽力填空題全數聽到相關訊息且都答對，僅是最基礎的聽力要求，需具備這樣的條件後再刷聽力 TPO 才是不耗費真題且檢視自己實力之道。

・藉由對字彙、文法和一定程度的閱讀能力，才具備能夠答好這類試題的能力。這部分的練習和聽力強化練習都是很基礎的練習。程度基礎的考生要掌握這兩個部分再去刷 TPO 試題，才不會有太大程度的落差或無法在時限內完成閱讀試題或完全聽不太懂聽力試題內容。

same as that of the officer who steers the ship. At Police Court, it is revealed that Compeyson eventually falls into the river and is found dead. Compeyson and Arthur, Miss Havisham's brother, all pay the price. Arthur dies from serious illness right before the **20.** _____ of both Magwitch and Compeyson.

Miss Havisham's distorted mind resulting from the harm caused by Compeyson and Arthur could totally be cured if she knew the notion of "what comes around goes around" and "unjust is doomed to **21.** _____." Karma will eventually do the justice for her. Miss Havisham eventually comes to her senses right before her death that she has done quite a **22.** _____ to another human being, Estella.

"That she had done a **23.** _____ thing in taking an **24.** _____ child to mould into the form that her wild **25.** _____, spurned affection, and wounded pride, found **26.** _____ in, I knew full well......

A	normal	**B**	deception
C	refugee	**D**	assistance
E	grievous	**F**	capsizing
G	destruction	**H**	sentence
I	satisfaction	**J**	enormous
K	pursuit	**L**	impressionable
M	separate	**N**	gravity
O	erudite	**P**	whim

Q	damage	**R**	heavily
S	cloak	**T**	circulation
U	smash	**V**	susceptibility
W	lavish	**X**	guidance
Y	resentment	**Z**	vengeance

參考答案

1. V	**2.** K
3. N	**4.** J
5. P	**6.** I
7. X	**8.** O
9. B	**10.** W
11. A	**12.** T
13. M	**14.** R
15. U	**16.** C
17. D	**18.** S
19. F	**20.** H
21. G	**22.** Q
23. E	**24.** L
25. Y	**26.** Z

Part 1
Part 2
Part 3 字彙實力檢測
Part 4
Part 5
Part 6

INSTRUCTIONS

INSTRUCTIONS

▶ 摘要能力 TEST 8

| Instruction | [MP3 016]

　　考生可以藉由重新聞讀英文文章後提筆撰寫 200-250 字的摘要或是在閱讀文章後，以口說的方式摘要出一段英文重要訊息具備在職場能夠摘要一段英文會議內容的能力，提升職場競爭力。

▶ 參考答案

　　Three novels act as the reflection of the reality, and In *Vanity Fair*, Mr. Sedley's poor investment makes him bankrupt.

　　Mr. Sedley in *Vanity Fair*, and Mr. Thornton's condition in *North and South* shares the same vein. To both Mr. Thornton and Henry, Margaret's inherited money can be of great assistance for their careers.

　　Margaret in *North and South* and Philip in *Of Human Bondage* are considered lucky, but Philip's inability to use the money makes his life as not great as it should have been.

　　It can be concluded that investment money should come from the sources that will not influence one's living; otherwise, there is going to be a disaster. No matter how lucky a person can be, not being able to control the spending can result in serious damage in life (like Philip). Being too speculative can also have the same fate like Mr. Sedley, losing enormous wealth and his hard-to-build enterprise. Working industriously and diligently can still end up like Mr. Thornton, lacking enough money to keep the company afloat. Predictions of one's life trajectory are too unlikely, but what we can do is do our part and not investing recklessly or dreaming of becoming a rich billionaire in a day.

Part 1
Part 2
Part 3
Part 4
摘要能力題
Part 5
Part 6

獨家規劃摘要「讀＋寫」和「讀＋說」 大幅提升新托福口說和寫作的答題能力

・考生須具備兩大關鍵技能，也就是閱讀完一大段訊息後，能夠有一定水準的寫作能力，摘要出關鍵重點。另外一部分就是，再讀完一段訊息後，口述摘要一段訊息給聽者聽。掌握這兩部分的考生均能輕而易舉答好新托福整合題。

Part 1
Part 2
Part 3
Part 4
Part 5
影子跟讀和中譯
Part 6

conviction that three years at the first job are quite an important step for your next job.

在《人性枷鎖》中，經過深思熟慮，菲利普的第一個人生決定是成為梅塞爾事務所的實習生。他的伯父和朋友們相信，在梅塞爾事務所任職期間，菲利普將學到足夠的專業技能，足以讓他自立並謀生。「每一種職業、每一門生意都需要花時間學習或經驗，更糟的是還需要投入金錢。」然而，菲利普就像一些二十多歲的年輕人一樣，還未了解一個惱人的道理，第一份工作做滿三年對你下一份工作來說是相當重要的一步。

❶ inferior 次的；較差的
❷ glamorous 富有魅力的
❸ disastrous 災難性的
❹ deliberation 深思熟慮

❺ tenure 任期
❻ mortifying 惱人的
❼ conviction 確信，信念
❽ important 重要的

Bad advice from one of his friends also dissipates his valuable twentysomething years. "I cannot imagine you sitting in an office over a ledger." "My feeling is that one should look upon life as an adventure, one should burn with the hard, gem-like flame, and one should take risks, one should expose oneself to danger." His friend's belief in Philip's ability in art does not equal with how the reality views about him as a person. Despite the Vicar's disagreement for Philip's life trajectory change, Philip insists on going to Paris to learn art. Still Philip has

176

to wait for a year to get his small inheritance from his father.

他其中一位朋友的糟糕建議也浪費掉了他寶貴的 20 多歲時光。「我無法想像你竟坐在辦公室裡，埋首於一本本帳冊之中。我覺得人生就像一場冒險，應像寶石般的火焰熊熊燃燒，勇於接受挑戰，危難當前亦不畏懼。」他的朋友對菲利普藝術才華有信念並不等於現實世界對他所評價出的能力。儘管牧師不同意菲利普改變人生軌跡，但菲利普堅持去巴黎學習藝術。菲利普仍需要等待一年才能從他父親那裡得到他的小額遺產。

❶ dissipate 浪費，揮霍
❷ adventure 冒險，冒險精神
❸ reality 現實；真實
❹ Vicar 教區牧師

❺ disagreement 意見不合
❻ trajectory 軌跡；軌線
❼ insist 堅持
❽ inheritance 遺產；遺贈

Aunt Louisa gives Philip her savings, an amount worth around a hundred pounds to pay for Philip's living expenses in Paris. Her generosity only lasts for a short time, and soon is replaced by the young man's visions in Paris. Eventually, the suggestion of the great artist proves that Philip's uncle is right all along. "Take your courage in both hands and try your luck at something else" The heart-felt, visceral advice ends Philip's two-year journey in Paris and terminates his dream of becoming an artist.

177

閱讀內容中英對照
且便於考生演練影子跟讀練習

· 基礎備考考生能藉由中英對照輔助自學，改善使用 TPO 且無中譯和解析等輔助的問題。並逐步藉由書中的規劃達到能獨立撰寫各單項的 TPO 試題。考生更能藉由這個篇章對照練習影子跟讀練習，提升專注力。程度更佳的考生，可以在僅播放聽力訊息的情況下獨立演練跟讀練習。

INSTRUCTIONS

具鑑別度的模擬試題測驗
需掌握多項閱讀技巧來答每一題

· 收錄更具鑑別度的考題能有效區隔考生語文
能力是否位於更高的分數段，並運用各種閱
讀能力，包含理解整個段落上下文的文意或
搭配推測能力去答對字彙題。或是考生是否
掌握關鍵字、句意、主題句、句子整體描述
的概念和轉折、文法（掌握代名詞指代）、
寫作和閱讀間的關聯性等協助定位和判答

Education seems to be the key to amending people's mind. **As the story progresses, the devil demands the creation of an identity similar to him so that he can find someone to love and to be loved. Victor at first concurs another attempt to create one for him, then out of the blue shifting into thinking that manufacturing the spouse for him equates with producing a monster. He can barely handle the devil, let alone dealing with two bad-looking creatures.**

21 Which of the sentences below best expresses the essential information in the highlighted sentence in the passage? Incorrect answer choices change the meaning in important ways or leave out essential information.
 (A) Victor really needs to learn the skills of dealing with the formidable devil so that he can manufacture monsters without any worry.
 (B) Victor is so afraid of creating another creature not good-looking that so he does not want to risk ingredients and take time to create a new one.
 (C) Victor's endorsement rests on wanting his creation to feel loved, but on a second thought, the consequence of bringing another can be disastrous.
 (D) Victor's thinking patterns are eccentric in a sense that

he cannot think in the devil's shoe to create a new creature to love his creation.

A lot of murder crimes relating to love can be evaded if proper education and giving others more love have seriously been paid attention to. One does not have to take rejections too seriously. As a saying goes, "things that seem disastrous at the time usually do work out for the rest." Sometimes it does mean that God has a better idea, wanting to give you something much better.

22 According to the passage, why does the author mention "things that seem disastrous at the time usually do work out for the rest."?
 (A) to show the importance of a good education
 (B) to show there is bound to be a good arrangement
 (C) to show societal problems will become more rampant
 (D) to highlight consequences relating to disasters

Part 1
Part 2
Part 3
Part 4
Part 5
Part 6
新托福全真模擬試題

QR Code download

TENTS

PART

03 閱讀、文法和字彙整合強化

字彙實力檢測

PART
04 口說和寫作摘要一主題整合強化

摘要能力題

CONTENTS

PART
05 聽力SHADOWING和翻譯閱讀整合強化

影子跟讀和中譯

CONTENTS

CONTENTS

There are numerous love songs that are gripping and make people resonate. Among them, topics related to "love someone who truly loves you" and "choose the person you love" are the most popular. How to make the right choice and select the ideal life partner can be quite difficult. Often a lot of sayings on social media platforms and views of those celebrities in the show are misleading and are often rife with claims that don't stand up to scrutiny. Luckily, by reading British romance novels, like *Far from the Madding Crowd*, we can have a better understanding about making smarter choices.

Three promising guys in *Far from the Madding Crowd* can be seen as the summarized version of the real life. Three candidates are Oak, Boldwood, and Troy.

As anyone can remember from high school and college, most girls would go for the handsome and bad boy types, simply because they want to be tamed. They deem the guy with principles and integrity as boring and easily controlled, but that pushes them away from real happiness. That is also the main reason why Oak is not accepted by heroine, Bathsheba at the very beginning

Part 1
資訊歸納題

Part 2

Part 3

Part 4

Part 5

Part 6

of the novel. Oak has several admirable traits that make him an ideal husband for Bathsheba. He is kind-hearted and has a real passion for Bathsheba. Oak proclaims that he will work twice as hard after marriage.

So far, this has been about all the readers' perception of him. What about Boldwood's account about Oak? Near the very end of the novel, Boldwood has a heart-felt confession with Oak, when Boldwood has the sense that his prospect with Bathsheba is around the corner. "You have behaved like a man, and I, as a sort of successful rival-successful partly through your goodness of heart I should like definitely to show my sense of your friendship under what must have been a great pain to you."

As for Boldwood, he has a crazy devotion for Bathsheba that separates him apart from both Troy and Oak, and he is also the man who can wait for the girl for six years. At a much later time, a locked box that contains expensive silks, satins, poplins, velvets, muffs (sable and ermine), and a case of jewellery that includes four heavy gold bracelets and several lockets and rings can symbolize the importance of Bathsheba in Boldwood's heart.

In the middle part of the story, Bathsheba chooses

Troy to be her husband, and Troy seems to fall into the untamed type. Troy can be good for a diversion, but not for a long-lasting relationship. However, Troy does have his charm. Troy volunteers to sweep and shake bees into the hive to impress Bathsheba. Troy further demonstrates his swordsmanship in their next appointment, creating a special moment to imprint a kiss on Bathsheba. The sense of novelty and surprise prevails, making her act on impulse and without reason.

According to the author, Troy is good at concealment and superficiality so that ethical defects will not be perceived by women, whereas Oak stands in a sharp contrast with Troy because Oak's shortcomings can be apparently seen. Beneath the veneer of Troy, there are flaws most people will not notice. However, no matter how good one is at varnish, he will eventually show the true colors.

"Every voice in nature was unanimous in bespeaking change." Unprotected ricks equal to 750 pounds of food. The storm is coming closer, but Troy is nowhere to be seen. According to Oak, Troy is asleep in the barn, neglecting all the harm that the weather might do to the crop and the consequence that will cost their barn. Oak's

Part 1
資訊歸納題

Part 2

Part 3

Part 4

Part 5

Part 6

endeavor to protect the crop shows his true love for Bathsheba. He uses his actions to validate the love. Troy; however, demonstrates his indifference, making Bathsheba realize Troy as a person.

Boldwood loves Bathsheba deeply by wanting to provide her material comfort as a way to possess a beauty. Oak, on the other hand, wants to love Bathsheba by using all his life. Troy seems to have an agenda on Bathsheba because of Bathsheba's wealth and barn. Bathsheba at first gets married with Troy by choosing the one she truly loves, and till the end she figures out it is the one who truly loves her that she should be with. As a Chinese saying goes, "people look for him thousands of Baidu. Looking back suddenly, the man was there, in a dimly lit place." Perhaps Bathsheba just comes to the realization about this a bit too late. True love is always around us, but our perception prevents us from seeing it clearly.

 **資訊歸納題**

Complete the table below to summarize the information about four characters in *Far from the Madding Crowd* as discussed in the passage. Match the appropriate statements to the listed animals. **You may use the letter more than once**.

Boldwood	• •
Bathsheba	• •
Oak	• •
Troy	• •

Answer Choices

A. exhibits affections in a state of frenzy

B. whose feelings are swayed by unfamiliar experiences

C. whose flaws are conspicuous for not knowing how to hide

Part 1

資訊歸納題

Part 2

Part 3

Part 4

Part 5

Part 6

D. possesses praiseworthy characteristics to be one's suitable life partner

E. depicts one's benevolence genuinely

F. can be the distraction when it comes to a relationship

G. negligence of a potential danger that can do quite a harm

H. recognition of the meaning of true love after enough life experience

Troy: F, G

Oak: C, D

Bathsheba: B, H

Boldwood: A, E

Answers

"**I believe that I have no enemy on earth, and none surely would have been so wicked as to destroy me wantonly.**" A saying from *Frankenstein* seems to convey the message of Justine's viewpoint that men inherently possess a good heart. While various people may hold different views on this statement, Justine's conjecture about the devil who frames her is entirely correct. The devil has a good heart from the start, but Victor, the main character, resists acknowledging the devil as his creation or his own baby, resulting in a distorted mind for the devil. There has been some mental separation between the two. Acceptance and refusal are two antithetical concepts, and feeling loved is essential for anyone's personal development. The devil's atrocious behavior results from getting rejected and not being amended. Not getting loved makes someone feel neglected, unaccepted, and being excluded. All these factors engender serious psychological behavior that creates some of the social crimes.

Education seems to be the key to amending people's mind. As the story progresses, the devil

Part 1
資訊歸納題

Part 2

Part 3

Part 4

Part 5

Part 6

demands the creation of an identity similar to him so that he can find someone to love and to be loved. Victor at first concurs another attempt to create a new one for him, then out of the blue shifting into thinking that manufacturing the spouse for him equates with producing a monster. He can barely handle the devil, let alone dealing with two bad-looking creatures. The novel itself conveys several important messages essential for human beings to pay serious attention so that more societal problems can be avoided, thus making it especially great and eternally valuable.

A lot of murder crimes relating to love can be evaded if proper education and giving others more love have seriously been paid attention to. One does not have to take rejections too seriously. As a saying goes, **"things that seem disastrous at the time usually do work out for the rest."** Sometimes it does mean that God has a better idea, wanting to give you something much better.

As can be seen in another classic, *Middlemarch*, God certainly wants James to have not just someone better, but someone more suitable for him. In towns, neighbors and farmers have the predilection for Celia over Dorothea simply because Celia is more approachable, innocent, clever, and sophisticated. Dorothea has a quality of not self-admiring, thinking Celia is more charming than she is. James, on the other hand, has a crush on Dorothea. **"He felt that he had chosen the one who was in all respects the superior; and a man naturally likes to look forward to having the best."** However, James does not even have any chance with Dorothea.

His rival Mr. Casaubon does not have to do much and wins over the heart of Dorothea in such a short time. Luckily, James does not take this as a defeat or as something that will crush him. Getting rejected does not make someone a failure as most people would think. It is one's mindset that makes a man. Some would writhe under the idea of failure and rejection and then do the harm to the rival, hurt themselves, or cause quite a damage to someone you love. The thing is you do not have to act like that.

Other people, including Dorothea's uncle, are shocked at Dorothea's choice of a man, not choosing James as a husband. Celia has a feeling that James will be a great husband, but from her observations, they will not be a good fit. Dorothea's choice may be good for both of them. It should not be interpreted as seriously harming

Part 1
資訊歸納題

Part 2

Part 3

Part 4

Part 5

Part 6

someone. James claims that Dorothea should wait until she is mature enough to make the decision and is mad at Dorothea's choice, but eventually he gladly accepts this news. It does mean that more saccharine fruits are waiting for him definitely.

As the story progresses to a much later time, his feelings of getting rejected have gone already, having been replaced by getting engaged with Celia. **"His disregarded love had not turned to bitterness; its death had made sweet odors – floating memories that clung with a consecrating effect to Dorothea."** True love deserves some time to wait. Two classics *Middlemarch* and *Frankenstein*, should all be the required reading during high school, shaping those feelings so that more tragedy can be avoided.

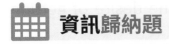 資訊歸納題

Directions

Complete the table below to summarize the information about *Frankenstein* and *Middlemarch* as discussed in the passage. Match the appropriate statements to the listed people. **You may use the letter more than once.**

Justine	•
Victor	•
the devil	•
James	•
Celia	•
Dorothea	•
Dorothea's uncle	•
Mr. Casaubon	•

A. alteration of a promise due to some considerations

B. the seed of a dreadful trait sows in the mind

C. willingness to believe people possess a kind heart

D. seeking for a manufacture due to the desire of getting loved

E. nice interpretations to evaluate someone objectively

F. appalled by the announcement of the major decision

G. less popular among villagers

H. unwillingness of giving the love results in a regrettable harm

I. effortlessly triumphs, even with another rivalry present

J. possesses the growth mindset that does not view refusal as a setback

Part 1
資訊歸納題

Part 2

Part 3

Part 4

Part 5

Part 6

Answers

Justine: C

Victor: A, H

the devil: B, D

James: J

Celia: E

Dorothea: G

Dorothea's uncle: F

Mr. Casaubon: I

"It would have been cruel in Miss Havisham, horribly cruel, to practice on the susceptibility of a poor boy, and to torture me through all these years with a vain hope and idle pursuit, if she had reflected on the gravity of what she did."

In *Great Expectations*, Miss Havisham's enormous wealth does not give her the joy that she is in desperate need of. Miss Havisham's use of the little girl, Estella, to torture the boy that she hires, on the other hand, fulfills her whim and the sense of satisfaction. As a saying goes, pain and conflict only bring more pain and conflict. Not letting go of the past rigorously hurts or erodes Miss Havisham's body and soul.

Miss Havisham's hurt can be traced back to an incident happening about twenty years ago. Pip's encounter with both Magwitch and Compeyson paves the way for a further development. Magwitch, a poor and unlucky guy, under the guidance of fortune, meets with self-pretentious, handsome, erudite Compeyson. The chance encounter leads Magwitch to learn the truth about Compeyson and his partner, Arthur. The

Part 1
資訊歸納題

Part 2

Part 3

Part 4

Part 5

Part 6

deception from a rich lady, which is believed to be Miss Havisham, earns them a great deal of fortune. However, Compeyson's lavish spending habits cannot keep up with the money he earns from doing the dirty things.

Doing bad things, and not getting caught for a while seems normal, but committing a list of crimes and not getting captured will be deemed unlikely. Pretty soon, both are taken to court for a trial. They both are charged with putting stolen notes in circulation. Compeyson demands that they go separate ways, and Compeyson smart thinking does work. Magwitch can only get Mr. Jaggers as a lawyer for the defense.

The "birth" issue and one's education also weigh heavily on criminals in court, making Compeyson's sentence the half of Magwitch's. Magwitch has been unfairly judged at the court and eventually gets 14 years in prison. They are in the same prison ship, but Magwitch cannot get closer to Compeyson. Fleeing the prison ship leads to the encounter of Pip, the main character, and Compeyson. This time Magwitch has enough time to smash Compeyson's face to get revenge.

Magwitch and Compeyson will try every way to bring

each other down. Compeyson can report there is a refugee that flees from the prison ship. Magwitch and Pip's flee then encounters The Hamburg, the steamer, sailing swiftly towards them. People on the steamer demand the assistance to capture the person wrapping with a cloak on Pip's ship. As Magwitch goes behind the person who tries to seize him, he has the time to tear off another person with a cloak on the steamer to verify whether his identity is Compeyson. Compeyson is in shock and then waddles. Thereafter, they have a struggle, falling into the river. Other guys trying to seize Magwitch eventually cause the capsizing of the Pip's ship. Magwitch is found seriously injured, and with no traces of Compeyson. Pip has no reason to doubt Magwitch's account of what just happened because it is the same as that of the officer who steers the ship. At Police Court, it is revealed that Compeyson eventually falls into the river and is found dead. Compeyson and Arthur, Miss Havisham's brother, all pay the price. Arthur dies from serious illness right before the sentence of both Magwitch and Compeyson.

Miss Havisham's distorted mind resulting from the harm caused by Compeyson and Arthur could totally be cured if she knew the notion of "what comes around

Part 1
資訊歸納題

Part 2

Part 3

Part 4

Part 5

Part 6

goes around" and "unjust is doomed to destruction." Karma will eventually do the justice for her. Miss Havisham eventually comes to her senses right before her death that she has done quite a damage to another human being, Estella.

"That she had done a grievous thing in taking an impressionable child to mould into the form that her wild resentment, spurned affection, and wounded pride, found vengeance in, I knew full well."

During her chat with Pip, Miss Havisham tries to seek inner peace. Forgiveness really is a cure for all bad things. Miss Havisham would have lived a much happier life, if she had mastered the art of forgiveness.

資訊歸納題

Directions

Complete the table below to summarize the information about *Great Expectations* as discussed in the passage. Match the appropriate statements to the listed people. **You may use the letter more than once.**

Estella	•
Compeyson	•
Arthur	•
Magwitch	•
Pip	•
Mr. Jaggers	•
Miss Havisham	•
Compeyson and Arthur	•
Compeyson and Magwitch	•

Answer Choices

A. alteration of one's countenance due to rage

B. the chief cause of another's unwholesome behavior

C. procure lesser punishment due to erudition

D. a tool for someone to seek for ultimate revenge

E. cannot live to witness the verdict of his former crime partner

F. awareness of the previous action that can have an impact on someone

G. don a cloak on the boat

H. disintegration of the mind leads to morbid behavior

I. due to consistency, one has to think that the depiction is believable

Part 1

資訊歸納題

Part 2

Part 3

Part 4

Part 5

Part 6

Answers

Estella: D

Compeyson: C

Arthur: E

Magwitch: A

Pip: I

Mr. Jaggers: 卌

Miss Havisham: F, H

Compeyson and Arthur: B

Compeyson and Magwitch: G

In our daily life, we rarely take the idea or wisdom from time-enduring classics into account, so we are still struggling in several aspects of our life. The storylines of *Vanity Fair* ring alarmingly true to most readers. By taking an in-depth look into how Becky capitalizes every opportunity to get the desired outcome, we can probably have a better life.

Not having parents and being poor are two main factors that put heroine of *Vanity Fair*, Becky Sharp into a disadvantaged position. Since most girls have their parents' assistance to settle matters with the young man to change the fate, Becky has to do this all on her own, and one does not have to be extremely clever to know the truth that getting married with a wealthy husband will more or less make one's later life a lot smoother. The chance event comes when one of her wealthy friends, Amelia invites her to stay at her house for a week before Becky moves on to do the private tutor job.

Becky soon finds out a golden opportunity that Amelia's brother, Joseph is still single. Becky is ready to

Part 1

資訊歸納題

Part 2

Part 3

Part 4

Part 5

Part 6

put the move on Joseph, but she is not yet ready. Mr. Sedley deliberately wants Becky to try some curry with cayenne pepper and a chili that Becky obviously cannot put up with, and then Mr. Sedley enjoys this show along with his son, Joseph, and also informs his son that Becky has set her sights on him. Then all things have been in Becky's favor, but George Osborne considers Becky and Joseph a mesalliance, frightening Joseph for a bit. Osborne's intervention ends Becky's prospect of marrying with Joseph outright.

However, this setback does not dissuade young Rebecca from reaching her goal. It does mean she has not yet mastered the art of deception. Becky embarks on her journey of being the governess of Sir Pitt's two daughters, making her much closer to a real celebrity circle. Her goal has been constant: to find a rich husband. Winning the heart over Sir Pitt's two daughters and being baronet's confidence at Queen's Crawley are the first step towards Rebecca's success, and the mastery of the hypocrisy the second, the marriage with Rawdon Crawley the third.

Distinguished brilliance can certainly make up for poor birth as in the case of Becky. Becky earns the accolade from Miss Crawley that she has more brains than half the shire, and "as her equal." Sir Pitt wants Becky to be his bride by saying **"you've got more brains in your little vinger than any baronet's wife in the country."**, but Becky's true success is to tie the knot with Rawdon Crawley, who will inherit most of Miss Crawley's fortune. Rawdon Crawley's viewpoints about Becky are concordant with those of his aunt, Miss Crawley and his father, Sir Pitt. He has met multiple clippers, but has never encountered someone as witty as his wife, Becky. These correspond to several notions mentioned in one of the bestsellers, *The Wealth Elite*. It is not about the inheritance or Luck. One does need to have the exact DNA to keep money or acquire more wealth. In one of the British classics, *Treasure Island*, an idea relating to this has also been put forward at the very end of the chapter that it is not the amount of the money that you get. It is about one's nature.

The following development does not let Rawdon Crawley down as Becky exhibits more of her inborn talent. Becky seizes the moment during the war to make a fortune by selling a horse to Joseph. Wealthy people aspiring to flee also lack the key transportation, the horse. Even Lord Bareacres is willing to pay the price for

Part 1
資訊歸納題

Part 2

Part 3

Part 4

Part 5

Part 6

two horses under this circumstance. The sum is enormous enough to be considered a fortune to Becky. With the money and the sale of the residue of Rawdon's effects, and her pension as a widow, she will be financially independent, not having to worry about money for her entire life. Later, it is believed that the value of two horses equals a luxurious life in Paris a year for both Rawdon Crawley and Becky.

The couple's reunion after war brings more joyful news, as concealment of cash, checks, watches, and other valuables in Becky's coat reveals themselves. Becky has had unprecedented success even in Paris. It can be concluded that despite Becky's poorness and lack of the background, she possesses an admirable quality against adversity and cruel fate, surpassing her classmates, Amelia, born into a wealthy family and with the worth of the 10,000 pounds, where she has none. **"So in fetes, pleasures, and prosperity, the winter of 1815-16 passed away with Mrs. Rawdon Crawley, who accommodated herself to polite life as if her ancestors had been people of fashion for centuries past – and who from her wit, talent, and energy, indeed merited a place of honor in Vanity Fair."**

 **資訊歸納題**

Complete the table below to summarize the information about *Vanity Fair* as discussed in the passage. Match the appropriate statements to the listed people. **You may use the letter more than once.**

George Osborne	●
Rawdon Crawley	●
Sir Pitt	●
Amelia	●
Joseph	●
Mr. Sedley	●
Becky	●
Miss Crawley	●
Lord Bareacres	●

Answer Choices

A. whose charm on winning over the heart of the best pales next to his son

B. get enormous wealth by seizing the moment

42

Part 1

資訊歸納題

Part 2

Part 3

Part 4

Part 5

Part 6

C. being difficult with someone

D. a bachelor who gets fixed on, but gladly accepted

E. do the meddling to terminate someone's future hope

F. will get the inheritance from a close relative

G. a bachelor who gets targeted, but easily disturbed

H. without sustenance, one needs to be independent

I. getting exploited under an unusual circumstance

J. being inherently wealthy, but getting gradually surpassed by her counterpart

Answers

George Osborne: E

Rawdon Crawley: D, F

Sir Pitt: A

Amelia: J

Joseph: G

Mr. Sedley: C

Becky: B, H

Miss Crawley:

Lord Bareacres: I

People are so focusing on "birth" that they forget it is a series of choices that eventually make or break someone. Bad decisions in every key life moment can drag someone down the path, leading to an inferior outcome. The term "birth" will be just glamorous from the start and disastrous in the end.

In *Of Human Bondage*, with some deliberation, Philip's first life decision is to be an intern at the office of Messers. Herbert Carter & Co. in which his uncle and friends believe that under the tenure, Philip will learn professional skills enough for him to stand on his own feet and make a living. **"Every profession, and every trade, required length of time, and what was worse, money."** However, Philip is just like some of the twentysomethings, and not yet understands the mortifying conviction that three years at the first job are quite an important step for your next job.

Bad advice from one of his friends also dissipates his valuable twentysomething years. **"I cannot imagine you sitting in an office over a ledger." "My feeling is that one should look upon life as an adventure, one**

Part 1
資訊歸納題

Part 2

Part 3

Part 4

Part 5

Part 6

should burn with the hard, gem-like flame, and one should take risks, one should expose oneself to danger." His friend's belief in Philip's ability in art does not equal with how the reality views about him as a person. Despite the Vicar's disagreement for Philip's life trajectory change, Philip insists on going to Paris to learn art. Still Philip has to wait for a year to get his small inheritance from his father.

Aunt Louisa gives Philip her savings, an amount worth around a hundred pounds to pay for Philip's living expenses in Paris. Her generosity only lasts for a short time, and soon is replaced by the young man's visions in Paris. Eventually, the suggestion of the great artist proves that Philip's uncle is right all along. "Take your courage in both hands and try your luck at something else" The heart-felt, visceral advice ends Philip's two-year journey in Paris and terminates his dream of becoming an artist.

Perseverance is what Philip obviously lacks. His next step is to follow in his father's footsteps to become a doctor. With the qualification of entering a medical school, he chooses St. Luke's. For people entering on the medical profession, there are all kinds, and readers have yet to know how Philip will become. Philip believes that with his intelligence that he will scrape through the test, but in fact he fails at the anatomy examination, making him among the list of the incompetent. Love affairs distract Philip too much attention, when he should be focusing on the study. His worst decision is to involve himself with the stock market. Even though at first, he does have several wins, he eventually pays a hefty price for that. He writes a letter to his uncle asking for money, but is turned down. Without enough money, he has to find the job to pay daily expenses and discontinue his medical studies. He cannot believe that he screws things up, changing his entire life trajectory.

In Philip's case, the birth does not make his life wonderful. His father's small inheritance should have been a great assistance for him, but his poor decision effaces what has been given to him.

In *The History of Tom Jones, a Founding*, Tom's birth does not give him the upper hand when he is not able to live with his co-father. Good education and wealthy family from birth do not make Tom capable of standing on his own feet. Instead, he lacks professional skills needed for survival, ultimately accepting 50 pounds from Lady Bellaston.

Part 1
資訊歸納題

Part 2

Part 3

Part 4

Part 5

Part 6

So for those who are still jealous of your friends' rich parents, you might as well have to focus on what you can do at every key decision, making it tremendously beneficial to the next step of your life. Once you have become greater and greater, you will find that the world is a better place. You will even notice that Goddess of Fate makes a light smile at you.

 資訊歸納題

Directions

Complete the table below to summarize the information about *Of Human Bondage* and *The History of Tom Jones, a Founding* as discussed in the passage. Match the appropriate statements to the listed people. **You may use the letter more than once.**

Philip	•
Vicar	•
Aunt Louisa	•
the great artist	•
Lady Bellaston	•
Tom	•
Philip and Tom	•

A. inborn advantages do not become great assistance

B. adopting the advice from an acquaintance, further squandering valuable time

C. offering truthful, cruel advice to someone

D. willingness to sacrifice for another's greatness

E. cannot be financially independent

F. objection for one's career change because of practical concerns

G. not being grateful for one's magnanimity

H. acceptance of money from someone due to several concerns

I. refusal of giving someone the money for the sake of one's future

Answers

Philip: B, G

Vicar: F, I

Aunt Louisa: D

the great artist: C

Lady Bellaston: 卌

Tom: E

Philip and Tom: A, H

The fact that no third person must directly touch on other people's love affairs is a fundamental respect for people who are in love, yet meddling, out of curiosity, protection and other factors is commonly seen in reality. Among them, parents can be said to be the most frequent disturbance to their kid's marriage or love affairs. Parents may hold different ideas when it comes to this topic. Regret has often happened after years of marriage with someone, making it reasonable for parents to interfere. Gerald in *Gone with the Wind* has chosen to inform his child, Scarlett, whereas Mr. Brooke, Dorothea's uncle has adopted a liberal approach. However, the outcome for both Scarlett and Dorothea has remained the same, making us wonder what should someone do when there is actually a need to make an interference.

"It is as fatal as a murder or any other horror that divides people." However, in *Drop Dead Diva*, Jane's coworker Owen and Kim, have decided to meddle in Jane's love affairs when they know Ian Holt, a cold-blooded killer is dating their colleague. Kim, who used to have some quarrels with Jane, because at the law

Part 1

資訊歸納題

Part 2

Part 3

Part 4

Part 5

Part 6

firm they are in direct competition with Jane, now is willing to pay US 10,000 dollars to Ian Holt for him to go away. Ian Holt rejects the offer and then is met with Owen's direct opposition of his conduct. It seems that Kim and Owen are doing the right things, but they are still not in the relationship with either one of them. It's best if Kim and Owen just stay out of this.

To go deeper into the story, Grayson comes closer to getting married to Jane, but unfortunately, he dies after an operation in the hospital. Grayson hits the return button, so that he gets a second chance to live. Ironically, his soul is placed in Ian Holt's body, making his identity questionable for others.

The janitor outside the cell tells Jane that a ruthless killer like Ian Holt does not have the right to get a second chance. Jane, now being Ian's lawyer, argues on Ian's behalf that there should be a stay of execution and she believes that Ian is innocent. Despite the fact that there are no new facts sustaining a stay, Ian comes up with the idea that there should be a new death warrant. Without the new death warrant, the new execution will be postponed, making Ian capable of living for another 24 hours. Having an excogitation of sufficient reason to get

Ian acquitted in a day is insane. Owen and Jane can only surmise the idea that makes Ian stay life imprison. However, Ian demands they fight for a claim of actual guiltlessness because letters and other evidence makes Ian truly believe his innocence.

During the penalty of the trial, the victim's wife Cheryl did testify on Ian's behalf that he was innocent. Cheryl implored the judge that Ian, a man convicted of killing her husband, should be set free. Cheryl's testimony does make Owen and Jane rethink about things happening during the night at the club. They eventually figure out the real killer is Breeman, resulting in a happy ending for Jane and Ian. After the release, Jane and Ian's love affair may sound like an eccentric combination. Even though Ian's name has been cleared, others might still think Ian has mistaken his gratitude for Jane as true love. Jane cannot handle her grief with the loss of Grayson, so she starts the relationship with Ian.

In *Middlemarch*, there is a great divide between Dorothea and Will if they have to be with each other. The long-enduring unsolved problems for all generations: The rich and the poor. There is bound to be a great hindrance for the two, even if Dorothea does not care about the

Part 1
資訊歸納題

Part 2

Part 3

Part 4

Part 5

Part 6

money. It is true that destitution will soon wear out two people's love after their marriage. Like what's stated before, the best thing we can do is congratulations for any couple and let nature take its course. After all, it is not your marriage, so mind your own business. People's relationships will soon end the moment one of the parties cannot endure, and there is no need for one to act like a judge, arbitrating trivial matters happening in other people's marriage.

 資訊歸納題

Directions

Complete the table below to summarize the information about *Drop Dead Diva* and *Middlemarch* as discussed in the passage. Match the appropriate statements to the listed people. **You may use the letter more than once.**

Mr. Brooke	•
Gerald	•
Dorothea	•
Scarlett	•
Ian Holt	•

Jane	•
Kim and Owen	•
Grayson	•
Cheryl	•
Owen and Jane	•
Dorothea and Will	•

Answer Choices

A. to be seen as odd by societal conventions

B. make a deposition that someone is entirely guiltless

C. make a decision to intervene out of protection

D. willingness to put down the past because of sensing potential danger

E. to tie the knot, a great sacrifice needed to be made

F. maintain suspension of the death penalty

G. to be reborn into a new life under an unusual occasion

H. conceive an idea that the litigant is not entirely satisfied

Part 1
資訊歸納題

Part 2

Part 3

Part 4

Part 5

Part 6

I. suggest lawyers go with inculpability defense

J. conceive a different concept because of a declaration made during the court

K. conceive a notion that turns over a situation

Answers

Mr. Brooke: 卌
Gerald: 卌
Dorothea: 卌
Scarlett: 卌
Ian Holt: K, I
Jane: F
Kim: D
Kim and Owen: C
Grayson: G
Cheryl: B
Owen and Jane: H
Dorothea and Will: A, E
Ian Holt and Jane: A

Most people have less of outward vision, focusing their attention on how to be financially independent, but in today's world, downsizing among large, profit-driven companies is so common, lots of people are not able to secure high-paying jobs as they have been used to. What makes things worse is that prices of commodities are getting increasingly higher, resulting in not having enough cash to live an ideal life. Some sit in their rented apartments in lethargic melancholy, whereas others fix their minds on getting the inheritance from parents so that they do not have to worry about money.

In *North and South*, Margaret is lucky enough to get a large inheritance, making her an even better pick among single men. However, not all cases of inheritance end up with a pleasant result. In *Drop Dead Diva*, Violet Harwood is an heiress with a great deal of fortune. Unluckily, Violet Harwood's parents create a trust that is regulated by her brother. Without the approbation of the trustee, Violet Harwood is unable to use the money freely. Violet Harwood's plan of using her fortune on the shelter house has shattered because her brother controls the

Part 1
資訊歸納題

Part 2

Part 3

Part 4

Part 5

Part 6

expenses. Fortunately, Violet Harwood's lawyer comes up with the idea of the dead-hand clause.

The definition of the dead-hand clause is to prevent dead people from exercising control from the grave beyond a single generation. The trick is Violet Harwood's parents cannot mandate her to give the antique watch to someone who did not exist when they died, making the whole trust ineffective. "What's good for the goose is good for the gander", so the inheritance shall be distributed equally between Violet Harwood and her brother.

In *Middlemarch*, the idea of the dead-hand clause has also been used by Mr. Casaubon. "But well-being is not to be secured by ample, independent possession of property; on the contrary, occasions might arise in which such possession might expose her to the more danger."

It might be reasonable to deduce that Mr. Casaubon has the foresight to protect his wife from men's deception, but a closer inspection can reveal his agenda. The inheritance will be the control of his wife even after his death. Mrs. Casaubon will lose the inheritance if she is married with Will, making her unable to tie the knot with the person she truly loves. Mr. Casaubon's intent can also be perceived as an insult to his own wife, who remains loyal to him while he is alive. Mrs. Casaubon has never been a materialistic young lady. Eventually, she figures out true love transcends all things, including a great deal of inheritance, and has a happy ending with Will.

In *Wuthering Heights*, Edgar Linton is aware of Mr. Heathcliff's intention of claiming his private property and Thrushcross Grange. Originally, Edgar Linton wants Miss Cathy to use the property at her disposal, but later he ameliorates the will, putting it in the trust, for Miss Cathy to use and for her descendants to utilize after Miss Cathy dies. If Linton dies, the property will not go to Mr. Heathcliff. In *Wuthering Heights*, **"Earnshaw had mortgaged every yard of land he owned for cash to supply his mania for gaming; and he, Heathcliff, was the mortgagee."** Mr. Heathcliff not only gets Earnshaw's inheritance, Wuthering Heights, making Hareton, Earnshaw's son, moneyless, but also the estate of Edgar Linton. Even if Mr. Heathcliff's son, Linton dies, Catherine will not be the heir. Miss Cathy is reluctant to believe Mr. Heathcliff is a bad guy. According to the will of the previous Linton generation, Thrushcross Grange will only

Part 1
資訊歸納題

Part 2

Part 3

Part 4

Part 5

Part 6

be inherited by a male descendant, so Mr. Heathcliff's contemplation is foxy and smart enough to let his son Linton get married with Miss Cathy.

Resolving an inheritance issue is not as easy as it seems. Sometimes it involves several people who maliciously vie for the property in court. Margaret in *North and South* is probably the happiest person that gets the inherited money, lending it to Mr. Thornton for a loan. Mrs. Casaubon's great wisdom of not valuing the property too highly is also very admirable. It is true that more money only creates more problems. We can only pray that we will not be ending like Mr. Heathcliff, living unhappily till his death.

 資訊歸納題

Directions

Complete the table below to summarize the information about *North and South, Drop Dead Diva, Middlemarch,* and *Wuthering Heights* as discussed in the passage. Match the appropriate statements to the listed people. **You may use the letter more than once.**

Violet Harwood	•
Violet Harwood's brother	•
Margaret	•
Violet Harwood's lawyer	•
Violet Harwood's parents	•
Mr. Casaubon	•
Mrs. Casaubon	•
Edgar Linton	•
Mr. Heathcliff	•
Earnshaw's son	•

Answer Choices

A. penniless because of the extravagance from the previous generation

B. mandate a trustee to control the expenses of someone

C. control the expenses of someone because of the trust

D. shrewd enough to use the trust to protect inheritance for the offspring

E. sagacious enough to know the hazard underneath

F.   cannot control the expenses because of the trust

G.   clever enough to use the notion of the dead-hand clause

H.   cunning enough to let someone be the slave

I.   get forfeited the right if against the will

J.   making someone able to use the money from the trust

K.   crafty enough to steal someone's fortune

L.   gain popularity as a result of being wealthier

Answers

Violet Harwood: F
Violet Harwood's brother: C
Margaret: L
Violet Harwood's lawyer: G, J
Violet Harwood's parents: B
Mr. Casaubon: E, G
Mrs. Casaubon: I
Edgar Linton: D
Mr. Heathcliff: H, K
Earnshaw's son: A

Part 1
資訊歸納題

Part 2

Part 3

Part 4

Part 5

Part 6

61

Wealthy or poor, investment has been tightly linked with people's life. Poor people wish to multiply their money through numerous investment opportunities, whereas rich people set their sights on getting richer by utilizing lucrative information. As a saying goes, the purpose of a novel is a reflection of reality. Great lessons can be learned from the following three novels: *Of Human Bondage*, *North and South*, and *Vanity Fair.*

It is understood that a poor investment can lead someone to wait in line for a free soup quicker than one might think. In *Vanity Fair*, an inferior judgment in investment soon makes a rich person, like Mr. Sedley, bankrupt. **"Funds had risen when he calculated they would fall." "His bills were protested, his act of bankruptcy formal. The house and furniture of Russell Square were seized and sold up, and he and his family were thrust away."**

Similar to the situation of Mr. Sedley in *Vanity Fair*, Mr. Thornton's condition in *North and South* shares the same fate. Both start out as rich from the beginning of the novel, but eventually the vicissitude of life emerges.

Part 1
資訊歸納題

Part 2

Part 3

Part 4

Part 5

Part 6

Mr. Thornton's problem lies in his use of capital. Using it in new machinery and expansion results in not having enough cash for emergencies during a bad economy. During the economic recession, the value of all large stocks plunges, and Mr. Thornton's shares almost halve.

This corresponds to a wise saying from Nelly Dean in *Wuthering Heights* that no one can guarantee one's wealth throughout the entire life. One cannot always be rich, so using one's richness or wealth as a criterion when it comes to choosing a mate is not wise. Still, being rich is an irresistible quality in the market because wealth almost equal the sense of security. Henry in *North and South* provides us with the same insight. Margaret's inherited property is just a part of her. Even though it means that Margaret's money can instantly make him succeed, that should not be the criterion for choosing a life-partner. However, both Mr. Thornton and Henry have the contemplation of using Margaret's fortune to assist their own business. As in the case of Mr. Thornton, he lacks enough money to keep the company going, while Henry needs enough currency to start the law business.

It's true that **"those who are happy and successful themselves are too apt to make light of the misfortune**

of others." Ultimately, Margaret is willing to loan eighteen thousand and fifty-seven pounds to Mr. Thornton.

Reversed fate makes the story a happy ending, but not everyone is as lucky as Margaret in *North and South* and Philip in *Of Human Bondage*. Margaret inherits the money and property worth 42,000 pounds, while Philip has an inheritance enough for him to finish medical school, making his fate much better than the rest of his classmates. Philip can focus all his attention on the study. Inheritance or extra money through other means can be good or bad really depends on the use of the person. In the case of Philip, it is definitely a bad thing. However, Philip squanders some of the money on girls instead of spending it on what's necessary, and worst of all, he gambles his tuition fees and money for the daily use on the stock market. **"History was being made, and the process was so significant that it seemed absurd that it should touch the life of an obscure medical student."** Selling shares now during the market plunge would mean that he can only have 80 pounds left, making him unable to continue his medical school.

It can be concluded that investment money should

Part 1
資訊歸納題

Part 2

Part 3

Part 4

Part 5

Part 6

come from the sources that will not influence one's living; otherwise, there is going to be a disaster. No matter how lucky a person can be, not being able to control the spending can result in serious damage in life (like Philip). Being too speculative can also have the same fate like Mr. Sedley, losing enormous wealth and his hard-to-build enterprise. Working industriously and diligently can still end up like Mr. Thornton, lacking enough money to keep the company afloat. Predictions of one's life trajectory are too unlikely, but what we can do is do our part and not investing recklessly or dreaming of becoming a rich billionaire in a day.

 資訊歸納題

Directions

Complete the table below to summarize the information about *Of Human Bondage*, *North and South*, and *Vanity Fair* as discussed in the passage. Match the appropriate statements to the listed animals. **You may use the letter more than once.**

Mr. Thornton	•
Mr. Sedley	•

Philip	•
Henry	•
Margaret	•
Nelly Dean	•
Henry and Mr. Thornton	•
Margaret and Philip	•

Answer Choices

A. a lack of moderation in expenditure will be detrimental

B. factors other than hardworking ruin the entire future

C. discontinuation on the study due to lack of money

D. serendipity turns the life into a much smoother sailing

E. money should not be the sole consideration when it comes to choosing a mate

F. confiscation of the property due to bad investment

G. chancy behavior can make one end up with nothing

H. an even better pick after getting the inheritance

Part 1
資訊歸納題

Part 2

Part 3

Part 4

Part 5

Part 6

I.   constancy in wealth throughout the entire life is impossible

J.   careers need another's assistance to turn around

Answers

Mr. Thornton: B

Mr. Sedley: F, G

Philip: A, C

Henry: E

Margaret: H

Nelly Dean: I

Henry and Mr. Thornton: J

Margaret and Philip: D

聽讀整合 TEST 1

There are **1.**_____ love songs that are gripping and make people **2.**_____. Among them, topics related to "love someone who truly loves you" and "choose the person you love" are the most popular. How to make the right choice and select the ideal life partner can be quite difficult. Often a lot of sayings on social media **3.**_____ and views of those **4.**_____ in the show are misleading and are often rife with claims that don't stand up to **5.**_____. Luckily, by reading British romance novels, like *Far from the Madding Crowd*, we can have a better understanding about making smarter choices.

Three promising guys in *Far from the Madding Crowd* can be seen as the **6.**_____ version of the real life. Three candidates are Oak, Boldwood, and Troy.

As anyone can remember from high school and college, most girls would go for the handsome and bad boy types, simply because they want to be **7.**_____. They deem the guy with **8.**_____ and integrity as boring and easily controlled, but that pushes them away from real happiness. That is also the main reason why Oak is not accepted by heroine, Bathsheba at the very beginning of the novel. Oak has several **9.**_____ traits that make him an **10.**_____ husband for Bathsheba. He is kind-hearted and has a real passion for Bathsheba. Oak proclaims that he will work twice as hard after marriage.

So far, this has been about all the readers' **11.**_____ of him.

Part 1

Part 2

聽
力
填
空
題

Part 3

Part 4

Part 5

Part 6

What about Boldwood's account about Oak? Near the very end of the novel, Boldwood has a heart-felt **12.**_____ with Oak, when Boldwood has the sense that his **13.**_____ with Bathsheba is around the corner. "You have behaved like a man, and I, as a sort of successful rival- successful partly through your goodness of heart I should like definitely to show my sense of your **14.**_____ under what must have been a great pain to you."

As for Boldwood, he has a crazy **15.**_____ for Bathsheba that separates him apart from both Troy and Oak, and he is also the man who can wait for the girl for six years. At a much later time, a locked box that contains **16.**_____ silks, satins, poplins, velvets, muffs (sable and ermine), and a case of jewellery that includes four heavy gold **17.**_____ and several lockets and rings can symbolize the importance of Bathsheba in Boldwood's heart.

In the middle part of the story, Bathsheba chooses Troy to be her husband, and Troy seems to fall into the **18.**_____ type. Troy can be good for a **19.**_____, but not for a long-lasting relationship. However, Troy does have his charm. Troy volunteers to sweep and shake bees into the hive to impress Bathsheba. Troy further demonstrates his **20.**_____ in their next appointment, creating a special moment to **21.**_____ a kiss on Bathsheba. The sense of **22.**_____ and surprise prevails, making her act on **23.**_____ and without reason.

According to the author, Troy is good at **24.**_____ and **25.**_____ so that ethical defects will not be perceived by women, whereas Oak stands in a sharp contrast with Troy because Oak's **26.**_____ can be apparently seen. Beneath the **27.**_____ of Troy, there are flaws most people will not notice. However, no matter how good one is at varnish, he will eventually show the true colors.

"Every voice in nature was **28.**_____ in bespeaking change." Unprotected ricks equal to 750 pounds of food. The storm is coming closer, but Troy is nowhere to be seen. According to Oak, Troy is asleep in the barn, **29.**_____ all the harm that the weather might do to the crop and the consequence that will cost their barn. Oak's **30.**_____ to protect the crop shows his true love for Bathsheba. He uses his actions to validate the love. Troy; however, demonstrates his **31.**_____, making Bathsheba realize Troy as a person.

Boldwood loves Bathsheba deeply by wanting to provide her material comfort as a way to possess a **32.**_____. Oak, on the other hand, wants to love Bathsheba by using all his life. Troy seems to have an **33.**_____ on Bathsheba because of Bathsheba's wealth and barn. Bathsheba at first gets married with Troy by choosing the one she truly loves, and till the end she figures out it is the one who truly loves her that she should be with. As a Chinese saying goes, **"people look for him thousands of Baidu. Looking back suddenly, the man was there, in a 34.**_____ **lit place."** Perhaps Bathsheba just comes to the realization about this a bit too late. True love is always around us, but our perception prevents us from seeing it clearly.

Part 1

Part 2
聽
力
填
空
題

Part 3

Part 4

Part 5

Part 6

聽讀整合 參考答案

Test 1

1. numerous
2. resonate
3. platforms
4. celebrities
5. scrutiny
6. summarized
7. tamed
8. principles
9. admirable
10. ideal
11. perception
12. confession
13. prospect
14. friendship
15. devotion
16. expensive
17. bracelets
18. untamed
19. diversion
20. swordsmanship
21. imprint
22. novelty
23. impulse
24. concealment
25. superficiality
26. shortcomings
27. veneer
28. unanimous
29. neglecting
30. endeavor
31. indifference
32. beauty
33. agenda
34. dimly

"I believe that I have no enemy on earth, and none surely would have been so 1._____ as to destroy me 2._____." A saying from *Frankenstein* seems to convey the message of Justine's viewpoint that men **3._____** possess a good heart. While various people may hold different views on this statement, Justine's **4._____** about the devil who frames her is entirely correct. The devil has a good heart from the start, but Victor, the main character, resists **5._____** the devil as his **6._____** or his own baby, resulting in a **7._____** mind for the devil. There has been some mental separation between the two. Acceptance and refusal are two **8._____** concepts, and feeling loved is essential for anyone's personal development. The devil's **9._____** behavior results from getting rejected and not being **10._____**. Not getting loved makes someone feel neglected, unaccepted, and being excluded. All these factors engender serious **11._____** behavior that creates some of the social crimes.

Education seems to be the key to amending people's mind. As the story progresses, the devil demands the creation of an identity similar to him so that he can find someone to love and to be loved. Victor at first **12._____** another attempt to create a new one for him, then out of the blue shifting into thinking that **13._____** the spouse for him **14._____** with producing a monster. He can barely handle the devil, let alone dealing with two bad-looking creatures. The novel itself conveys several important messages **15.____** for human beings to pay serious attention so that more **16.____** problems can be avoided, thus making it especially great and eternally **17.____**.

A lot of **18.____** crimes relating to love can be **19.____** if proper education and giving others more love have seriously been paid attention to. One does not have to take **20.____** too seriously. As a saying goes, **"things that seem 21.____ at the time usually do work out for the rest."** Sometimes it does mean that God has a better idea, wanting to give you something much better.

As can be seen in another classic, *Middlemarch*, God certainly wants James to have not just someone better, but someone more suitable for him. In towns, neighbors and farmers have the **22.____** for Celia over Dorothea simply because Celia is more **23.____**, innocent, clever, and sophisticated. Dorothea has a quality of not self-admiring, thinking Celia is more charming than she is. James, on the other hand, has a crush on Dorothea. **"He felt that he had chosen the one who was in all respects the 24.____; and a man 25.____ likes to look forward to having the best."** However, James does not even have any chance with Dorothea.

His **26.____** Mr. Casaubon does not have to do much and wins over the heart of Dorothea in such a short time. Luckily, James does not take this as a **27.____** or as something that will crush him. Getting rejected does not make someone a failure as most people would think. It is one's mindset that makes a man. Some would writhe under the idea of failure and rejection

Part 1

Part 2

聽力填空題

Part 3

Part 4

Part 5

Part 6

and then do the harm to the rival, hurt themselves, or cause quite a damage to someone you love. The thing is you do not have to act like that.

Other people, including Dorothea's uncle, are **28.**_____ at Dorothea's choice of a man, not choosing James as a husband. Celia has a feeling that James will be a great husband, but from her **29.**_____, they will not be a good fit. Dorothea's choice may be good for both of them. It should not be **30.**_____ as seriously harming someone. James claims that Dorothea should wait until she is mature enough to make the decision and is mad at Dorothea's choice, but eventually he gladly accepts this news. It does mean that more **31.**_____ fruits are waiting for him definitely.

As the story progresses to a much later time, his feelings of getting rejected have gone already, having been replaced by getting engaged with Celia. "His **32.**_____ **love had not turned to 33.**_____**; its death had made sweet odors – 34.**_____ **memories that clung with a 35.**_____**effect to Dorothea."** True love deserves some time to wait. Two classics *Middlemarch* and *Frankenstein*, should all be the required reading during high school, shaping those hurt feelings so that more **36.**_____ can be avoided.

Part 1

Part 2
聽
力
填
空
題

Part 3

Part 4

Part 5

Part 6

Test 2

1. wicked
2. wantonly
3. inherently
4. conjecture
5. acknowledging
6. creation
7. distorted
8. antithetical
9. atrocious
10. amended
11. psychological
12. concurs
13. manufacturing
14. equates
15. essential
16. societal
17. valuable
18. murder
19. evaded
20. rejections
21. disastrous
22. predilection
23. approachable
24. superior
25. naturally
26. rival
27. defeat
28. shocked
29. observations
30. interpreted
31. saccharine
32. disregarded
33. bitterness
34. floating
35. consecrating
36. tragedy

"It would have been cruel in Miss Havisham, horribly cruel, to practice on the **1.**_____ of a poor boy, and to torture me through all these years with a vain hope and idle **2.**_____, if she had reflected on the **3.**_____ of what she did."

In *Great Expectations*, Miss Havisham's **4.**_____ wealth does not give her the joy that she is in **5.**_____ need of. Miss Havisham's use of the little girl, Estella, to torture the boy that she hires, on the other hand, fulfills her **6.**_____ and the sense of **7.**_____ . As a saying goes, pain and conflict only bring more pain and conflict. Not letting go of the past rigorously hurts or **8.**_____ Miss Havisham's body and soul.

Miss Havisham's hurt can be traced back to an incident happening about twenty years ago. Pip's **9.**_____ with both Magwitch and Compeyson paves the way for a further development. Magwitch, a poor and unlucky guy, under the **10.**_____ of fortune, meets with self-pretentious, handsome, **11.**_____ Compeyson. The chance encounter leads Magwitch to learn the truth about Compeyson and his partner, Arthur. The **12.**_____ from a rich lady, which is believed to be Miss Havisham, earns them a great deal of fortune. However, Compeyson's **13.**_____ spending habits cannot keep up with the money he earns from doing the dirty things.

Doing bad things, and not getting caught for a while seems **14.**_____ , but committing a list of crimes and not getting

Part 1

Part 2

聽
力
填
空
題

Part 3

Part 4

Part 5

Part 6

captured will be deemed unlikely. Pretty soon, both are taken to court for a trial. They both are charged with putting stolen notes in **15.**_____. Compeyson demands that they go **16.**_____ ways, and Compeyson smart thinking does work. Magwitch can only get Mr. Jaggers as a lawyer for the defense.

The "birth" issue and one's education also weigh **17.**_____ on criminals in court, making Compeyson's sentence the half of Magwitch's. Magwitch has been **18.**_____ judged at the court and eventually gets 14 years in prison. They are in the same prison ship, but Magwitch cannot get closer to Compeyson. Fleeing the prison ship leads to the encounter of Pip, the main character, and Compeyson. This time Magwitch has enough time to **19.**_____ Compeyson's face to get revenge.

Magwitch and Compeyson will try every way to bring each other down. Compeyson can report there is a **20.**_____ that flees from the prison ship. Magwitch and Pip's flee then encounters The Hamburg, the steamer, sailing swiftly towards them. People on the steamer demand the **21.**_____ to capture the person wrapping with a cloak on Pip's ship. As Magwitch goes behind the person who tries to seize him, he has the time to tear off another person with a **22.**_____ on the steamer to verify whether his identity is Compeyson. Compeyson is in shock and then waddles. Thereafter, they have a struggle, falling into the river. Other guys trying to seize Magwitch eventually cause the **23.**_____ of the Pip's ship. Magwitch is found seriously **24.**_____, and with no traces of Compeyson. Pip has no **25.**_____ to doubt Magwitch's account of what just happened because it is the same as that of the officer who steers the ship.

At Police Court, it is revealed that Compeyson eventually falls into the river and is found **26.**_____. Compeyson and Arthur, Miss Havisham's brother, all pay the price. Arthur dies from serious illness right before the **27.**_____ of both Magwitch and Compeyson.

Miss Havisham's **28.**_____ mind resulting from the harm caused by Compeyson and Arthur could totally be cured if she knew the notion of "what comes around goes around" and "unjust is doomed to **29.**_____." Karma will eventually do the justice for her. Miss Havisham eventually comes to her senses right before her death that she has done quite a **30.**_____ to another human being, Estella.

"That she had done a **31.**_____ thing in taking an **32.**_____ child to mould into the form that her wild **33.**_____, spurned affection, and wounded pride, found **34.**_____ in, I knew full well."

During her chat with Pip, Miss Havisham tries to seek inner peace. Forgiveness really is a cure for all bad things. Miss Havisham would have lived a much happier life, if she had mastered the art of forgiveness.

Part 1

Part 2
聽力填空題

Part 3

Part 4

Part 5

Part 6

聽讀整合 參考答案

Test 3

1. susceptibility
2. pursuit
3. gravity
4. enormous
5. desperate
6. whim
7. satisfaction
8. erodes
9. encounter
10. guidance
11. erudite
12. deception
13. lavish
14. normal
15. circulation
16. separate
17. heavily
18. unfairly
19. smash
20. refugee
21. assistance
22. cloak
23. capsizing
24. injured
25. reason
26. dead
27. sentence
28. distorted
29. destruction
30. damage
31. grievous
32. impressionable
33. resentment
34. vengeance

聽讀整合 TEST 4

In our daily life, we rarely take the idea or **1.**_____ from time-enduring classics into account, so we are still struggling in several aspects of our life. The **2.**_____ of *Vanity Fair* ring **3.**_____ true to most readers. By taking an in-depth look into how Becky capitalizes every **4.**_____ to get the desired outcome, we can probably have a better life.

Not having parents and being poor are two main factors that put heroine of *Vanity Fair*, Becky Sharp into a **5.**_____ position. Since most girls have their parents' assistance to **6.**_____ matters with the young man to change the fate, Becky has to do this all on her own, and one does not have to be **7.**_____ clever to know the truth that getting married with a wealthy husband will more or less make one's later life a lot **8.**_____. The chance event comes when one of her **9.**_____ friends, Amelia invites her to stay at her house for a week before Becky moves on to do the private tutor job.

Becky soon finds out a **10.**_____ opportunity that Amelia's brother, Joseph is still single. Becky is ready to put the move on Joseph, but she is not yet ready. Mr. Sedley **11.**_____ wants Becky to try some curry with cayenne pepper and a chili that Becky **12.**_____ cannot put up with, and then Mr. Sedley enjoys this show along with his son, Joseph, and also informs his son that Becky has set her sights on him. Then all things have been in Becky's favor, but George Osborne considers Becky and Joseph a **13.**_____, frightening Joseph for a bit. Osborne's

Part 1

Part 2

聽
力
填
空
題

Part 3

Part 4

Part 5

Part 6

intervention ends Becky's prospect of marrying with Joseph **14.**_____.

However, this setback does not **15.**_____ young Rebecca from reaching her goal. It does mean she has not yet mastered the art of **16.**_____. Becky embarks on her journey of being the **17.**_____ of Sir Pitt's two daughters, making her much closer to a real **18.**_____ circle. Her goal has been **19.**_____: to find a rich husband. Winning the heart over Sir Pitt's two daughters and being baronet's **20.**_____ at Queen's Crawley are the first step towards Rebecca's success, and the mastery of the **21.**_____ the second, the marriage with Rawdon Crawley the third.

Distinguished **22.**_____ can certainly make up for poor birth as in the case of Becky. Becky earns the **23.**_____ from Miss Crawley that she has more brains than half the shire, and "as her equal." Sir Pitt wants Becky to be his bride by saying **"you've got more brains in your little vinger than any baronet's wife in the country."**, but Becky's true success is to tie the knot with Rawdon Crawley, who will inherit most of Miss Crawley's fortune. Rawdon Crawley's viewpoints about Becky are **24.**_____ with those of his aunt, Miss Crawley and his father, Sir Pitt. He has met multiple clippers, but has never encountered someone as witty as his wife, Becky. These correspond to several notions mentioned in one of the bestsellers, *The Wealth Elite*. It is not about the **25.**_____ or Luck. One does need to have the exact DNA to keep money or acquire more wealth. In one of the British classics, *Treasure Island*, an idea relating to this has also been put forward at the very end of the chapter that it is not the amount of the money that you get. It is about one's **26.**_____.

The following development does not let Rawdon Crawley down as Becky exhibits more of her **27.**_____ talent. Becky seizes the moment during the war to make a fortune by selling a horse to Joseph. Wealthy people aspiring to flee also lack the key **28.**_____, the horse. Even Lord Bareacres is willing to pay the price for two horses under this circumstance. The sum is enormous enough to be considered a fortune to Becky. With the money and the sale of the **29.**_____ of Rawdon's effects, and her pension as a widow, she will be financially independent, not having to worry about money for her entire life. Later, it is believed that the value of two horses equals a **30.**_____ life in Paris a year for both Rawdon Crawley and Becky.

The couple's reunion after war brings more joyful news, as concealment of cash, checks, watches, and other valuables in Becky's coat reveals themselves. Becky has had **31.**_____ success even in Paris. It can be concluded that despite Becky's poorness and lack of the background, she possesses an admirable quality against **32.**_____ and cruel fate, surpassing her classmates, Amelia, born into a wealthy family and with the worth of the 10,000 pounds, where she has none. **"So in fetes, pleasures, and prosperity, the winter of 1815-16 passed away with Mrs. Rawdon Crawley, who accommodated herself to polite life as if her ancestors had been people of fashion for centuries past – and who from her wit, talent, and energy, indeed merited a place of honor in Vanity Fair."**

Part 1

Part 2
聽力填空題

Part 3

Part 4

Part 5

Part 6

聽讀整合 參考答案

Test 4

1. wisdom
2. storylines
3. alarmingly
4. opportunity
5. disadvantaged
6. settle
7. extremely
8. smoother
9. wealthy
10. golden
11. deliberately
12. obviously
13. mesalliance
14. outright
15. dissuade
16. deception
17. governess
18. celebrity
19. constant
20. confidence
21. hypocrisy
22. brilliance
23. accolade
24. concordant
25. inheritance
26. nature
27. inborn
28. transportation
29. residue
30. luxurious
31. unprecedented
32. adversity

聽讀整合 TEST 5

People are so focusing on "birth" that they forget it is a series of **1.**_____ that eventually make or break someone. Bad **2.**_____ in every key life moment can drag someone down the path, leading to an **3.**_____ outcome. The term "birth" will be just **4.**_____ from the start and disastrous in the end.

In *Of Human Bondage*, with some **5.**_____, Philip's first life decision is to be an **6.**_____ at the office of Messers. Herbert Carter & Co. in which his uncle and friends believe that under the **7.**_____, Philip will learn professional skills enough for him to stand on his own feet and make a living. **"Every profession, and every trade, 8.**_____ **length of time, and what was worse, money."** However, Philip is just like some of the twentysomethings, and not yet understands the **9.**_____ conviction that three years at the first job are quite an important step for your next job.

Bad advice from one of his friends also **10.**_____ his valuable twentysomething years. **"I cannot imagine you sitting in an office over a ledger." "My feeling is that one should look upon life as an 11.**_____**, one should burn with the hard, gem-like flame, and one should take risks, one should expose oneself to danger."** His friend's belief in Philip's ability in art does not equal with how the reality views about him as a person. Despite the Vicar's **12.**_____ for Philip's life **13.**_____ change, Philip insists on going to Paris to learn art. Still Philip has to wait for a year to get his small inheritance from his father.

Part 1

Part 2

聽
力
填
空
題

Part 3

Part 4

Part 5

Part 6

Aunt Louisa gives Philip her savings, an amount worth around a hundred pounds to pay for Philip's living **14.**_____ in Paris. Her **15.**_____ only lasts for a short time, and soon is replaced by the young man's visions in Paris. Eventually, the **16.**_____ of the great artist proves that Philip's uncle is right all along. "Take your courage in both hands and try your luck at something else" The heart-felt, **17.**_____ advice ends Philip's two-year journey in Paris and **18.**_____ his dream of becoming an artist.

Perseverance is what Philip obviously lacks. His next step is to follow in his father's **19.**_____ to become a doctor. With the **20.**_____ of entering a medical school, he chooses St. Luke's. For people entering on the medical profession, there are all kinds, and readers have yet to know how Philip will become. Philip believes that with his **21.**_____ that he will scrape through the test, but in fact he fails at the **22.**_____ examination, making him among the list of the **23.**_____. Love affairs distract Philip too much attention, when he should be focusing on the study. His worst decision is to involve himself with the stock market. Even though at first, he does have several wins, he eventually pays a **24.**_____ price for that. He writes a letter to his uncle asking for money, but is turned down. Without enough money, he has to find the job to pay daily expenses and **25.**_____ his medical studies. He cannot believe that he screws things up, changing his entire life trajectory.

In Philip's case, the birth does not make his life **26.**_____. His father's small inheritance should have been a great assistance for him, but his poor decision **27.**_____ what has been given to him.

In *The History of Tom Jones, a Founding*, Tom's birth does not give him the upper hand when he is not able to live with his **28.**_____. Good education and wealthy family from birth do not make Tom capable of standing on his own feet. Instead, he lacks **29.**_____ skills needed for survival, ultimately accepting 50 pounds from Lady Bellaston.

So for those who are still **30.**_____ of your friends' rich parents, you might as well have to focus on what you can do at every key decision, making it **31.**_____ beneficial to the next step of your life. Once you have become greater and greater, you will find that the world is a better place. You will even notice that Goddess of Fate makes a **32.**_____ smile at you.

聽讀整合　參考答案

Test 5

1. choices
2. decisions
3. inferior
4. glamorous
5. deliberation
6. intern
7. tenure
8. required
9. mortifying
10. dissipates
11. adventure
12. disagreement
13. trajectory
14. expenses
15. generosity
16. suggestion

17. visceral
19. footsteps
21. intelligence
23. incompetent
25. discontinue
27. effaces
29. professional
31. tremendously

18. terminates
20. qualification
22. anatomy
24. hefty
26. wonderful
28. co-father
30. jealous
32. light

Part 1

Part 2
聽力填空題

Part 3

Part 4

Part 5

Part 6

聽讀整合 TEST 6

The fact that no third person must **1.**_____ touch on other people's love affairs is a fundamental **2.**_____ for people who are in love, yet meddling, out of **3.**_____, protection and other factors is **4.**_____ seen in reality. Among them, parents can be said to be the most frequent **5.**_____ to their kid's marriage or love affairs. Parents may hold different ideas when it comes to this topic. Regret has often happened after years of marriage with someone, making it reasonable for parents to **6.**_____. Gerald in *Gone with the Wind* has chosen to inform his child, Scarlett, whereas Mr. Brooke, Dorothea's uncle has adopted a **7.**_____ approach. However, the **8.**_____ for both Scarlett and Dorothea has remained the same, making us wonder what should someone do when there is actually a need to make an interference.

"It is as fatal as a murder or any other 9._____ **that divides people."** However, in *Drop Dead Diva*, Jane's coworker Owen and Kim, have decided to meddle in Jane's love affairs when they know Ian Holt, a cold-blooded killer is dating their colleague. Kim, who used to have some **10.**_____ with Jane, because at the law firm they are in direct **11.**_____ with Jane, now is willing to pay US 10,000 dollars to Ian Holt for him to go away. Ian Holt rejects the offer and then is met with Owen's direct **12.**_____ of his conduct. It seems that Kim and Owen are doing the right things, but they are still not in the **13.**_____ with either one of them. It's best if Kim and Owen just stay out of this.

Part 1

Part 2
聽
力
填
空
題

Part 3

Part 4

Part 5

Part 6

To go deeper into the story, Grayson comes closer to getting married to Jane, but unfortunately, he dies after an **14.**_____ in the hospital. Grayson hits the return **15.**_____, so that he gets a second chance to live. Ironically, his soul is placed in Ian Holt's body, making his identity **16.**_____ for others.

The **17.**_____ outside the cell tells Jane that a **18.**_____ killer like Ian Holt does not have the right to get a second chance. Jane, now being Ian's lawyer, argues on Ian's **19.**_____ that there should be a stay of **20.**_____ and she believes that Ian is innocent. Despite the fact that there are no new facts sustaining a stay, Ian comes up with the idea that there should be a new death warrant. Without the new death warrant, the new execution will be **21.**_____, making Ian capable of living for another 24 hours. Having an **22.**_____ of sufficient reason to get Ian **23.**_____ in a day is insane. Owen and Jane can only **24.**_____ the idea that makes Ian stay life imprison. However, Ian demands they fight for a claim of actual **25.**_____ because letters and other evidence makes Ian truly believe his innocence.

During the penalty of the trial, the victim's wife Cheryl did **26.**_____ on Ian's behalf that he was innocent. Cheryl implored the judge that Ian, a man convicted of killing her husband, should be set free. Cheryl's **27.**_____ does make Owen and Jane rethink about things happening during the night at the club. They eventually figure out the real killer is Breeman, resulting in a happy ending for Jane and Ian. After the **28.**_____, Jane and Ian's love affair may sound like an **29.**_____ combination. Even though Ian's name has been cleared, others might still think Ian has mistaken his **30.**_____ for Jane as true love. Jane cannot handle her **31.**_____ with the loss of Grayson, so she starts the relationship with Ian.

In *Middlemarch*, there is a great divide between Dorothea and Will if they have to be with each other. The long-enduring **32.**_____ problems for all generations: The rich and the poor. There is bound to be a great hindrance for the two, even if Dorothea does not care about the money. It is true that **33.**_____ will soon wear out two people's love after their marriage. Like what's stated before, the best thing we can do is congratulations for any couple and let nature take its course. After all, it is not your marriage, so mind your own business. People's relationships will soon end the moment one of the parties cannot endure, and there is no need for one to act like a judge, **34.**_____ trivial matters happening in other people's marriage.

聽讀整合 參考答案

Test 6

1. directly
2. respect
3. curiosity
4. commonly
5. disturbance
6. interfere
7. liberal
8. outcome
9. horror
10. quarrels
11. competition
12. opposition

13. relationship
14. operation
15. button
16. questionable
17. janitor
18. ruthless
19. behalf
20. execution
21. postponed
22. excogitation
23. acquitted
24. surmise
25. guiltlessness
26. testify
27. testimony
28. release
29. eccentric
30. gratitude
31. grief
32. unsolved
33. destitution
34. arbitrating

Part 1

Part 2

聽
力
填
空
題

Part 3

Part 4

Part 5

Part 6

Most people have less of **1.**_____ vision, focusing their attention on how to be financially independent, but in today's world, **2.**_____ among large, profit-driven companies is so common, lots of people are not able to secure high-paying jobs as they have been used to. What makes things worse is that prices of **3.**_____ are getting increasingly higher, resulting in not having enough cash to live an ideal life. Some sit in their rented **4.**_____ in **5.**_____ melancholy, whereas others fix their minds on getting the inheritance from parents so that they do not have to worry about money.

In *North and South*, Margaret is lucky enough to get a large **6.**_____, making her an even better pick among single men. However, not all cases of inheritance end up with a **7.**_____ result. In *Drop Dead Diva*, Violet Harwood is an heiress with a great deal of fortune. Unluckily, Violet Harwood's parents create a trust that is **8.**_____ by her brother. Without the approbation of the trustee, Violet Harwood is unable to use the money freely. Violet Harwood's plan of using her fortune on the shelter house has **9.**_____ because her brother controls the expenses. Fortunately, Violet Harwood's lawyer comes up with the idea of the dead-hand clause.

The **10.**_____ of the dead-hand clause is to prevent dead people from exercising control from the grave beyond a single generation. The trick is Violet Harwood's parents cannot **11.**_____ her to give the **12.**_____ watch to someone who

Part 1

Part 2

聽力填空題

Part 3

Part 4

Part 5

Part 6

did not exist when they died, making the whole trust **13.**_____
. "What's good for the goose is good for the gander", so the
inheritance shall be **14.**_____ equally between Violet Harwood
and her brother.

In *Middlemarch*, the idea of the dead-hand clause has also been
used by Mr. Casaubon. "But well-being is not to be **15.**_____
by ample, independent **16.**_____ of property; on the contrary,
occasions might arise in which such possession might expose her
to the more danger."

It might be reasonable to **17.**_____ that Mr. Casaubon has the
18._____ to protect his wife from men's **19.**_____, but a
closer inspection can reveal his **20.**_____. The inheritance will
be the control of his wife even after his death. Mrs. Casaubon
will lose the inheritance if she is married with Will, making her
unable to tie the knot with the person she truly loves. Mr.
Casaubon's intent can also be **21.**_____ as an insult to his own
wife, who remains loyal to him while he is alive. Mrs. Casaubon
has never been a **22.**_____ young lady. Eventually, she figures
out true love **23.**_____ all things, including a great deal of
inheritance, and has a happy ending with Will.

In *Wuthering Heights*, Edgar Linton is aware of Mr. Heathcliff's
24._____ of claiming his private property and Thrushcross
Grange. Originally, Edgar Linton wants Miss Cathy to use the
property at her **25.**_____, but later he **26.**_____ the will,
putting it in the trust, for Miss Cathy to use and for her
descendants to utilize after Miss Cathy dies. If Linton dies, the
property will not go to Mr. Heathcliff. In *Wuthering Heights*,

"Earnshaw had **27.**_____ every yard of land he owned for cash to supply his mania for gaming; and he, Heathcliff, was the **28.**_____." Mr. Heathcliff not only gets Earnshaw's inheritance, Wuthering Heights, making Hareton, Earnshaw's son, **29.**_____, but also the estate of Edgar Linton. Even if Mr. Heathcliff's son, Linton dies, Catherine will not be the heir. Miss Cathy is reluctant to believe Mr. Heathcliff is a bad guy. According to the will of the previous Linton generation, Thrushcross Grange will only be **30.**_____ by a male descendant, so Mr. Heathcliff's **31.**_____ is foxy and smart enough to let his son Linton get married with Miss Cathy.

Resolving an inheritance issue is not as easy as it seems. Sometimes it involves several people who **32.**_____ vie for the property in court. Margaret in *North and South* is probably the happiest person that gets the **33.**_____ money, lending it to Mr. Thornton for a loan. Mrs. Casaubon's great wisdom of not valuing the property too highly is also very **34.**_____. It is true that more money only creates more problems. We can only pray that we will not be ending like Mr. Heathcliff, living unhappily till his death.

Part 1

Part 2
聽
力
填
空
題

Part 3

Part 4

Part 5

Part 6

Test 7

1. outward
2. downsizing
3. commodities
4. apartments
5. lethargic
6. inheritance
7. pleasant
8. regulated
9. shattered
10. definition
11. mandate
12. antique
13. ineffective
14. distributed
15. secured
16. possession
17. deduce
18. foresight
19. deception
20. agenda
21. perceived
22. materialistic
23. transcends
24. intention
25. disposal
26. ameliorates
27. mortgaged
28. mortgagee
29. moneyless
30. inherited
31. contemplation
32. maliciously
33. inherited
34. admirable

Wealthy or poor, **1.**_____ has been tightly linked with people's life. Poor people wish to multiply their money through **2.**_____ investment opportunities, whereas rich people set their sights on getting richer by utilizing **3.**_____ information. As a saying goes, the purpose of a novel is a **4.**_____ of reality. Great lessons can be learned from the following three novels: *Of Human Bondage*, *North and South*, and *Vanity Fair*.

It is understood that a poor investment can lead someone to wait in line for a free **5.**_____ quicker than one might think. In *Vanity Fair*, an inferior judgment in investment soon makes a rich person, like Mr. Sedley, bankrupt. **"Funds had risen when he 6._____ they would fall." "His bills were protested, his act of 7._____ formal. The house and furniture of Russell Square were seized and sold up, and he and his family were thrust away."**

Similar to the situation of Mr. Sedley in *Vanity Fair*, Mr. Thornton's condition in *North and South* shares the same fate. Both start out as rich from the beginning of the novel, but eventually the **8.**_____ of life emerges. Mr. Thornton's problem lies in his use of **9.**_____. Using it in new machinery and **10.**_____ results in not having enough cash for emergencies during a bad economy. During the economic **11.**_____, the value of all large stocks plunges, and Mr. Thornton's shares almost halve.

This corresponds to a wise saying from Nelly Dean in *Wuthering*

Part 1

Part 2

聽
力
填
空
題

Part 3

Part 4

Part 5

Part 6

Heights that no one can **12.**_____ one's wealth throughout the entire life. One cannot always be rich, so using one's richness or wealth as a **13.**_____ when it comes to choosing a mate is not wise. Still, being rich is an **14.**_____ quality in the market because wealth almost equals the sense of **15.**_____. Henry in *North and South* provides us with the same insight. Margaret's inherited property is just a part of her. Even though it means that Margaret's money can instantly make him **16.**_____, that should not be the criterion for choosing a life-partner. However, both Mr. Thornton and Henry have the **17.**_____ of using Margaret's **18.**_____ to assist their own business. As in the case of Mr. Thornton, he lacks enough money to keep the company going, while Henry needs enough **19.**_____ to start the law business.

It's true that **"those who are happy and successful themselves are too apt to make light of the 20.**_____ **of others."** Ultimately, Margaret is willing to loan eighteen thousand and fifty-seven pounds to Mr. Thornton.

21._____ fate makes the story a happy ending, but not everyone is as lucky as Margaret in *North and South* and Philip in *Of Human Bondage*. Margaret inherits the money and **22.**_____ worth 42,000 pounds, while Philip has an inheritance enough for him to finish medical school, making his fate much better than the rest of his classmates. Philip can focus all his attention on the study. Inheritance or extra money through other means can be good or bad really depends on the use of the person. In the case of Philip, it is definitely a bad thing. However, Philip **23.**_____

some of the money on girls instead of spending it on what's **24.**_____, and worst of all, he gambles his tuition fees and money for the daily use on the stock market. **"History was being made, and the process was so 25.**_____ **that it seemed absurd that it should touch the life of an 26.**_____ **medical student."** Selling shares now during the market **27.**_____ would mean that he can only have 80 pounds left, making him unable to continue his medical school.

It can be concluded that investment money should come from the sources that will not **28.**_____ one's living; otherwise, there is going to be a disaster. No matter how lucky a person can be, not being able to control the spending can result in serious damage in life (like Philip). Being too **29.**_____ can also have the same fate like Mr. Sedley, losing enormous wealth and his hard-to-build enterprise. Working **30.**_____ and diligently can still end up like Mr. Thornton, lacking enough money to keep the company **31.**_____. **32.**_____ of one's life trajectory are too unlikely, but what we can do is do our part and not investing recklessly or dreaming of becoming a rich billionaire in a day.

聽讀整合 參考答案

Test 8

1. investment
2. numerous
3. lucrative
4. reflection
5. soup
6. calculated

7. bankruptcy
9. capital
11. recession
13. criterion
15. security
17. contemplation
19. currency
21. Reversed
23. squanders
25. significant
27. plunge
29. speculative
31. afloat

8. vicissitude
10. expansion
12. guarantee
14. irresistible
16. succeed
18. fortune
20. misfortune
22. property
24. necessary
26. obscure
28. influence
30. industriously
32. Predictions

Part 1

Part 2
聽力填空題

Part 3

Part 4

Part 5

Part 6

TEST 1

There are **1.**_____ love songs that are gripping and make people **2.**_____. Among them, topics related to "love someone who truly loves you" and "choose the person you love" are the most popular. How to make the right choice and select the ideal life partner can be quite difficult. Often a lot of sayings on social media **3.**_____ and views of those **4.**_____ in the show are misleading and are often rife with claims that don't stand up to **5.**_____. Luckily, by reading British romance novels, like *Far from the Madding Crowd*, we can have a better understanding about making smarter choices. Three promising guys in *Far from the Madding Crowd* can be seen as the **6.**_____ version of the real life. Three candidates are Oak, Boldwood, and Troy.

As anyone can remember from high school and college, most girls would go for the handsome and bad boy types, simply because they want to be **7.**_____. They deem the guy with **8.**_____ and integrity as boring and easily controlled, but that pushes them away from real happiness. That is also the main reason why Oak is not accepted by heroine, Bathsheba at the very beginning of the novel. Oak has several **9.**_____ traits that make him an ideal husband for Bathsheba. He is kind-hearted and has a real passion for Bathsheba. Oak proclaims that he will work twice as hard after marriage.

So far, this has been about all the readers' **10.**_____ of him. What about Boldwood's account about Oak? Near the very end of the novel, Boldwood has a heart-felt **11.**_____ with Oak, when Boldwood has the sense that his **12.**_____ with Bathsheba is around the corner. "You have behaved like a man, and I, as a sort of successful rival- successful partly through your goodness of heart I should like definitely to show my sense of your friendship under what must have been a great pain to you." As for Boldwood, he has a crazy **13.**_____ for Bathsheba that separates him apart from both Troy and Oak, and he is also the man who can wait for the girl for six years. At a much later time, a locked box that contains expensive silks, satins, poplins, velvets, muffs (sable and ermine), and a case of jewellery that includes four heavy gold, bracelets and several lockets and rings can symbolize the importance of Bathsheba in Boldwood's heart.

In the middle part of the story, Bathsheba chooses Troy to be her husband, and Troy seems to fall into the **14.**_____ type. Troy can be good for a **15.**_____, but not for a long-lasting relationship. However, Troy does have his charm. Troy volunteers to sweep and shake bees into the hive to impress Bathsheba. Troy further demonstrates his **16.**_____ in their next appointment, creating a special moment to **17.**_____ a kiss on Bathsheba. The sense of **18.**_____ and surprise prevails, making her act on **19.**_____ and without reason.

According to the author, Troy is good at **20.**_____ and superficiality so that ethical defects will not be perceived by women, whereas Oak stands in a sharp contrast with Troy because Oak's **21.**_____ can be apparently seen. Beneath the **22.**_____ of Troy, there are flaws most people will not notice.

Part 1

Part 2

Part 3

字彙實力檢測。

Part 4

Part 5

Part 6

However, no matter how good one is at varnish, he will eventually show the true colors. "Every voice in nature was **23.**_____ in bespeaking change." Unprotected ricks equal to 750 pounds of food. The storm is coming closer, but Troy is nowhere to be seen. According to Oak, Troy is asleep in the barn, **24.**_____ all the harm that the weather might do to the crop and the consequence that will cost their barn. Oak's **25.**_____ to protect the crop shows his true love for Bathsheba. He uses his actions to validate the love. Troy; however, demonstrates his indifference, making Bathsheba realize Troy as a person.

Boldwood loves Bathsheba deeply by wanting to provide her material comfort as a way to possess a beauty. Oak, on the other hand, wants to love Bathsheba by using all his life. Troy seems to have an **26.**_____ on Bathsheba because of Bathsheba's wealth and barn. Bathsheba at first gets married with Troy by choosing the one she truly loves, and till the end she figures out it is the one who truly loves her that she should be with......

A	swordsmanship	**B**	diversion
C	shortcomings	**D**	neglecting
E	principles	**F**	imprint
G	scrutiny	**H**	prospect
I	concealment	**J**	confession
K	summarized	**L**	admirable
M	numerous	**N**	tamed

Part 1

Part 2

Part 3
字彙實力檢測

Part 4

Part 5

Part 6

O	unanimous	**P**	novelty
Q	devotion	**R**	platforms
S	resonate	**T**	veneer
U	perception	**V**	celebrities
W	untamed	**X**	impulse
Y	endeavor	**Z**	agenda

參考答案

1. M	**2.** S
3. R	**4.** V
5. G	**6.** K
7. N	**8.** E
9. L	**10.** U
11. J	**12.** H
13. Q	**14.** W
15. B	**16.** A
17. F	**18.** P
19. X	**20.** I
21. C	**22.** T
23. O	**24.** D
25. Y	**26.** Z

TEST 2

"I believe that I have no enemy on earth, and none surely would have been so 1._____ as to destroy me 2._____." A saying from *Frankenstein* seems to convey the message of Justine's viewpoint that men **3._____** possess a good heart. While various people may hold different views on this statement, Justine's **4._____** about the devil who frames her is entirely correct. The devil has a good heart from the start, but Victor, the main character, resists **5._____** the devil as his **6._____** or his own baby, resulting in a **7._____** mind for the devil. There has been some mental separation between the two. Acceptance and refusal are two **8._____** concepts, and feeling loved is essential for anyone's personal development. The devil's **9._____** behavior results from getting rejected and not being amended. Not getting loved makes someone feel neglected, unaccepted, and being excluded. All these factors engender serious **10._____** behavior that creates some of the social crimes.

Education seems to be the key to amending people's mind. As the story progresses, the devil demands the creation of an identity similar to him so that he can find someone to love and to be loved. Victor at first **11._____** another attempt to create a new one for him, then out of the blue shifting into thinking that **12._____** the spouse for him **13._____** with producing a monster. He can barely handle the devil, let alone dealing with two bad-looking creatures. The novel itself conveys several important messages essential for human beings to pay serious attention so that more **14._____** problems can be avoided, thus making it especially great and eternally **15._____**. A lot of murder crimes relating to love can be evaded if proper education and giving others more love have seriously been paid attention to. One does not have to take **16._____** too seriously. As a saying goes, **"things that seem 17._____ at the time usually do work out for the rest."** Sometimes it does mean that God has a better idea, wanting to give you something much better.

As can be seen in another classic, *Middlemarch*, God certainly wants James to have not just someone better, but someone more suitable for him. In towns, neighbors and farmers have the **18._____** for Celia over Dorothea simply because Celia is more **19._____**, innocent, clever, and sophisticated. Dorothea has a quality of not self-admiring, thinking Celia is more charming than she is. James, on the other hand, has a crush on Dorothea. **"He felt that he had chosen the one who was in all respects the 20._____ ; and a man 21._____ likes to look forward to having the best."** However, James does not even have any chance with Dorothea. His rival Mr. Casaubon does not have to do much and wins over the heart of Dorothea in such a short time. Luckily, James does not take this as a defeat or as something that will crush him. Getting rejected does not make someone a failure as most people would think. It is one's mindset that makes a man. Some would writhe under the idea of failure and rejection and then do the harm to the rival, hurt themselves, or cause quite a damage to someone you love. The thing is you

Part 1

Part 2

Part 3

字彙實力檢測

Part 4

Part 5

Part 6

do not have to act like that. Other people, including Dorothea's uncle, are shocked at Dorothea's choice of a man, not choosing James as a husband. Celia has a feeling that James will be a great husband, but from her **22._____**, they will not be a good fit. Dorothea's choice may be good for both of them. It should not be interpreted as seriously harming someone. James claims that Dorothea should wait until she is mature enough to make the decision and is mad at Dorothea's choice, but eventually he gladly accepts this news. It does mean that more **23._____** fruits are waiting for him definitely.

As the story progresses to a much later time, his feelings of getting rejected have gone already, having been replaced by getting engaged with Celia. **"His 24._____ love had not turned to 25._____ ; its death had made sweet odors – floating memories that clung with a 26._____ effect to Dorothea."** True love deserves some time to wait......

A	atrocious	**B**	saccharine
C	superior	**D**	disregarded
E	valuable	**F**	inherently
G	acknowledging	**H**	creation
I	disastrous	**J**	equates
K	approachable	**L**	wantonly
M	antithetical	**N**	rejections
O	concurs	**P**	distorted

Part 1

Part 2

Part 3
字彙實力檢測

Part 4

Part 5

Part 6

Q	predilection	**R**	psychological
S	naturally	**T**	conjecture
U	observations	**V**	manufacturing
W	wicked	**X**	societal
Y	consecrating	**Z**	bitterness

參考答案

1. W	**2.** L
3. F	**4.** T
5. G	**6.** H
7. P	**8.** M
9. A	**10.** R
11. O	**12.** V
13. J	**14.** X
15. E	**16.** N
17. I	**18.** Q
19. K	**20.** C
21. S	**22.** U
23. B	**24.** D
25. Z	**26.** Y

"It would have been cruel in Miss Havisham, horribly cruel, to practice on the **1.**_____ of a poor boy, and to torture me through all these years with a vain hope and idle **2.**_____, if she had reflected on the **3.**_____ of what she did."

In *Great Expectations*, Miss Havisham's **4.**_____ wealth does not give her the joy that she is in desperate need of. Miss Havisham's use of the little girl, Estella, to torture the boy that she hires, on the other hand, fulfills her **5.**_____ and the sense of **6.**_____
. As a saying goes, pain and conflict only bring more pain and conflict. Not letting go of the past rigorously hurts or erodes Miss Havisham's body and soul.

Miss Havisham's hurt can be traced back to an incident happening about twenty years ago. Pip's encounter with both Magwitch and Compeyson paves the way for a further development. Magwitch, a poor and unlucky guy, under the **7.**_____ of fortune, meets with self-pretentious, handsome, **8.**_____ Compeyson. The chance encounter leads Magwitch to learn the truth about Compeyson and his partner, Arthur. The **9.**_____ from a rich lady, which is believed to be Miss Havisham, earns them a great deal of fortune. However, Compeyson's **10.**_____ spending habits cannot keep up with the money he earns from doing the dirty things.

Doing bad things, and not getting caught for a while seems **11.**_____, but committing a list of crimes and not getting captured will be deemed unlikely. Pretty soon, both are taken to court for a trial. They both are charged with putting stolen notes in **12.**_____. Compeyson demands that they go **13.**_____ ways, and Compeyson smart thinking does work. Magwitch can only get Mr. Jaggers as a lawyer for the defense.

The "birth" issue and one's education also weigh **14.**_____ on criminals in court, making Compeyson's sentence the half of Magwitch's. Magwitch has been unfairly judged at the court and eventually gets 14 years in prison. They are in the same prison ship, but Magwitch cannot get closer to Compeyson. Fleeing the prison ship leads to the encounter of Pip, the main character, and Compeyson. This time Magwitch has enough time to **15.**_____ Compeyson's face to get revenge.

Magwitch and Compeyson will try every way to bring each other down. Compeyson can report there is a **16.**_____ that flees from the prison ship. Magwitch and Pip's flee then encounters The Hamburg, the steamer, sailing swiftly towards them. People on the steamer demand the **17.**_____ to capture the person wrapping with a cloak on Pip's ship. As Magwitch goes behind the person who tries to seize him, he has the time to tear off another person with a **18.**_____ on the steamer to verify whether his identity is Compeyson. Compeyson is in shock and then waddles. Thereafter, they have a struggle, falling into the river. Other guys trying to seize Magwitch eventually cause the **19.**_____ of the Pip's ship. Magwitch is found seriously injured, and with no traces of Compeyson. Pip has no reason to doubt Magwitch's account of what just happened because it is the

Part 1

Part 2

Part 3

字彙實力檢測

Part 4

Part 5

Part 6

same as that of the officer who steers the ship. At Police Court, it is revealed that Compeyson eventually falls into the river and is found dead. Compeyson and Arthur, Miss Havisham's brother, all pay the price. Arthur dies from serious illness right before the **20.**_____ of both Magwitch and Compeyson.

Miss Havisham's distorted mind resulting from the harm caused by Compeyson and Arthur could totally be cured if she knew the notion of "what comes around goes around" and "unjust is doomed to **21.**_____." Karma will eventually do the justice for her. Miss Havisham eventually comes to her senses right before her death that she has done quite a **22.**_____ to another human being, Estella.

"That she had done a **23.**_____ thing in taking an **24.**_____ child to mould into the form that her wild **25.**_____, spurned affection, and wounded pride, found **26.**_____ in, I knew full well......

A	normal	**B**	deception
C	refugee	**D**	assistance
E	grievous	**F**	capsizing
G	destruction	**H**	sentence
I	satisfaction	**J**	enormous
K	pursuit	**L**	impressionable
M	separate	**N**	gravity
O	erudite	**P**	whim

Part 1

Part 2

Part 3

字彙實力檢測

Part 4

Part 5

Part 6

Q damage	**R** heavily
S cloak	**T** circulation
U smash	**V** susceptibility
W lavish	**X** guidance
Y resentment	**Z** vengeance

參考答案

1. V	**2.** K
3. N	**4.** J
5. P	**6.** I
7. X	**8.** O
9. B	**10.** W
11. A	**12.** T
13. M	**14.** R
15. U	**16.** C
17. D	**18.** S
19. F	**20.** H
21. G	**22.** Q
23. E	**24.** L
25. Y	**26.** Z

TEST 4

In our daily life, we rarely take the idea or wisdom from time-enduring classics into account, so we are still struggling in several aspects of our life. The **1.**_____ of *Vanity Fair* ring **2.**_____ true to most readers. By taking an in-depth look into how Becky capitalizes every opportunity to get the desired outcome, we can probably have a better life. Not having parents and being poor are two main factors that put heroine of *Vanity Fair*, Becky Sharp into a **3.**_____ position. Since most girls have their parents' assistance to **4.**_____ matters with the young man to change the fate, Becky has to do this all on her own, and one does not have to be extremely clever to know the truth that getting married with a wealthy husband will more or less make one's later life a lot smoother. The chance event comes when one of her **5.**_____ friends, Amelia invites her to stay at her house for a week before Becky moves on to do the private tutor job.

Becky soon finds out a **6.**_____ opportunity that Amelia's brother, Joseph is still single. Becky is ready to put the move on Joseph, but she is not yet ready. Mr. Sedley **7.**_____ wants Becky to try some curry with cayenne pepper and a chili that Becky **8.**_____ cannot put up with, and then Mr. Sedley enjoys this show along with his son, Joseph, and also informs his son that Becky has set her sights on him. Then all things have been in Becky's favor, but George Osborne considers Becky and Joseph a **9.**_____, frightening Joseph for a bit. Osborne's intervention ends Becky's prospect of marrying with Joseph **10.**_____.

Part 1

Part 2

Part 3

字彙實力檢測

Part 4

Part 5

Part 6

However, this setback does not **11.**_____ young Rebecca from reaching her goal. It does mean she has not yet mastered the art of **12.**_____. Becky embarks on her journey of being the **13.**_____ of Sir Pitt's two daughters, making her much closer to a real **14.**_____ circle. Her goal has been **15.**_____: to find a rich husband. Winning the heart over Sir Pitt's two daughters and being baronet's **16.**_____ at Queen's Crawley are the first step towards Rebecca's success, and the mastery of the **17.**_____ the second, the marriage with Rawdon Crawley the third.

Distinguished **18.**_____ can certainly make up for poor birth as in the case of Becky. Becky earns the **19.**_____ from Miss Crawley that she has more brains than half the shire, and "as her equal." Sir Pitt wants Becky to be his bride by saying **"you've got more brains in your little vinger than any baronet's wife in the country."**, but Becky's true success is to tie the knot with Rawdon Crawley, who will inherit most of Miss Crawley's fortune. Rawdon Crawley's viewpoints about Becky are **20.**_____ with those of his aunt, Miss Crawley and his father, Sir Pitt. He has met multiple clippers, but has never encountered someone as witty as his wife, Becky. These correspond to several notions mentioned in one of the bestsellers, *The Wealth Elite*. It is not about the **21.**_____ or Luck. One does need to have the exact DNA to keep money or acquire more wealth. In one of the British classics, *Treasure Island*, an idea relating to this has also been put forward at the very end of the chapter that it is not the amount of the money that you get. It is about one's **22.**_____.

The following development does not let Rawdon Crawley down as Becky exhibits more of her inborn talent. Becky seizes the moment during the war to make a fortune by selling a horse to Joseph. Wealthy people aspiring to flee also lack the key **23.**_____ , the horse. Even Lord Bareacres is willing to pay the price for two horses under this circumstance. The sum is enormous enough to be considered a fortune to Becky. With the money and the sale of the **24.**_____ of Rawdon's effects, and her pension as a widow, she will be financially independent, not having to worry about money for her entire life. Later, it is believed that the value of two horses equals a **25.**_____ life in Paris a year for both Rawdon Crawley and Becky.

The couple's reunion after war brings more joyful news, as concealment of cash, checks, watches, and other valuables in Becky's coat reveals themselves. Becky has had **26.**_____ success even in Paris. Becky possesses an admirable quality against adversity and cruel fate, surpassing her classmates, Amelia, born into a wealthy family and with the worth of the 10,000 pounds, where she has none......

A alarmingly	**B** deception
C obviously	**D** outright
E governess	**F** settle
G storylines	**H** mesalliance
I brilliance	**J** dissuade
K confidence	**L** wealthy

Part 1

Part 2

Part 3
字彙實力檢測

Part 4

Part 5

Part 6

M	inheritance	**N**	constant
O	concordant	**P**	golden
Q	residue	**R**	disadvantaged
S	transportation	**T**	celebrity
U	nature	**V**	accolade
W	hypocrisy	**X**	deliberately
Y	unprecedented	**Z**	luxurious

參考答案

1. G	**2.** A
3. R	**4.** F
5. L	**6.** P
7. X	**8.** C
9. H	**10.** D
11. J	**12.** B
13. E	**14.** T
15. N	**16.** K
17. W	**18.** I
19. V	**20.** O
21. M	**22.** U
23. S	**24.** Q
25. Z	**26.** Y

People are so focusing on "birth" that they forget it is a series of choices that eventually make or break someone. Bad decisions in every key life moment can drag someone down the path, leading to an **1.**_____ outcome. The term "birth" will be just **2.**_____ from the start and disastrous in the end.

In *Of Human Bondage*, with some **3.**_____, Philip's first life decision is to be an **4.**_____ at the office of Messers. Herbert Carter & Co. in which his uncle and friends believe that under the **5.**_____, Philip will learn professional skills enough for him to stand on his own feet and make a living. **"Every profession, and every trade, 6.**_____ **length of time, and what was worse, money."** However, Philip is just like some of the twentysomethings, and not yet understands the **7.**_____ conviction that three years at the first job are quite an important step for your next job.

Bad advice from one of his friends also **8.**_____ his valuable twentysomething years. **"I cannot imagine you sitting in an office over a ledger." "My feeling is that one should look upon life as an 9.**_____**, one should burn with the hard, gem-like flame, and one should take risks, one should expose oneself to danger."** His friend's belief in Philip's ability in art does not equal with how the reality views about him as a person. Despite the Vicar's **10.**_____ for Philip's life **11.**_____ change, Philip insists on going to Paris to learn art. Still Philip has to wait for a

Part 1

Part 2

Part 3

字彙實力檢測

Part 4

Part 5

Part 6

year to get his small inheritance from his father.

Aunt Louisa gives Philip her savings, an amount worth around a hundred pounds to pay for Philip's living **12.**_____ in Paris. Her **13.**_____ only lasts for a short time, and soon is replaced by the young man's visions in Paris. Eventually, the **14.**_____ of the great artist proves that Philip's uncle is right all along. "Take your courage in both hands and try your luck at something else" The heart-felt, **15.**_____ advice ends Philip's two-year journey in Paris and **16.**_____ his dream of becoming an artist.

Perseverance is what Philip obviously lacks. His next step is to follow in his father's **17.**_____ to become a doctor. With the **18.**_____ of entering a medical school, he chooses St. Luke's. For people entering on the medical profession, there are all kinds, and readers have yet to know how Philip will become. Philip believes that with his **19.**_____ that he will scrape through the test, but in fact he fails at the **20.**_____ examination, making him among the list of the **21.**_____. Love affairs distract Philip too much attention, when he should be focusing on the study. His worst decision is to involve himself with the stock market. Even though at first, he does have several wins, he eventually pays a hefty price for that. He writes a letter to his uncle asking for money, but is turned down. Without enough money, he has to find the job to pay daily expenses and **22.**_____ his medical studies. He cannot believe that he screws things up, changing his entire life trajectory.

In Philip's case, the birth does not make his life **23.**_____. His father's small inheritance should have been a great assistance for him, but his poor decision **24.**_____ what has been given to him.

In *The History of Tom Jones, a Founding*, Tom's birth does not give him the upper hand when he is not able to live with his co-father. Good education and wealthy family from birth do not make Tom capable of standing on his own feet. Instead, he lacks **25.**_____ skills needed for survival, ultimately accepting 50 pounds from Lady Bellaston.

So for those who are still jealous of your friends' rich parents, you might as well have to focus on what you can do at every key decision, making it tremendously beneficial to the next step of your life. Once you have become greater and greater, you will find that the world is a better place. You will even notice that Goddess of Fate makes a **32.**_____ smile at you.

A	qualification	**B**	glamorous
C	trajectory	**D**	deliberation
E	tenure	**F**	adventure
G	visceral	**H**	intern
I	footsteps	**J**	disagreement
K	mortifying	**L**	required
M	wonderful	**N**	intelligence
O	dissipates	**P**	expenses
Q	effaces	**R**	suggestion

Part 1

Part 2

Part 3

字彙實力檢測

Part 4

Part 5

Part 6

S anatomy

T generosity

U professional

V terminates

W incompetent

X discontinue

Y light

Z inferior

參考答案

1. Z		**2.** B	
3. D		**4.** H	
5. E		**6.** L	
7. K		**8.** O	
9. F		**10.** J	
11. C		**12.** P	
13. T		**14.** R	
15. G		**16.** V	
17. I		**18.** A	
19. N		**20.** S	
21. W		**22.** X	
23. M		**24.** Q	
25. U		**26.** Y	

The fact that no third person must **1.**_____ touch on other people's love affairs is a fundamental **2.**_____ for people who are in love, yet meddling, out of curiosity, protection and other factors is **3.**_____ seen in reality. Among them, parents can be said to be the most frequent **4.**_____ to their kid's marriage or love affairs. Parents may hold different ideas when it comes to this topic. Regret has often happened after years of marriage with someone, making it reasonable for parents to **5.**_____. Gerald in *Gone with the Wind* has chosen to inform his child, Scarlett, whereas Mr. Brooke, Dorothea's uncle has adopted a **6.**_____ approach. However, the **7.**_____ for both Scarlett and Dorothea has remained the same, making us wonder what should someone do when there is actually a need to make an interference.

"It is as fatal as a murder or any other 8._____ **that divides people."** However, in *Drop Dead Diva*, Jane's coworker Owen and Kim, have decided to meddle in Jane's love affairs when they know Ian Holt, a cold-blooded killer is dating their colleague. Kim, who used to have some **9.**_____ with Jane, because at the law firm they are in direct **10.**_____ with Jane, now is willing to pay US 10,000 dollars to Ian Holt for him to go away. Ian Holt rejects the offer and then is met with Owen's direct **11.**_____ of his conduct. It seems that Kim and Owen are doing the right things, but they are still not in the **12.**_____ with either one of them. It's best if Kim and Owen just stay out of this.

Part 1

Part 2

Part 3

字彙實力檢測

Part 4

Part 5

Part 6

To go deeper into the story, Grayson comes closer to getting married to Jane, but unfortunately, he dies after an **13.**_____ in the hospital. Grayson hits the return button, so that he gets a second chance to live. Ironically, his soul is placed in Ian Holt's body, making his identity **14.**_____ for others.

The **15.**_____ outside the cell tells Jane that a **16.**_____ killer like Ian Holt does not have the right to get a second chance. Jane, now being Ian's lawyer, argues on Ian's behalf that there should be a stay of **17.**_____ and she believes that Ian is innocent. Despite the fact that there are no new facts sustaining a stay, Ian comes up with the idea that there should be a new death warrant. Without the new death warrant, the new execution will be **18.**_____, making Ian capable of living for another 24 hours. Having an **19.**_____ of sufficient reason to get Ian **20.**_____ in a day is insane. Owen and Jane can only **21.**_____ the idea that makes Ian stay life imprison. However, Ian demands they fight for a claim of actual **22.**_____ because letters and other evidence makes Ian truly believe his innocence.

During the penalty of the trial, the victim's wife Cheryl did **23.**_____ on Ian's behalf that he was innocent. Cheryl implored the judge that Ian, a man convicted of killing her husband, should be set free. Cheryl's **24.**_____ does make Owen and Jane rethink about things happening during the night at the club. They eventually figure out the real killer is Breeman, resulting in a happy ending for Jane and Ian. After the release, Jane and Ian's love affair may sound like an **25.**_____ combination. Even though Ian's name has been cleared, others might still think Ian has mistaken his gratitude for Jane as true love. Jane cannot handle her grief with the loss of Grayson, so she starts the relationship with Ian.

In *Middlemarch*, there is a great divide between Dorothea and Will if they have to be with each other. The long-enduring unsolved problems for all generations: The rich and the poor. There is bound to be a great hindrance for the two, even if Dorothea does not care about the money. It is true that **26.**_____ will soon wear out two people's love after their marriage. Like what's stated before, the best thing we can do is congratulations for any couple and let nature take its course. After all, it is not your marriage, so mind your own business. People's relationships will soon end the moment one of the parties cannot endure, and there is no need for one to act like a judge, arbitrating trivial matters happening in other people's marriage.

A	interfere	B	quarrels
C	postponed	D	testimony
E	outcome	F	competition
G	acquitted	H	procedure
I	eccentric	J	surmise
K	ruthless	L	horror
M	destitution	N	testify
O	directly	P	excogitation
Q	janitor	R	opposition

Part 1

Part 2

Part 3
字彙實力檢測

Part 4

Part 5

Part 6

S	disturbance	**T**	relationship
U	execution	**V**	commonly
W	guiltlessness	**X**	questionable
Y	liberal	**Z**	respect

參考答案

1. O	**2.** Z
3. V	**4.** S
5. A	**6.** Y
7. E	**8.** L
9. B	**10.** F
11. R	**12.** T
13. H	**14.** X
15. Q	**16.** K
17. U	**18.** C
19. P	**20.** G
21. J	**22.** W
23. N	**24.** D
25. I	**26.** M

TEST 7

Most people have less of **1.**_____ vision, focusing their attention on how to be financially independent, but in today's world, **2.**_____ among large, profit-driven companies is so common, lots of people are not able to secure high-paying jobs as they have been used to. What makes things worse is that prices of **3.**_____ are getting increasingly higher, resulting in not having enough cash to live an ideal life. Some sit in their rented apartments in **4.**_____ melancholy, whereas others fix their minds on getting the inheritance from parents so that they do not have to worry about money. In *North and South*, Margaret is lucky enough to get a large inheritance, making her an even better pick among single men. However, not all cases of inheritance end up with a pleasant result. In *Drop Dead Diva*, Violet Harwood is an heiress with a great deal of fortune. Unluckily, Violet Harwood's parents create a trust that is **5.**_____ by her brother. Without the approbation of the trustee, Violet Harwood is unable to use the money freely. Violet Harwood's plan of using her fortune on the shelter house has **6.**_____ because her brother controls the expenses. Fortunately, Violet Harwood's lawyer comes up with the idea of the dead-hand clause.

The definition of the dead-hand clause is to prevent dead people from exercising control from the grave beyond a single generation. The trick is Violet Harwood's parents cannot mandate her to give the **7.**_____ watch to someone who did not exist when they died, making the whole trust **8.**_____ . "What's

Part 1

Part 2

Part 3

字彙實力檢測

Part 4

Part 5

Part 6

good for the goose is good for the gander", so the inheritance shall be **9.**_____ equally between Violet Harwood and her brother. In *Middlemarch*, the idea of the dead-hand clause has also been used by Mr. Casaubon. "But well-being is not to be **10.**_____ by ample, independent **11.**_____ of property; on the contrary, occasions might arise in which such possession might expose her to the more danger."

It might be reasonable to **12.**_____ that Mr. Casaubon has the **13.**_____ to protect his wife from men's **14.**_____, but a closer inspection can reveal his agenda. The inheritance will be the control of his wife even after his death. Mrs. Casaubon will lose the inheritance if she is married with Will, making her unable to tie the knot with the person she truly loves. Mr. Casaubon's intent can also be **15.**_____ as an insult to his own wife, who remains loyal to him while he is alive. Mrs. Casaubon has never been a **16.**_____ young lady. Eventually, she figures out true love **17.**_____ all things, including a great deal of inheritance, and has a happy ending with Will.

In *Wuthering Heights*, Edgar Linton is aware of Mr. Heathcliff's **18.**_____ of claiming his private property and Thrushcross Grange. Originally, Edgar Linton wants Miss Cathy to use the property at her disposal, but later he **19.**_____ the will, putting it in the trust, for Miss Cathy to use and for her descendants to utilize after Miss Cathy dies. If Linton dies, the property will not go to Mr. Heathcliff. In *Wuthering Heights*, **"Earnshaw had 20._____ every yard of land he owned for cash to supply his mania for gaming; and he, Heathcliff, was the 21._____."** Mr.

Heathcliff not only gets Earnshaw's inheritance, Wuthering Heights, making Hareton, Earnshaw's son, **22.**_____, but also the estate of Edgar Linton. Even if Mr. Heathcliff's son, Linton dies, Catherine will not be the heir. Miss Cathy is reluctant to believe Mr. Heathcliff is a bad guy. According to the will of the previous Linton generation, Thrushcross Grange will only be inherited by a male descendant, so Mr. Heathcliff's **23.**_____ is foxy and smart enough to let his son Linton get married with Miss Cathy. Resolving an inheritance issue is not as easy as it seems. Sometimes it involves several people who **24.**_____ vie for the property in court. Margaret in *North and South* is probably the happiest person that gets the inherited money, lending it to Mr. Thornton for a loan. Mrs. Casaubon's great wisdom of not valuing the property too highly is also very **25.**_____. It is true that more money only creates more problems. We can only pray that we will not be ending like Mr. Heathcliff, living **26.**_____ till his death.

A possession		**B** ineffective	
C transcends		**D** distributed	
E deception		**F** deduce	
G perceived		**H** foresight	
I downsizing		**J** shattered	
K contemplation		**L** lethargic	
M mortgagee		**N** regulated	
O commodities		**P** mortgaged	

Part 1

Part 2

Part 3
字彙實力檢測

Part 4

Part 5

Part 6

Q	unhappily	R	maliciously
S	ameliorates	T	intention
U	materialistic	V	admirable
W	antique	X	moneyless
Y	secured	Z	outward

參考答案

1. Z	2. I
3. O	4. L
5. N	6. J
7. W	8. B
9. D	10. Y
11. A	12. F
13. H	14. E
15. G	16. U
17. C	18. T
19. S	20. P
21. M	22. X
23. K	24. R
25. V	26. Q

TEST 8

Wealthy or poor, **1.**_____ has been tightly linked with people's life. Poor people wish to multiply their money through numerous investment opportunities, whereas rich people set their sights on getting richer by utilizing **2.**_____ information. As a saying goes, the purpose of a novel is a **3.**_____ of reality. Great lessons can be learned from the following three novels: *Of Human Bondage*, *North and South*, and *Vanity Fair*.

It is understood that a poor investment can lead someone to wait in line for a free soup quicker than one might think. In *Vanity Fair*, an inferior judgment in investment soon makes a rich person, like Mr. Sedley, bankrupt. **"Funds had risen when he 4.**_____ **they would fall." "His bills were protested, his act of 5.**_____ **formal. The house and furniture of Russell Square were seized and sold up, and he and his family were thrust away."** Similar to the situation of Mr. Sedley in *Vanity Fair*, Mr. Thornton's condition in *North and South* shares the same fate. Both start out as rich from the beginning of the novel, but eventually the **6.**_____ of life emerges. Mr. Thornton's problem lies in his use of **7.**_____. Using it in new machinery and **8.**_____ results in not having enough cash for emergencies during a bad economy. During the economic **9.**_____, the value of all large stocks plunges, and Mr. Thornton's shares almost halve.

This corresponds to a wise saying from Nelly Dean in *Wuthering Heights* that no one can guarantee one's wealth throughout the

Part 1

Part 2

Part 3

字彙實力檢測

Part 4

Part 5

Part 6

entire life. One cannot always be rich, so using one's richness or wealth as a criterion when it comes to choosing a mate is not wise. Still, being rich is an **10.**_____ quality in the market because wealth almost equals the sense of **11.**_____ . Henry in *North and South* provides us with the same insight. Margaret's inherited property is just a part of her. Even though it means that Margaret's money can instantly make him succeed, that should not be the criterion for choosing a life-partner. However, both Mr. Thornton and Henry have the **12.**_____ of using Margaret's **13.**_____ to assist their own business. As in the case of Mr. Thornton, he lacks enough money to keep the company going, while Henry needs enough **14.**_____ to start the law business.

It's true that **"those who are happy and successful themselves are too apt to make light of the 15.**_____ **of others."** Ultimately, Margaret is willing to loan eighteen thousand and fifty-seven pounds to Mr. Thornton.

16._____ fate makes the story a happy ending, but not everyone is as lucky as Margaret in *North and South* and Philip in *Of Human Bondage*. Margaret inherits the money and **17.**_____ worth 42,000 pounds, while Philip has an inheritance enough for him to finish medical school, making his fate much better than the rest of his classmates. Philip can focus all his attention on the study. Inheritance or extra money through other means can be good or bad really depends on the use of the person. In the case of Philip, it is definitely a bad thing. However, Philip **18.**_____ some of the money on girls instead of spending it on what's **19.**_____ , and worst of all, he gambles his tuition fees and money for the daily use on the stock market. **"History was being made, and the process was so 20._____ that it seemed absurd that it should touch the life of an 21._____ medical student."** Selling shares now during the market plunge would mean that he can only have 80 pounds left, making him unable to continue his medical school.

It can be concluded that investment money should come from the sources that will not 22._____ one's living; otherwise, there is going to be a disaster. No matter how lucky a person can be, not being able to control the spending can result in serious damage in life (like Philip). Being too 23._____ can also have the same fate like Mr. Sedley, losing enormous wealth and his hard-to-build enterprise. Working 24._____ and diligently can still end up like Mr. Thornton, lacking enough money to keep the company 25._____. 26._____ of one's life trajectory are too unlikely, but what we can do is do our part and not investing recklessly or dreaming of becoming a rich billionaire in a day.

A lucrative		**B** contemplation	
C fortune		**D** reflection	
E currency		**F** misfortune	
G capital		**H** calculated	
I investment		**J** necessary	
K property		**L** expansion	
M vicissitude		**N** Reversed	
O speculative		**P** squanders	

Q	afloat	**R**	security
S	obscure	**T**	significant
U	Predictions	**V**	irresistible
W	industriously	**X**	influence
Y	recession	**Z**	bankruptcy

Part 1

Part 2

Part 3
字彙實力檢測

Part 4

Part 5

Part 6

參考答案

1. I	**2.** A
3. D	**4.** H
5. Z	**6.** M
7. G	**8.** L
9. Y	**10.** V
11. R	**12.** B
13. C	**14.** E
15. F	**16.** N
17. K	**18.** P
19. J	**20.** T
21. S	**22.** X
23. O	**24.** W
25. Q	**26.** U

▶▶ 摘要能力 TEST 1

| **Instruction** | MP3 **009**

　　考生可以藉由重新閱讀英文文章後提筆撰寫 200-250 字的摘要或是在閱讀文章後，以口說的方式摘要出一段英文重要訊息具備在職場能夠摘要一段英文會議內容的能力，提升職場競爭力。

NOTE

Part 1

Part 2

Part 3

Part 4

摘
要
能
力
題

Part 5

Part 6

▶▶ 參考答案

Young girls' criterion for guys are confined to appearances and certain characteristics, and is not based on personality. Praiseworthy traits pale next to untamed types, so Oak will not be chosen by the heroine.

Readers' perceptions of Oak are concordant with those of Boldwood. Oak possesses kind-heartedness, whereas Boldwood demonstrates an extreme passion. The value of Bathsheba in Boldwood's heart can be seen from luxurious items in the treasured box.

Bathsheba's choice of a man is not suitable for long term. Troy does have a way of wooing a woman by creating surprises, making Bathsheba overwhelmed. Oak cannot compete with Troy's maneuver, but time will tell the integrity of a man.

As a saying goes, actions speak louder than words. Troy's negligence of the barn and Oak's effort to protect are the contrast for Bathsheba to know who truly loves her. Three main characters demonstrate various love to Bathsheba, but true love is adjacent, awaiting us to eventually realize that.

▶▶ 摘要能力 TEST 2

| Instruction | MP3 010

　　考生可以藉由重新閱讀英文文章後提筆撰寫 200-250 字的摘要或是在閱讀文章後，以口説的方式摘要出一段英文重要訊息具備在職場能夠摘要一段英文會議內容的能力，提升職場競爭力。

Part 1

Part 2

Part 3

Part 4

摘要能力題

Part 5

Part 6

▶▶ **參考答案**

In *Frankenstein*, the topic that explores inborn goodness of a man makes us realize that the devil's benevolence is eventually gone because the way others are treating him. Not feeling loved and getting accepted make the devil's mind atypical and distorted.

Victor's other concerns for not creating the lover for the devil makes things worse, and if there is enough care, many societal problems can be avoided.

Guys plainly want to have the best, instead of thinking about suitability. Mr. Casaubon easily wins, but James is the one who possesses the growth mindset, not taking this as a failure.

Celia's observations demonstrate objectivity. Eventually, James gets the love he needs, removing past rejected pungency. True love is worth the wait.

▶▶ 摘要能力 TEST 3

| Instruction | MP3 011

　　考生可以藉由重新閱讀英文文章後提筆撰寫 200-250 字的摘要或是在閱讀文章後，以口說的方式摘要出一段英文重要訊息具備在職場能夠摘要一段英文會議內容的能力，提升職場競爭力。

NOTE

Part 1

Part 2

Part 3

Part 4

摘
要
能
力
題

Part 5

Part 6

▶▶ 參考答案

Lengthy narration can be narrowed into Arthur and Compeyson's move on Miss Havisham's money. Deception works earning them a great deal of fortune, but they cannot retain the fortune. However, Miss Havisham suffers and then uses Estella as a way to make her mind appeased.

As a saying goes, criminals will always get caught. The charge drags both Compeyson and Magwitch to court; however, one's schooling and birth are taken into account, making Compeyson's sentence lesser than it appears.

Compeyson and Magwitch's feud does not end until after their flee from the prison. Their encounter on the ship leads to the capsizing of the ship and Compeyson's falling into the river, ending the life of Compeyson. Compeyson and Arthur end up with a tragic outcome.

Two wise proverbs can totally save Miss Havisham from suffering the agony and Estella will have a happy childhood. Forgiveness really is the lesson for someone like Miss Havisham.

▶ 摘要能力 TEST 4

| Instruction | MP3 012

考生可以藉由重新閱讀英文文章後提筆撰寫 200-250 字的摘要或是在閱讀文章後，以口說的方式摘要出一段英文重要訊息具備在職場能夠摘要一段英文會議內容的能力，提升職場競爭力。

NOTE

Part 1

Part 2

Part 3

Part 4

摘要能力題

Part 5

Part 6

▶▶ 參考答案

Not having parents to assist makes Becky Sharp's future prospect disadvantageous. Still, knowing how to seize the moment makes her back on the track, when there is an invitation from a wealthy friend.

Becky's first setback is the interference from her friend's father, Mr. Sedley. Despite the fact that chance favors Becky at last, Osborne's intervention ends her dream. This does not deter Becky from getting to the top, and three goals of her will make her rich.

Becky's talent wins the heart of three aristocrats: Miss Crawley, Sir Pitt, and Rawdon Crawley. Becky's story is the living proof of success and is backed up by one of the bestsellers, *The Wealth Elite* and *Treasure Island*. One's inborn talent is the key.

Becky's exploitation of selling the horse makes her rich. With her inherited money and pension, and cash, she will not have to worry about money any more. Despite her lack of good birth from the start, Becky's natures make her transcend her counterpart, Amelia.

▶▶ 摘要能力 TEST 5

| Instruction | MP3 013

　　考生可以藉由重新閱讀英文文章後提筆撰寫 200-250 字的摘要或是在閱讀文章後，以口說的方式摘要出一段英文重要訊息具備在職場能夠摘要一段英文會議內容的能力，提升職場競爭力。

Part 1

Part 2

Part 3

Part 4

摘要能力題

Part 5

Part 6

▶▶ 參考答案

Making wise decisions is more important than having good birth, as can be seen in Philip's case. Philip's uncle and friends are well aware of the certain truth, recommending he cultivate his skills at an accounting firm.

Philip's friends encourage him to take risks in life; however, it is Philip who has to face the change of the life trajectory. Despite the hurdles and discouragement from his uncle, Philip gets enough money from his aunt, embarking on an adventure in Paris. In the end, the great artist's advice ceases his whim.

Philip's next step of becoming a doctor encounters a setback during the anatomy exam. Love and gambling in the stock market are the main distractions that causes him to postpone his medical studies. Philip's inability to make a good decision erases the advantage that has been given to him.

Tom's birth is another example because birth and education do not make him financially independent. One only needs to focus on making good decisions in every key stage of life.

▶▶ 摘要能力 TEST 6

| Instruction | MP3 014

　　考生可以藉由重新閱讀英文文章後提筆撰寫 200-250 字的摘要或是在閱讀文章後，以口說的方式摘要出一段英文重要訊息具備在職場能夠摘要一段英文會議內容的能力，提升職場競爭力。

Part 1

Part 2

Part 3

Part 4

Part 5

Part 6

▶▶ 參考答案

Two classics offer two different parentings, yet the problem of meddling in one's love affairs still lingers.

Dividing people makes people's life miserable, yet Owen and Kim have decided to intervene in Jane and Ian Holt through several gestures.

Jane's endeavor to save Ian Holt and Ian's clever way of earning himself one more day to live show something. Still, arguing for a claim of innocence is quite hard.

Cheryl's testimony for Ian's innocence makes Jane and Owen reconsider the whole thing, figuring out the real killer. Jane and Ian's love after the release seems odd for different reasons.

▶▶ 摘要能力 TEST 7

| **Instruction** | MP3 **015**

　　考生可以藉由重新閱讀英文文章後提筆撰寫 200-250 字的摘要
或是在閱讀文章後，以口說的方式摘要出一段英文重要訊息具備在職
場能夠摘要一段英文會議內容的能力，提升職場競爭力。

N O T E

Part 1

Part 2

Part 3

Part 4

摘要能力題

Part 5

Part 6

▶▶ 參考答案

Lots of reasons fuel people's craze to becoming rich. Some occupy their time earning more money, while others expect an inheritance from parents.

In *North and South*, Margaret's getting of the inheritance is the pleasant result, whereas in *Drop Dead Diva*, Violet Harwood's inheritance is controlled by the trustee. In the end, the lawyer conceives the dead-hand clause to make the money equally divided between Violet Harwood and her brother.

In *Middlemarch*, Mr. Casaubon's use of the dead-hand clause is to protect Mrs. Casaubon from getting deceived from other men, and acts as a way to control Mrs. Casaubon. Mrs. Casaubon at last is willing to make a sacrifice and gets married with the loved one.

In *Wuthering Heights*, there are lots of moves on protecting assets and claiming someone else's assets. Edgar Linton's protection of assets is decoded by Mr. Heathcliff because the heir has to be male. Mr. Heathcliff also makes himself a mortgagee, controlling the fate of Earnshaw's son.

▶▶ 摘要能力 TEST 8

| **Instruction** | MP3 **016**

　　考生可以藉由重新閱讀英文文章後提筆撰寫 200-250 字的摘要
或是在閱讀文章後，以口說的方式摘要出一段英文重要訊息具備在職
場能夠摘要一段英文會議內容的能力，提升職場競爭力。

N O T E

Part 1

Part 2

Part 3

Part 4

摘要能力題

Part 5

Part 6

▶▶ 參考答案

Three novels act as the reflection of the reality, and In *Vanity Fair*, Mr. Sedley's poor investment makes him bankrupt.

Mr. Sedley in *Vanity Fair*, and Mr. Thornton's condition in *North and South* shares the same vein. To both Mr. Thornton and Henry, Margaret's inherited money can be of great assistance for their careers.

Margaret in *North and South* and Philip in *Of Human Bondage* are considered lucky, but Philip's inability to use the money makes his life not as great as it should have been.

It can be concluded that investment money should come from the sources that will not influence one's living; otherwise, there is going to be a disaster. No matter how lucky a person can be, not being able to control the spending can result in serious damage in life (like Philip). Being too speculative can also have the same fate like Mr. Sedley, losing enormous wealth and his hard-to-build enterprise. Working industriously and diligently can still end up like Mr. Thornton, lacking enough money to keep the company afloat. Predictions of one's life trajectory are too unlikely, but what we can do is do our part and not investing recklessly or dreaming of becoming a rich billionaire in a day.

利用此篇章中英對照觀看並另外進行跟讀練習提升聽力專注力。

There are numerous love songs that are gripping and make people resonate. Among them, topics related to "love someone who truly loves you" and "choose the person you love" are the most popular. How to make the right choice and select the ideal life partner can be quite difficult. Often a lot of sayings on social media platforms and views of those celebrities in the show are misleading and are often rife with claims that don't stand up to scrutiny. Luckily, by reading British romance novels, like *Far from the Madding Crowd*, we can have a better understanding about making smarter choices.

無數情歌扣人心弦，讓人產生共鳴。這些歌曲中「愛一個真正愛你的人」和「擇你所愛的人」的話題最為流行。如何做出正確的選擇，挑選出理想的人生伴侶是關山難越的。往往社交媒體平台上不勝枚舉的說法和節目中的名人的觀點都具有誤導性，且常常充斥著經不起推敲的說法。幸運的是，透過閱讀像是《遠離塵囂》這樣的英國浪漫小說，我們可以有較好的體認以做出更明智的選擇。

Three promising guys in *Far from the Madding Crowd* can be seen as the summarized version of the real life. Three candidates

Part 1

Part 2

Part 3

Part 4

Part 5

影子跟讀和中譯

Part 6

are Oak, Boldwood, and Troy.

《遠離塵囂》中的三個前途似錦的男性可以看作是對現實生活的概括。三個候選人是歐克、包伍德和曹伊。

❶ resonate（使）共鳴；
（使）起回聲

❷ ideal 理想的，完美的

❸ platform 平臺，臺；講臺

❹ celebrities 名人

❺ misleading 使人誤解的；騙人的

❻ scrutiny 仔細的觀察[U]

❼ romance 戀愛，浪漫情調
[U]

❽ promising 有前途的，大有可為的

❾ summarize 總結，概述

❿ version（同一作品的不同）版本

As anyone can remember from high school and college, most girls would go for the handsome and bad boy types, simply because they want to be tamed. They deem the guy with principles and integrity as boring and easily controlled, but that pushes them away from real happiness. That is also the main reason why Oak is not accepted by heroine, Bathsheba at the very beginning of the novel. Oak has several admirable traits that make him an ideal husband for Bathsheba. He is kind-hearted and has a real passion for Bathsheba. Oak proclaims that he will work twice as hard after marriage.

任何人都記得高中和大學時，大多數女孩都會選擇帥氣和壞男孩類型，僅僅是因為她們想要被馴服。她們認為有原則和正直的人無趣且容易控制，但這使她們遠離真正的幸福。這也是小說一開始歐克不被女主角貝莎芭接受的主要原因。歐克有幾個令人欽佩的特質，使他成為貝莎芭的理想丈夫。他心地善良，對貝莎芭有著真正的熱情。歐克宣稱他婚後會加倍努力工作。

- -

❶ tamed 經馴養的，馴服的

❷ principles 原則；原理

❸ integrity 正直；廉正

❹ controlled 支配下的；被控制的

❺ heroine（小説、電影等的）女主角

❻ admirable 值得讚揚的；令人欽佩的

❼ passion 熱情，激情[U][C]

❽ proclaim 宣告；公布

- -

So far, this has been about all the readers' perception of him. What about Boldwood's account about Oak? Near the very end of the novel, Boldwood has a heart-felt confession with Oak, when Boldwood has the sense that his prospect with Bathsheba is around the corner. "You have behaved like a man, and I, as a sort of successful rival-successful partly through your goodness of heart I should like definitely to show my sense of your friendship under what must have been a great pain to you."

到目前為止，這都是關於讀者對他的看法。那麼關於包伍德對歐克的描述呢？在小說的最後，包伍德對歐克進行了一場發自內心的告白，

Part 1

Part 2

Part 3

Part 4

Part 5

影子跟讀和中譯

Part 6

這時包伍德感覺到他與貝莎芭的前景指日可待。「你的所作所為還像男子漢一樣光明磊落。而我作為一個勝出的情敵－ 我之所以能勝出有一部分是因為你心地善良－一定要對你之前不惜承受著極大的痛苦所表現出的善意略表感謝之意。」

As for Boldwood, he has a crazy devotion for Bathsheba that separates him apart from both Troy and Oak, and he is also the man who can wait for the girl for six years. At a much later time, a locked box that contains expensive silks, satins, poplins, velvets, muffs (sable and ermine), and a case of jewellery that includes four heavy gold bracelets and several lockets and rings can symbolize the importance of Bathsheba in Boldwood's heart.

至於包伍德，他對貝莎芭的痴迷讓他有別於曹伊和歐克，他也是那個可以等待女孩六年的男人。在更久之後，一個裝有昂貴的絲綢、緞子、府綢、天鵝絨、暖手筒（紫貂皮和白貂皮款）的上鎖盒子，以及一個裝有四個沉重的金手鐲和幾個掛墜盒和戒指的珠寶盒，都象徵著貝莎芭在包伍德的內心的地位。

❶ perception 感覺 [U]；看法

❷ account 記述，描述

❸ confession 承認；坦白

❹ prospect 指望；前景

❺ separate 個別的，不同的

❻ bracelet 手鐲；臂鐲

❼ locket 盒式項鏈墜

❽ symbolize 象徵，標誌

In the middle part of the story, Bathsheba chooses Troy to

be her husband, and Troy seems to fall into the untamed type. Troy can be good for a diversion, but not for a long-lasting relationship. However, Troy does have his charm. Troy volunteers to sweep and shake bees into the hive to impress Bathsheba. Troy further demonstrates his swordsmanship in their next appointment, creating a special moment to imprint a kiss on Bathsheba. The sense of novelty and surprise prevails, making her act on impulse and without reason.

故事的中段，貝莎芭選擇了曹伊做她的丈夫，而曹伊似乎屬於不易馴服的類型。曹伊可能適合短暫怡情的戀愛，但不符合長久穩定戀情。不過，曹伊也有他的魅力在。曹伊自願揮掃蜜蜂將其趕進蜂巢，以給貝莎芭留下好印象。曹伊在他們的下一次約會中進一步展示了他的劍術，創造了一個特殊的時刻，將一個吻銘刻在貝莎芭身上。新鮮感和驚奇感佔了上風，使她表現得不理性且衝動行事。

According to the author, Troy is good at concealment and superficiality so that ethical defects will not be perceived by women, whereas Oak stands in a sharp contrast with Troy because Oak's shortcomings can be apparently seen. Beneath the veneer of Troy, there are flaws most people will not notice. However, no matter how good one is at varnish, he will eventually show the true colors.

作者認為，曹伊擅長掩飾和表面功夫，不讓女性察覺到道德缺陷，而歐克就與曹伊形成鮮明對比，因為歐克的缺點可以一目了然。在曹伊的外表之下，存在著大多數人不會注意到的缺陷。然而，再好的偽裝，終究會露出真面目的。

Part 1

Part 2

Part 3

Part 4

Part 5

影子跟讀和中譯

Part 6

❶ untamed 野性的; 未受抑制的

❷ diversion 娛樂，消遣

❸ swordsmanship 劍術

❹ prevail 勝過；流行

❺ concealment 隱藏；隱瞞 [U]

❻ superficiality 表面情況；淺薄

❼ veneer 虛飾；外飾

❽ varnish 粉飾，掩飾

"Every voice in nature was unanimous in bespeaking change." Unprotected ricks equal to 750 pounds of food. The storm is coming closer, but Troy is nowhere to be seen. According to Oak, Troy is asleep in the barn, neglecting all the harm that the weather might do to the crop and the consequence that will cost their barn. Oak's endeavor to protect the crop shows his true love for Bathsheba. He uses his actions to validate the love. Troy; however, demonstrates his indifference, making Bathsheba realize Troy as a person.

「大自然裡的每個聲音都在預示即將發生的變化。」未受保護的乾草堆相當於 750 磅食物。暴風雨漸漸逼近，但曹伊卻不見踪影。根據歐克的說法，曹伊在穀倉裡睡著了，忽略了天氣可能對作物造成的所有傷害以及他們的穀倉將付出代價的後果。歐克保護莊稼的努力展現出了他對貝莎芭的真愛。他用自己的行動來證明愛。然而，曹伊卻表現出他的漠不關心，使貝莎芭意識到曹伊實際的為人。

❶ unanimous 全體一致的；
一致同意的

❷ unprotected 未受保護的

❸ neglect 忽視，忽略

❹ consequence 結果，後果

❺ endeavor 努力，力圖

❻ action 行動；行為

❼ validate 使有效；使生效

❽ indifference 漠不關心；冷
淡

Boldwood loves Bathsheba deeply by wanting to provide her material comfort as a way to possess a beauty. Oak, on the other hand, wants to love Bathsheba by using all his life. Troy seems to have an agenda on Bathsheba because of Bathsheba's wealth and barn. Bathsheba at first gets married with Troy by choosing the one she truly loves, and till the end she figures out it is the one who truly loves her that she should be with. As a Chinese saying goes, "people look for him thousands of Baidu. Looking back suddenly, the man was there, in a dimly lit place." Perhaps Bathsheba just comes to the realization about this a bit too late. True love is always around us, but our perception prevents us from seeing it clearly.

包伍德深愛貝莎芭，想提供她舒適的物質以此佔有美人。另一方面，歐克想用他的一生來愛貝莎芭。曹伊似乎因為貝莎芭的財富和穀倉而對她有所盤算。貝莎芭第一次和曹伊結婚，選擇了她真正愛的人，直到最後她才發現真正愛她的人才是她應該在一起的人。中國有句俗話，「眾里尋他千百度。驀然回首，那人卻在燈火闌珊處。」也許貝莎芭有點太晚才了解這點。真愛一直在我們身邊，只是我們的感受讓我們無法清楚分辨它。

Part 1

Part 2

Part 3

Part 4

Part 5

影子跟讀和中譯

Part 6

❶ material 物質的，有形的

❷ possess 擁有，持有

❸ agenda 計劃

❹ dimly 昏暗地；朦朧地

❺ realization 領悟；認識

❻ prevent 防止；阻止

利用此篇章中英對照觀看並另外進行跟讀練習提升聽力專注力。

"I believe that I have no enemy on earth, and none surely would have been so wicked as to destroy me wantonly." A saying from *Frankenstein* seems to convey the message of Justine's viewpoint that men inherently possess a good heart. While various people may hold different views on this statement, Justine's conjecture about the devil who frames her is entirely correct. The devil has a good heart from the start, but Victor, the main character, resists acknowledging the devil as his creation or his own baby, resulting in a distorted mind for the devil. There has been some mental separation between the two. Acceptance and refusal are two antithetical concepts, and feeling loved is essential for anyone's personal development. The devil's atrocious behavior results from getting rejected and not being amended. Not getting loved makes someone feel neglected, unaccepted, being excluded. All these factors engender serious psychological behavior that creates some of the social crimes.

「在這個世界上，我相信自己沒有任何敵人。沒有誰會如此惡毒，竟無端加害於我。」《科學怪人》中的一句敘述似乎傳達了賈斯婷對此訊息的看法，人與生俱來就是良善的。而不同的人對這樣的陳述會持著

Part 1

Part 2

Part 3

Part 4

Part 5

影子跟讀和中譯

Part 6

相異的觀點，賈斯婷對於誣陷她的惡魔的臆測是完全正確的。從一開始，惡魔本身就心存善念，但是主角維克特拒絕承認惡魔是他的創造物或他的小孩，導致了惡魔本身扭曲的心靈。兩人之間有著心靈隔閡在。接受和拒絕是兩個相對立的觀念，感到被愛對於一個人的個人成長是重要的。惡魔的暴行導因於受到拒絕並且並未修復。不被愛讓一個人感到受到忽略、不被接受和被排除在外。所有這些因素導致了造成某些社會犯罪的嚴重心理行為。

❶ wantonly 放縱地；嬉鬧地

❷ conjecture 推測，猜測

❸ antithetical 對立的

❹ engender 使產生；引起

Education seems to be the key to amending people's mind. As the story progresses, the devil demands the creation of an identity similar to him so that he can find someone to love and to be loved. Victor at first concurs another attempt to create a new one for him, then out of the blue shifting into thinking that manufacturing the spouse for him equates with producing a monster. He can barely handle the devil, let alone dealing with two bad-looking creatures. The novel itself conveys several important messages essential for human beings to pay serious attention so that more societal problems can be avoided, thus making it especially great and eternally valuable.

教育似乎是修復人們心靈的關鍵。隨著故事的進展，惡魔要求創造與他相似的個體，如此一來他就能找到一個人來愛並被愛著。維克特起初同意了再次試驗以創造一個新的個體給他，接著突然之間改變心意，因為替惡魔製造出一位伴侶等同於創造出一個猛獸。他幾乎無法應付惡魔了，更別說是要應對兩個醜陋的生物。小說本身傳達出幾個對於人類來說很重要的訊息，唯有注意到這樣的嚴重性，才能避免更多社會問題的發生。因此也讓這本小說特別偉大且具永恆價值。

A lot of murder crimes relating to love can be evaded if proper education and giving others more love have seriously been paid attention to. One does not have to take rejections too seriously. As a saying goes, **"things that seem disastrous at the time usually do work out for the rest."** Sometimes it does mean that God has a better idea, wanting to give you something much better.

有許多與愛情相關的謀殺罪是能夠避免的，如果適當的教育和給予其他人更多的關愛有一直受到大家重視。常言道：「**事情在當下看起來似乎糟透了，但是通常最後結果都適得其所。**」有時候這只是意謂著上天對這件事情有更好的看法，想要給予你比這個選擇還更棒的。

❶ concur 同意，一致　　　　❷ disastrous 災難性的

As can be seen in another classic, *Middlemarch*, God certainly wants James to have not just someone better, but someone more suitable for him. In towns, neighbors and farmers have the predilection for Celia over Dorothea simply because Celia is more approachable, innocent, clever, and sophisticated. Dorothea has a quality of not self-admiring, thinking Celia is more charming

158

Part 1

Part 2

Part 3

Part 4

Part 5
影子跟讀和中譯

Part 6

than she is. James, on the other hand, has a crush on Dorothea. **"He felt that he had chosen the one who was in all respects the superior; and a man naturally likes to look forward to having the best."** However, James does not even have any chance with Dorothea.

如同另一部經典《米德爾鎮的春天》所示，上天確實想要詹姆士不僅是有更好的伴侶，而是賦予一位更合適他的人。在小鎮上，比起多羅西亞，鄰居們和農夫們都偏好西利雅，僅因為西利雅更為平易近人、天真、聰明且世故。多羅西亞也有著不自戀的特質，認為西利雅比她更為有魅力。另一方面，詹姆士卻迷戀多羅西亞。「他覺得自己看上的那位布魯克小姐各方面都比較優秀。男人自然而然都想要擁有最好的。」然而，想要追求多羅西亞，詹姆士甚至沒有任何機會。

❶ suitable 適當的；合適的   ❸ self-admiring 自戀的

❷ predilection 嗜好；偏愛   ❹ superior 較好的，優秀的

His rival Mr. Casaubon does not have to do much and wins over the heart of Dorothea in such a short time. Luckily, James does not take this as a defeat or as something that will crush him. Getting rejected does not make someone a failure as most people would think. It is one's mindset that makes a man. Some would writhe under the idea of failure and rejection and then do the harm to the rival, hurt themselves, or cause quite a damage to someone you love. The thing is you do not have to act like that.

他的情敵卡索邦在短時間內不費吹灰之力就贏得了多羅西亞的芳心。幸運的是，詹姆士並未將此事當成是挫敗或者是會壓垮他的事情。事情並不像大家所想的那樣，被拒絕就讓一個人淪為敗犬。是一個人的心態造就了一個人。有些人會在失敗和拒絕的想法下掙扎，然後去傷害情敵、自殘或是對你所愛的對象造成很大程度的傷害。你不用因此而有這樣的行為出現。

- -

❶ rivalry 競爭；對抗　　　❷ writhe 如坐針氈

- -

Other people, including Dorothea's uncle, are shocked at Dorothea's choice of a man, not choosing James as a husband. Celia has a feeling that James will be a great husband, but from her observations, they will not be a good fit. Dorothea's choice may be good for both of them. It should not be interpreted as seriously harming someone. James claims that Dorothea should wait until she is mature enough to make the decision and is mad at Dorothea's choice, but eventually he gladly accepts this news. It does mean that more saccharine fruits are waiting for him definitely.

其他人包含多羅西亞的伯父對於多羅西亞沒有選擇詹姆士當丈夫都感到震驚。西利雅覺得詹姆士會是個好丈夫，但是就她的觀察來看，詹姆士和姐姐不會是天作之合。多羅西亞的選擇對於雙方來說都好。這個選擇不該解讀成嚴重的傷害了對方。詹姆士認為多羅西亞該等到更為成熟時在下決定，也對於她的選擇感到憤怒，但是最終他欣然接受了這個消息。這也意謂著更甜美的果實在等待著他。

Part 1

Part 2

Part 3

Part 4

Part 5

影子跟讀和中譯

Part 6

As the story progresses to a much later time, his feelings of getting rejected have gone already, having been replaced by getting engaged with Celia. **"His disregarded love had not turned to bitterness; its death had made sweet odors – floating memories that clung with a consecrating effect to Dorothea."** True love deserves some time to wait. Two classics *Middlemarch* and *Frankenstein*, should all be the required reading during high school, shaping those feelings so that more tragedy can be avoided.

　　隨著故事進展在更後期，詹姆士被拒絕的感受早已因為他和西利雅的訂婚而煙消雲散。「求婚被拒，卻沒有由愛生恨。他的愛情死亡之後，反倒散發出甜美的香氣，變成飄盪的記憶，淨化他對多羅西亞的情感。」真愛確實值得時間的等待。兩部經典作品《米德爾鎮的春天》和《科學怪人》都該成為高中的必讀書籍，形塑那些受到傷害的心靈，這樣一來對於更多的悲劇就能防患未然。

❶ observation 觀察；觀測

❷ interpret 解釋，詮釋

❸ saccharine 甜美的

❹ disregarded 受忽視的

❺ bitterness 苦味；痛苦

❻ floating 漂浮的；流動的

❼ consecrating 淨化的

❽ tragedy（一齣）悲劇

利用此篇章中英對照觀看並另外進行跟讀練習提升聽力專注力。

"It would have been cruel in Miss Havisham, horribly cruel, to practice on the susceptibility of a poor boy, and to torture me through all these years with a vain hope and idle pursuit, if she had reflected on the gravity of what she did."

「哈維森小姐如果早知道她所做的一切會有嚴重的後果，還這樣去玩弄一個貧窮孩子的感情，這麼多年來一直用渺茫的希望和徒勞的追求來折磨我，這實在是太殘忍了點，真的是太殘忍了。」

In *Great Expectations*, Miss Havisham's enormous wealth does not give her the joy that she is in desperate need of. Miss Havisham's use of the little girl, Estella, to torture the boy that she hires, on the other hand, fulfills her whim and the sense of satisfaction. As a saying goes, pain and conflict only bring more pain and conflict. Not letting go of the past rigorously hurts or erodes Miss Havisham's body and soul.

　　在《遠大前程》中，哈維森小姐的巨額財富並沒有給她帶來她迫切需要的快樂。 另一方面，哈維森小姐利用小女孩艾絲黛拉來折磨她僱用的男孩，滿足了她的幻想和滿足感。俗話說，痛苦和衝突只會帶來更多

Part 1

Part 2

Part 3

Part 4

Part 5

影子跟讀和中譯

Part 6

的痛苦和衝突。不放掉過去會嚴重傷害或侵蝕哈維森小姐的身心靈。

Miss Havisham's hurt can be traced back to an incident happening about twenty years ago. Pip's encounter with both Magwitch and Compeyson paves the way for a further development. Magwitch, a poor and unlucky guy, under the guidance of fortune, meets with self-pretentious, handsome, erudite Compeyson. The chance encounter leads Magwitch to learn the truth about Compeyson and his partner, Arthur. The deception from a rich lady, which is believed to be Miss Havisham, earns them a great deal of fortune. However, Compeyson's lavish spending habits cannot keep up with the money he earns from doing the dirty things.

哈維森小姐所受的傷害可以追溯到大約二十年前發生的一件事。皮普與馬格韋契和康佩森的相遇為進一步的發展鋪陳。貧窮倒霉的馬格韋契在命運的指引下，邂逅了自命不凡、英俊博學的康培生。一次偶然的相遇讓馬格韋契了解了關於康佩森和他的搭檔亞瑟的真相。欺騙富家女而獲取大量財富，而據說這個人就是哈維森小姐。然而，康佩森因為奢侈的消費習慣使得他從做骯髒事當中所賺取的錢瞠乎其後。

Doing bad things, and not getting caught for a while seems normal, but committing a list of crimes and not getting captured will be deemed unlikely. Pretty soon, both are taken to court for a trial. They both are charged with putting stolen notes in circulation. Compeyson demands that they go separate ways, and Compeyson smart thinking does work. Magwitch can only get Mr. Jaggers as a lawyer for the defense.

　　幹壞事一時不被逮捕看似正常，但有一連串的犯罪行為不被抓到就是枝末生根。 很快地，兩人都被送上法庭接受審判。他們都被控讓盜取的紙幣流通到市面上。 康佩森要求他們分道揚鑣，而康佩森的聰明想法確實奏效了。馬格韋契只能請賈格斯先生擔任辯護律師。

- -

❶ erudite 博學的　　　　　　　❷ lavish 非常慷慨的；浪費的

- -

The "birth" issue and one's education also weigh heavily on criminals in court, making Compeyson's sentence the half of Magwitch's. Magwitch has been unfairly judged at the court and eventually gets 14 years in prison. They are in the same prison ship, but Magwitch cannot get closer to Compeyson. Fleeing the prison ship leads to the encounter of Pip, the main character, and Compeyson. This time Magwitch has enough time to smash Compeyson's face to get revenge.

　　在法庭上，「出身」這個議題和一個人所受的教育也對罪犯所受的判決產生了重大的影響，使得康佩森的刑期只有馬格韋契的一半。馬格韋契在法庭上受到不公平的審判，最終被判入獄 14 年。他們在同一艘監獄船上，但馬格韋契無法靠近康培生。逃離囚船導致主角皮普和康佩生的偶遇。這回馬格韋契有足夠時間砸康佩生的臉以進行復仇。

　　Magwitch and Compeyson will try every way to bring each

Part 1

Part 2

Part 3

Part 4

Part 5

影子跟讀和中譯

Part 6

other down. Compeyson can report there is a refugee that flees from the prison ship. Magwitch and Pip's flee then encounters The Hamburg, the steamer, sailing swiftly towards them. People on the steamer demand the assistance to capture the person wrapping with a cloak on Pip's ship. As Magwitch goes behind the person who tries to seize him, he has the time to tear off another person with a cloak on the steamer to verify whether his identity is Compeyson. Compeyson is in shock and then waddles. Thereafter, they have a struggle, falling into the river. Other guys trying to seize Magwitch eventually cause the capsizing of the Pip's ship. Magwitch is found seriously injured, and with no traces of Compeyson. Pip has no reason to doubt Magwitch's account of what just happened because it is the same as that of the officer who steers the ship. At Police Court, it is revealed that Compeyson eventually falls into the river and is found dead. Compeyson and Arthur, Miss Havisham's brother, all pay the price. Arthur dies from serious illness right before the sentence of both Magwitch and Compeyson.

　　馬格韋契和康佩生千方百計地想要扳倒對方。康佩生可以舉發說有一名逃亡者從監獄船上逃了出來。馬格韋契和皮普的逃亡碰見漢堡號，這艘汽船正迅速駛向他們。輪船上的人要求協助逮捕皮普船上披著斗篷的人。當馬格韋契走到試圖抓住他的人身後時，他有時間在汽船上撕下另一位披著斗篷的人，以驗證他的身份是否是康培生。康佩生先是感到震驚，然後搖搖欲墜。此後，他們進行搏鬥，掉進河裡。其他試圖抓住馬格韋契的人最終導致了皮普的船傾覆。馬格韋契被發現身受重傷，且沒有康佩森的蛛絲馬跡。皮普沒有理由懷疑馬格韋契對剛才所發生的事情的描述，因為這與掌舵的官員的描述是如出一轍的。在警察法庭，揭露出康佩生最終掉進了河裡，發現時已經一命嗚呼。康佩生和哈維森小姐的弟弟亞瑟都為此付出了代價。亞瑟在馬格韋契和康佩生都被判刑前就死於重病。

---

❶ refugee 難民；流亡者　　❸ seize 沒收；扣押

❷ steamer 汽船，輪船　　❹ capsizing 翻覆

Miss Havisham's distorted mind resulting from the harm caused by Compeyson and Arthur could totally be cured if she knew the notion of "what comes around goes around" and "unjust is doomed to destruction." Karma will eventually do the justice for her. Miss Havisham eventually comes to her senses right before her death that she has done quite a damage to another human being, Estella.

哈維森小姐因康佩生和亞瑟的傷害而產生的扭曲心靈可以全然治癒，如果她知道「善有善報、惡有惡報」和「多行不義必自斃」的概念。業力最終會為她伸張正義。哈維森小姐在死前終於意識到她對另一個人艾絲黛拉造成了相當大的傷害。

"That she had done a grievous thing in taking an impressionable child to mould into the form that her wild resentment, spurned affection, and wounded pride, found vengeance in, I knew full well."

Part 1

Part 2

Part 3

Part 4

Part 5

影子跟讀和中譯

Part 6

「她做了一件嚴重的事情，她由於自己的情感被人玩弄，自尊受到傷害，心中充滿狂亂的怨恨，就因此將一個敏感無辜的女孩，塑造成自己的模樣，想要讓這個女孩長大之後，為她報仇雪恨。」

During her chat with Pip, Miss Havisham tries to seek inner peace. Forgiveness really is a cure for all bad things. Miss Havisham would have lived a much happier life, if she had mastered the art of forgiveness.

在與皮普聊天時，哈維森小姐試圖尋求內心的平靜。寬恕真的是治癒所有壞事的良藥。如果哈維森小姐掌握了寬恕的法門，她會過著更加快樂的日子。

❶ grievous 令人悲痛的

❷ impressionable 易受影響的

❸ resentment 忿怒，怨恨

❹ spurned 摒棄；藐視

❺ affection 愛，情愛

❻ wounded 受傷的

❼ vengeance 報復；報仇

❽ forgiveness 原諒

利用此篇章中英對照觀看並另外進行跟讀練習提升聽力專注力。

In our daily life, we rarely take the idea or wisdom from time-enduring classics into account, so we are still struggling in several aspects of our life. The storylines of *Vanity Fair* ring alarmingly true to most readers. By taking an in-depth look into how Becky capitalizes every opportunity to get the desired outcome, we can probably have a better life.

　　在我們日常生活中，我們鮮少將能受時間檢驗的經典作品中的想法和智慧列入考量，所以我們在生活幾個面向上掙扎喘息。《浮華世界》的故事情節對於大多數的讀者來說聽起來非常真實。藉由深入了解蓓琪利用每個機會得到想要的結果，我們可能可以有更好的生活。

Not having parents and being poor are two main factors that put heroine of *Vanity Fair*, Becky Sharp into a disadvantaged position. Since most girls have their parents' assistance to settle matters with the young man to change the fate, Becky has to do this all on her own, and one does not have to be extremely clever to know the truth that getting married with a wealthy husband will more or less make one's later life a lot smoother. The chance event comes when one of her wealthy friends, Amelia invites her

Part 1

Part 2

Part 3

Part 4

Part 5

影子跟讀和中譯

Part 6

to stay at her house for a week before Becky moves on to do the private tutor job.

　　沒有父母和貧窮是讓《浮華世界》女主角蓓琪‧夏普置身於不利處境的兩個主要因素。既然大多數的女孩們都有他們的父母協助張羅與年輕男性的婚事以此來改變命運，蓓琪卻必須要自力更生，而一個人並不需要極其聰明才能了解到，與一個富有的丈夫結婚或多或少會讓一個人往後的人生更加順暢這樣的真理。當艾美麗雅邀請蓓琪在前往從事私人教師工作之前先待在她家一週，偶然的機運出現了。

Becky soon finds out a golden opportunity that Amelia's brother, Joseph is still single. Becky is ready to put the move on Joseph, but she is not yet ready. Mr. Sedley deliberately wants Becky to try some curry with cayenne pepper and a chili that Becky obviously cannot put up with, and then Mr. Sedley enjoys this show along with his son, Joseph, and also informs his son that Becky has set her sights on him. Then all things have been in Becky's favor, but George Osborne considers Becky and Joseph a mesalliance, frightening Joseph for a bit. Osborne's intervention ends Becky's prospect of marrying with Joseph outright.

　　蓓琪很快察覺到黃金機遇，也就是艾美麗雅的哥哥喬瑟夫仍孑然一身。蓓琪準備要對喬瑟夫展開行動，但是她並未真的作好準備。薩德利先生故意要蓓琪試下她顯然無法承受的一些辣咖哩和辣椒，而接著薩德利先生和他兒子喬瑟夫就一起看好戲，薩德利先生還告知他兒子，蓓琪看上他了。然後一切事情都對蓓琪有利，但是喬治‧奧斯朋認為蓓琪和喬瑟夫門不當戶不對，有點打草驚蛇到喬瑟夫。奧斯朋的干涉徹底結束了蓓琪和喬瑟夫結婚前景。

❶ cayenne（紅）辣椒

❷ mesalliance 門不當戶不對的婚姻

However, this setback does not dissuade young Rebecca from reaching her goal. It does mean she has not yet mastered the art of deception. Becky embarks on her journey of being the governess of Sir Pitt's two daughters, making her much closer to a real celebrity circle. Her goal has been constant: to find a rich husband. Winning the heart over Sir Pitt's two daughters and being baronet's confidence at Queen's Crawley are the first step towards Rebecca's success, and the mastery of the hypocrisy the second, the marriage with Rawdon Crawley the third.

　　然而，這次挫折並沒有阻止年輕的雷貝卡實現她的目標。這確實意謂著她還沒有掌握欺騙的藝術。蓓琪開始了她成為皮特爵士兩個女兒的家庭教師的旅程，這使她更接近一個真正的著名圈子。她的目標一直不變：找一個有錢的丈夫。贏得皮特爵士的兩個女兒的心，並且在皇后克勞利成為準男爵的心腹是雷貝卡成功的第一步，第二步是掌握虛偽，第三步是與洛頓‧克勞利成婚。

❶ baronet 從男爵

❷ confidence 心腹

Distinguished brilliance can certainly make up for poor birth

Part 1

Part 2

Part 3

Part 4

Part 5

影子跟讀和中譯

Part 6

as in the case of Becky. Becky earns the accolade from Miss Crawley that she has more brains than half the shire, and "as her equal." Sir Pitt wants Becky to be his bride by saying **"you've got more brains in your little vinger than any baronet's wife in the country."**, but Becky's true success is to tie the knot with Rawdon Crawley, who will inherit most of Miss Crawley's fortune. Rawdon Crawley's viewpoints about Becky are concordant with those of his aunt, Miss Crawley and his father, Sir Pitt. He has met multiple clippers, but has never encountered someone as witty as his wife, Becky. These correspond to several notions mentioned in one of the bestsellers, *The Wealth Elite*. It is not about the inheritance or Luck. One does need to have the exact DNA to keep money or acquire more wealth. In one of the British classics, *Treasure Island*, an idea relating to this has also been put forward at the very end of the chapter that it is not the amount of the money that you get. It is about one's nature.

　　傑出的才華當然可以彌補蓓琪的不良出身。蓓琪贏得了克勞利小姐的讚譽，稱她比半個郡的人都聰明，而且「和她並駕齊驅」。皮特爵士希望蓓琪成為他的新娘，他說：「**你的小肚子比這個國家任何準男爵的妻子都聰明。**」但蓓琪真正的成功是與洛頓‧克勞利喜結良緣，後者將繼承克勞利小姐的大部分財產。洛頓‧克勞利 (Rawdon Crawley) 對蓓琪的看法與他的姨媽克勞利小姐和他的父親皮特爵士 (Sir Pitt) 的看法毫無二致。他見過很多窈窕淑女，但從未遇到過像他的妻子蓓琪這樣機智的人。這些與暢銷書之一《財富精英》中提到的幾個概念相對應。這與繼承或運氣無關。人的確要有確切的 DNA 來留住金錢或獲得更多財富。在英國的經典之作《金銀島》中，在書籍最末章也提出了一個與此相關的觀點，重點不是你所獲得的金錢的多寡，而是一個人的本來的天賦。

The following development does not let Rawdon Crawley down as Becky exhibits more of her inborn talent. Becky seizes the moment during the war to make a fortune by selling a horse to Joseph. Wealthy people aspiring to flee also lack the key transportation, the horse. Even Lord Bareacres is willing to pay the price for two horses under this circumstance. The sum is enormous enough to be considered a fortune to Becky. With the money and the sale of the residue of Rawdon's effects, and her pension as a widow, she will be financially independent, not having to worry about money for her entire life. Later, it is believed that the value of two horses equals a luxurious life in Paris a year for both Rawdon Crawley and Becky.

接下來的發展也不負洛頓‧克勞利所望，因為蓓琪展示了更多天賦。蓓琪在戰時趁機向喬瑟夫賣馬發了財。渴望逃離的富人也缺乏關鍵的交通工具，即馬匹。在這種情況下，就算是巴雷克雷斯大人也願意以這樣的價格購買兩匹馬。這筆錢對蓓琪來說是一筆巨款。有了這筆錢和洛頓遺留下來的財產變賣，再加上寡婦的撫卹金，她就可以經濟獨立了，一輩子都不用為錢發愁。後來，人們認為兩匹馬的價值相當於洛頓‧克勞利和蓓琪在巴黎一年的奢華生活。

The couple's reunion after war brings more joyful news, as concealment of cash, checks, watches, and other valuables in Becky's coat reveals themselves. Becky has had unprecedented

Part 1

Part 2

Part 3

Part 4

Part 5

影子跟讀和中譯

Part 6

success even in Paris. It can be concluded that despite Becky's poorness and lack of the background, she possesses an admirable quality against adversity and cruel fate, surpassing her classmates, Amelia, born into a wealthy family and with the worth of the 10,000 pounds, where she has none. **"So in fetes, pleasures, and prosperity, the winter of 1815-16 passed away with Mrs. Rawdon Crawley, who accommodated herself to polite life as if her ancestors had been people of fashion for centuries past – and who from her wit, talent, and energy, indeed merited a place of honor in Vanity Fair."**

　　戰後這對夫婦的重逢帶來了更多喜訊，因為蓓琪外套揭露了當中所隱藏的現金、支票、手錶和其他貴重物品。即使在巴黎，蓓琪也取得了空前的成功。可以得出的結論是，儘管蓓琪家境貧寒、缺乏背景，艾美麗雅出身豪門，就擁有一萬英鎊的身價，而她卻是一無所有，但她在逆境和殘酷命運面前卻有著令人欽佩的特質，超越了她的同學艾美麗雅。「就這樣，洛頓・克勞利太太在熱鬧的宴會中愉快度過一八一五至一八一六年的冬天，聲勢水漲船高。她在社交圈如魚得水，好像她歷代祖先都是貴族似的。她機智聰穎，精通許多才藝，活力四射，的確值得在浮華世界佔有一席之地。」

利用此篇章中英對照觀看並另外進行跟讀練習提升聽力專注力。

People are so focusing on "birth" that they forget it is a series of choices that eventually make or break someone. Bad decisions in every key life moment can drag someone down the path, leading to an inferior outcome. The term "birth" will be just glamorous from the start and disastrous in the end.

人們如此專注於「出身」以至於他們忘了最終成敗是一個人的一系列的選擇。在每個關鍵的人生時刻做出錯誤的決定都會拖累一個人，導致了糟糕的結果。「出身」這個詞從一開始就很迷人，到最後卻是災難性的。

In *Of Human Bondage*, with some deliberation, Philip's first life decision is to be an intern at the office of Messers. Herbert Carter & Co. in which his uncle and friends believe that under the tenure, Philip will learn professional skills enough for him to stand on his own feet and make a living. **"Every profession, and every trade, required length of time, and what was worse, money."** However, Philip is just like some of the twentysomethings, and not yet understands the mortifying conviction that three years at the first job are quite an important step for your next job.

Part 1
Part 2
Part 3
Part 4
Part 5
影子跟讀和中譯
Part 6

在《人性枷鎖》中，經過深思熟慮，菲利普的第一個人生決定是成為梅塞爾事務所的實習生。他的伯父和朋友們相信，在梅塞爾事務所任職期間，菲利普將學到足夠的專業技能，足以讓他自立並謀生。「**每一種職業、每一門生意都需要花時間學習或經營，更糟的是還需要投入金錢。**」然而，菲利普就像一些二十多歲的年輕人一樣，還未了解到一個惱人的道理，第一份工作做滿三年對你下一份工作來說是相當重要的一步。

❶ inferior 次的；較差的

❷ glamorous 富有魅力的

❸ disastrous 災難性的

❹ deliberation 深思熟慮

❺ tenure 任期

❻ mortifying 惱人的

❼ conviction 確信，信念

❽ important 重要的

Bad advice from one of his friends also dissipates his valuable twentysomething years. **"I cannot imagine you sitting in an office over a ledger." "My feeling is that one should look upon life as an adventure, one should burn with the hard, gem-like flame, and one should take risks, one should expose oneself to danger."** His friend's belief in Philip's ability in art does not equal with how the reality views about him as a person. Despite the Vicar's disagreement for Philip's life trajectory change, Philip insists on going to Paris to learn art. Still Philip has to wait for a year to get his small inheritance from his father.

他其中一位朋友的糟糕建議也浪費掉了他寶貴的 20 多歲時光。「我無法想像你竟坐在辦公室裡，埋首於一本本帳冊之中。我覺得人生就像一場冒險，應像寶石般的火焰熊熊燃燒，勇於接受挑戰，危難當前亦不畏懼。」他的朋友對菲利普藝術才華有信念並不等於現實世界對他所評價出的能力。儘管牧師不同意菲利普改變人生軌跡，但菲利普堅持去巴黎學習藝術。菲利普仍需要等待一年才能從他父親那裡得到他的小額遺產。

- -

❶ dissipate 浪費，揮霍　　❺ disagreement 意見不合

❷ adventure 冒險，冒險精神　❻ trajectory 軌跡; 軌線

❸ reality 現實；真實　　　❼ insist 堅持

❹ Vicar 教區牧師　　　　❽ inheritance 遺產；遺贈

- -

Aunt Louisa gives Philip her savings, an amount worth around a hundred pounds to pay for Philip's living expenses in Paris. Her generosity only lasts for a short time, and soon is replaced by the young man's visions in Paris. Eventually, the suggestion of the great artist proves that Philip's uncle is right all along. **"Take your courage in both hands and try your luck at something else"** The heart-felt, visceral advice ends Philip's two-year journey in Paris and terminates his dream of becoming an artist.

露易莎伯母把她的積蓄給了菲利普，這筆錢的價值大約一百英鎊，用於支付菲利普在巴黎的生活費用。她的慷慨只持續了很短的時間，很

Part 1

Part 2

Part 3

Part 4

Part 5

影子跟讀和中譯

Part 6

快就被年輕人對巴黎的憧憬所取代。最終，一位偉大藝術家的建議證明了菲利普伯父一直都是對的。「好好拿出勇氣，趁早轉行試試看吧！」這句發自內心深處且真誠的忠告結束了菲利普兩年的巴黎之旅，也終結了他成為藝術家的夢想。

❶ savings 存款；積蓄

❷ generosity 慷慨 [U]

❸ replace 取代

❹ vision 幻想，憧憬

❺ suggestion 建議，提議

❻ courage 膽量，勇氣

❼ visceral 出自內心深處的

❽ terminate 結束；終止

Perseverance is what Philip obviously lacks. His next step is to follow in his father's footsteps to become a doctor. With the qualification of entering a medical school, he chooses St. Luke's. For people entering on the medical profession, there are all kinds, and readers have yet to know how Philip will become. Philip believes that with his intelligence that he will scrape through the test, but in fact he fails at the anatomy examination, making him among the list of the incompetent. Love affairs distract Philip too much attention, when he should be focusing on the study. His worst decision is to involve himself with the stock market. Even though at first, he does have several wins, he eventually pays a hefty price for that. He writes a letter to his uncle asking for money, but is turned down. Without enough money, he has to find the job to pay daily expenses and discontinue his medical studies. He cannot believe that he screws things up, changing his entire life trajectory.

　　毅力顯然是菲利普所缺乏的。他的下一步是追隨父親的腳步成為一名醫生。有了進入醫學院的資格，他選擇了聖盧克醫學院。進入醫學界的人五花八門，菲利普會有什麼樣的成就，讀者還無法得知。菲利普相信以他的聰明才智可以勉強通過考試，但實際上他未能通過解剖學考試，躋身該屆學生中無能者之列。戀愛的事分散了菲利普太多的注意力，而他本應專注於學習。他最糟糕的決定是讓自己涉足股市。儘管一開始，他確實贏了幾次，但他最終為此付出了沉重的代價。他寫信向伯父要錢，但被拒絕了。沒有足夠的錢，他不得不找工作來支付日常開銷且中斷學業。他無法相信自己把事情搞砸了，改變了他整個人生的軌跡。

❶ perseverance 堅持不懈　　　　❺ intelligence 智能；智慧

❷ footstep 腳步，步伐　　　　　❻ anatomy 解剖學[U]

❸ qualification 資格，能力　　　❼ incompetent 不能勝任的

❹ profession 職業[C]　　　　　　❽ distract 使分心

　　In Philip's case, the birth does not make his life wonderful. His father's small inheritance should have been a great assistance for him, but his poor decision effaces what has been given to him.

　　就菲利普而言，出身並沒有使他的生活變得美好。他父親的小額遺產本應對他有很大幫助，但他的錯誤決定抹殺了所賦予他的一切。

In *The History of Tom Jones, a Founding,* Tom's birth does not give him the upper hand when he is not able to live with his co-father. Good education and wealthy family from birth do not make Tom capable of standing on his own feet. Instead, he lacks professional skills needed for survival, ultimately accepting 50 pounds from Lady Bellaston.

在《湯姆‧瓊斯》中,當湯姆不再與他的養父住在一起時,他的出身並沒有讓他佔上風。良好的教育和富裕的家庭並未讓湯姆有自力更生的能力。相反地,他缺乏生存所需的專業技能,最終還從貝拉斯頓夫人那裡接受了 50 磅。

So for those who are still jealous of your friends' rich parents, you might as well have to focus on what you can do at every key decision, making it tremendously beneficial to the next step of your life. Once you have become greater and greater, you will find that the world is a better place. You will even notice that Goddess of Fate makes a light smile at you.

所以對於那些還在嫉妒朋友具有有錢父母的人來說,不妨在每一個關鍵的決定上都把注意力放在自己能做的事情上,這對你人生的下一步助益良多。一旦你變得越來越棒,你也會發現世界變得更美好了。你甚至會注意到命運女神對你微微一笑。

Part 1
Part 2
Part 3
Part 4
Part 5
影子跟讀和中譯
Part 6

利用此篇章中英對照觀看並另外進行跟讀練習提升聽力專注力。

The fact that no third person must directly touch on other people's love affairs is a fundamental respect for people who are in love, yet meddling, out of curiosity, protection and other factors is commonly seen in reality. Among them, parents can be said to be the most frequent disturbance to their kid's marriage or love affairs. Parents may hold different ideas when it comes to this topic. Regret has often happened after years of marriage with someone, making it reasonable for parents to interfere. Gerald in *Gone with the Wind* has chosen to inform his child, Scarlett, whereas Mr. Brooke, Dorothea's uncle has adopted a liberal approach. However, the outcome for both Scarlett and Dorothea has remained the same, making us wonder what should someone do when there is actually a need to make an interference.

局外人不該直接干涉別人的感情事，這是對戀愛中的人最起碼的尊重，但在現實中出於好奇、保護等因素，干預的情況屢見不鮮。其中，父母可以說是對孩子婚姻或是戀愛時的干擾是最頻繁常見的。談到這個話題時，父母可能會有不同的看法。後悔常常會發生於與某人結婚多年後，因此父母的干預是合乎情理的。《亂世佳人》中的傑拉爾德選擇了告知他的孩子思嘉麗，而多蘿西亞的叔叔布魯克先生則採取了自由之道。然而，思嘉麗和多蘿西亞的結局是如出一轍的，讓我們不禁想到，當真正有需要干涉時，應該要怎麼做。

Part 1

Part 2

Part 3

Part 4

Part 5
影子跟讀和中譯

Part 6

❶ fundamental 基礎的　　❺ reasonable 合理的

❷ meddling 干涉　　❻ interfere 干預

❸ commonly 通常地，一般地　　❼ liberal 自由主義的

❹ disturbance 擾亂；打擾

"It is as fatal as a murder or any other horror that divides people." However, in *Drop Dead Diva*, Jane's coworker Owen and Kim, have decided to meddle in Jane's love affairs when they know Ian Holt, a cold-blooded killer is dating their colleague. Kim, who used to have some quarrels with Jane, because at the law firm they are in direct competition with Jane, now is willing to pay US 10,000 dollars to Ian Holt for him to go away. Ian Holt rejects the offer and then is met with Owen's direct opposition of his conduct. It seems that Kim and Owen are doing the right things, but they are still not in the relationship with either one of them. It's best if Kim and Owen just stay out of this.

「將別人拆散就跟殺人或其他恐怖罪行一樣要人命。」然而，在《美女上錯身》中，珍的同事歐文和金在認識伊恩·霍爾特後決定干涉珍的愛情，伊恩·霍爾特是一個冷血殺手，正在和他們的同事約會。以前和珍有過一些爭吵的金，因為在律師事務所他們和簡是直接的競爭關係，

現在願意付給伊恩・霍爾特一萬美元讓他走人。伊恩・霍爾特拒絕了這個提議，然後歐文直接反對他的行為。看起來金和歐文正在做正確的事情，但他們仍然沒有與他們中的任何一人交往。金和歐文最好不要插手干預。

1 horror 恐怖，震驚

2 cold-blooded 冷血的

3 colleague 同事，同僚

4 quarrel 爭吵；不和

5 competition 競爭，角逐

6 direct 直接的

7 opposition 反對；反抗

8 relationship 戀愛關係

To go deeper into the story, Grayson comes closer to getting married to Jane, but unfortunately, he dies after an operation in the hospital. Grayson hits the return button, so that he gets a second chance to live. Ironically, his soul is placed in Ian Holt's body, making his identity questionable for others.

更深一步去了解故事會發現格雷森差點和珍結婚，但不幸的是，他在醫院接受手術後去世了。格雷森按下了返回鍵這樣他就有了第二次活下去的機會。具有諷刺意味的是，他的靈魂被安置在伊恩・霍爾特的身體裡，讓其他人懷疑他的身份。

The janitor outside the cell tells Jane that a ruthless killer like Ian Holt does not have the right to get a second chance. Jane, now being Ian's lawyer, argues on Ian's behalf that there should be a stay of execution and she believes that Ian is innocent.

Part 1

Part 2

Part 3

Part 4

Part 5

影子跟讀和中譯

Part 6

Despite the fact that there are no new facts sustaining a stay, Ian comes up with the idea that there should be a new death warrant. Without the new death warrant, the new execution will be postponed, making Ian capable of living for another 24 hours. Having an excogitation of sufficient reason to get Ian acquitted in a day is insane. Owen and Jane can only surmise the idea that makes Ian stay life imprison. However, Ian demands they fight for a claim of actual guiltlessness because letters and other evidence makes Ian truly believe his innocence.

　　牢房外的看門人告訴珍，像伊恩·霍爾特這樣冷酷無情的殺手是沒有獲得第二次機會的權利。珍現在則是伊恩的律師，代表伊恩辯稱應該要暫緩執行死刑，她認為伊恩是無辜的。儘管沒有新的證據來支持暫緩執行死刑，但伊恩還是提出了應該有「新的死刑令」的想法。沒有新的死刑令，新的死刑執行將被推遲，這讓伊恩可以再活 24 小時。要在一天內想到足夠的事證讓伊恩無罪釋放是瘋狂的。歐文和珍只能想出讓伊恩被判終身監禁的主意。然而，伊恩要求他們須主張「真正無罪」，因為信件和其他證據讓伊恩真正相信自己是清白的。

❶ operation 手術

❷ procedure 程序；手續

❸ questionable 可疑的

❹ janitor 門警，看門人

❺ ruthless 無情的，殘忍的

❻ execution 處死刑；死刑

❼ sustain 支撐；承受

❽ warrant 授權令；逮捕狀

❾ postpone 使延期，延遲

❿ excogitation 想到

During the penalty of the trial, the victim's wife Cheryl did testify on Ian's behalf that he was innocent. Cheryl implored the judge that Ian, a man convicted of killing her husband, should be set free. Cheryl's testimony does make Owen and Jane rethink about things happening during the night at the club. They eventually figure out the real killer is Breeman, resulting in a happy ending for Jane and Ian. After the release, Jane and Ian's love affair may sound like an eccentric combination. Even though Ian's name has been cleared, others might still think Ian has mistaken his gratitude for Jane as true love. Jane cannot handle her grief with the loss of Grayson, so she starts the relationship with Ian.

在審判的刑罰期間,受害人的妻子綺麗兒確實曾為伊恩作證,證明他是無辜的。綺麗兒懇求法官釋放殺害她丈夫的男子伊恩。綺麗兒的證詞確實讓歐文和珍重新考慮了在俱樂部之夜所發生的事情。他們最終查明真正的兇手是布里曼,讓珍和伊恩有了幸福的結局。在獲釋後,珍和伊恩的戀情聽起來可能有些古怪。即使伊恩洗脫了罪名,但其他人可能仍會認為伊恩將他對珍的感激誤認為是真愛。珍無法處理失去格雷森的悲傷,而因此開始與伊恩談戀愛。

In *Middlemarch*, there is a great divide between Dorothea and Will if they have to be with each other. The long-enduring unsolved problems for all generations: The rich and the poor. There is bound to be a great hindrance for the two, even if Dorothea does not care about the money. It is true that destitution will soon wear out two people's love after their

Part 1

Part 2

Part 3

Part 4

Part 5

影子跟讀和中譯

Part 6

marriage. Like what's stated before, the best thing we can do is congratulations for any couple and let nature take its course. After all, it is not your marriage, so mind your own business. People's relationships will soon end the moment one of the parties cannot endure, and there is no need for one to act like a judge, arbitrating trivial matters happening in other people's marriage.

　　在《米德爾鎮的春天》中，多蘿西亞和威爾之間存在很大的分歧，如果他們要在一起的話。對所有世代來說，這是長久以來未解的難題：富人與窮人。就算多蘿西亞不在乎錢，這對兩人來說勢必會有很大的阻礙。誠然，婚後貧困很快就會磨滅兩人的愛情。就像之前所說的，我們能做的最好的事就是祝賀任何一對夫婦，並讓事情發展順其自然。畢竟，這不是你的婚姻，所以管好你自己的事。人與人之間的關係，當其中一方不能忍受的時候，很快就會結束，沒有必要像法官一樣，去仲裁別人婚姻中發生的瑣事。

❶ penalty 處罰；刑罰

❷ testify 作證

❸ implore 懇求

❹ testimony 證詞，證言

❺ eccentric 古怪的

❻ gratitude 感恩，感謝

❼ grief 悲痛，悲傷

❽ unsolved 未解決的

❾ hindrance 妨礙，障礙

❿ destitution 窮困；缺乏

TEST 7 影子跟讀和中譯 MP3 007

利用此篇章中英對照觀看並另外進行跟讀練習提升聽力專注力。

Most people have less of outward vision, focusing their attention on how to be financially independent, but in today's world, downsizing among large, profit-driven companies is so common, lots of people are not able to secure high-paying jobs as they have been used to. What makes things worse is that prices of commodities are getting increasingly higher, resulting in not having enough cash to live an ideal life. Some sit in their rented apartments in lethargic melancholy, whereas others fix their minds on getting the inheritance from parents so that they do not have to worry about money.

大多數的人不太留意外在景物,他們的注意力集中在如何在財務上獨立,但在當今世界,大型、以利潤為導向的公司的裁員非常普遍,很多人無法像他們過往那樣過慣獲得高薪工作。更糟糕的是,商品價格越來越高,導致沒有足夠的現金過上理想的生活。有的人悶悶不樂地坐在租來的公寓裡,有的人一心想著從父母那裡得到遺產,這樣他們就不用為錢發愁了。

Part 1
Part 2
Part 3
Part 4
Part 5 影子跟讀和中譯
Part 6

❶ downsizing 裁員   ❷ lethargic 無生氣的

In *North and South*, Margaret is lucky enough to get a large inheritance, making her an even better pick among single men. However, not all cases of inheritance end up with a pleasant result. In *Drop Dead Diva*, Violet Harwood is an heiress with a great deal of fortune. Unluckily, Violet Harwood's parents create a trust that is regulated by her brother. Without the approbation of the trustee, Violet Harwood is unable to use the money freely. Violet Harwood's plan of using her fortune on the shelter house has shattered because her brother controls the expenses. Fortunately, Violet Harwood's lawyer comes up with the idea of the dead-hand clause.

在《北與南》，瑪格麗特幸運地得到了一大筆遺產，使她成為單身男人中的佼佼者。然而，並非所有的繼承案例都以令人愉快的結果告終。在《美女上錯身》中，維奧萊特·哈伍德是一位擁有大量財富的女繼承人。不幸的是，維奧萊特·哈伍德的父母創建了一個由她哥哥監管的信託。沒有受託人的認可，維奧萊特·哈伍德無法隨意使用這筆錢。因為她的哥哥控制了花費，維奧萊特·哈伍德(Violet Harwood)用她的財產來建造庇護所的計劃破滅了。幸運的是，維奧萊特·哈伍德的律師提出了「死手條款」的想法。

❶ pleasant 令人愉快的　　　❸ approbation 許可，認可

❷ heiress 女繼承人　　　　❹ trustee 受託管理人

The definition of the dead-hand clause is to prevent dead people from exercising control from the grave beyond a single generation. The trick is Violet Harwood's parents cannot mandate her to give the antique watch to someone who did not exist when they died, making the whole trust ineffective. "What's good for the goose is good for the gander", so the inheritance shall be distributed equally between Violet Harwood and her brother.

　　死手條款的定義是為了防止死者從墳墓中行使超過一代人的控制權。訣竅在於維奧萊特·哈伍德的父母不能強制她將古董手錶交給他們死時不存在的人從而使整個信託無效。「必須一視同仁」，所以遺產將在維奧萊特·哈伍德和她的哥哥之間進行平均分配。

In *Middlemarch*, the idea of the dead-hand clause has also been used by Mr. Casaubon. "But well-being is not to be secured by ample, independent possession of property; on the contrary, occasions might arise in which such possession might expose her to the more danger."

　　在《米德爾鎮的春天》中，死手條款的想法也被卡索邦使用過。「但不是擁有充裕、獨立的財產生活就有保障。相反地，她擁有財產反

而會給她招來更多危險。」

Part 1

Part 2

Part 3

Part 4

Part 5

影子跟讀和中譯

Part 6

❶ definition 定義　　　　❸ ineffective 無效果的

❷ exercising 行使　　　　❹ gander 雄鵝

It might be reasonable to deduce that Mr. Casaubon has the foresight to protect his wife from men's deception, but a closer inspection can reveal his agenda. The inheritance will be the control of his wife even after his death. Mrs. Casaubon will lose the inheritance if she is married with Will, making her unable to tie the knot with the person she truly loves. Mr. Casaubon's intent can also be perceived as an insult to his own wife, who remains loyal to him while he is alive. Mrs. Casaubon has never been a materialistic young lady. Eventually, she figures out true love transcends all things, including a great deal of inheritance, and has a happy ending with Will.

卡索邦有先見之明以保護妻子免受男人所騙，這個推測似乎是合乎情理的，不過，在仔細審視後，可以察覺出這是他的謀劃。即使在他死後，遺產是用於掌控他的妻子。卡索邦太太若與威爾結婚的話，則將失去遺產，使她無法與心愛之人喜結連理。卡索邦的意圖也可以被視為對他自己妻子的侮辱，他在世時仍然忠誠於他。卡索邦太太從來都不是一個物質主義者。最終，她發現真愛超越一切，包括大量的遺產，並與威爾有一個幸福快樂的結局。

In *Wuthering Heights*, Edgar Linton is aware of Mr. Heathcliff's intention of claiming his private property and Thrushcross Grange. Originally, Edgar Linton wants Miss Cathy to use the property at her disposal, but later he ameliorates the will, putting it in the trust, for Miss Cathy to use and for her descendants to utilize after Miss Cathy dies. If Linton dies, the property will not go to Mr. Heathcliff. In *Wuthering Heights*, **"Earnshaw had mortgaged every yard of land he owned for cash to supply his mania for gaming; and he, Heathcliff, was the mortgagee."** Mr. Heathcliff not only gets Earnshaw's inheritance, Wuthering Heights, making Hareton, Earnshaw's son, moneyless, but also the estate of Edgar Linton. Even if Mr. Heathcliff's son, Linton dies, Catherine will not be the heir. Miss Cathy is reluctant to believe Mr. Heathcliff is a bad guy. According to the will of the previous Linton generation, Thrushcross Grange will only be inherited by a male descendant, so Mr. Heathcliff's contemplation is foxy and smart enough to let his son Linton get married with Miss Cathy.

在《呼嘯山莊》中，埃德加·林頓(Edgar Linton)知道希斯克利夫有意奪取他的私有財產和畫眉山莊。本來，埃德加·林頓想讓凱西小姐使用她所支配的財產，後來他更改了遺囑，將其委託給凱西小姐使用，並在凱西小姐死後供她的後代使用。如果林頓死了，財產就不會歸希斯克利夫先生所有。在《呼嘯山莊》中，恩蕭為了賭博早已把他所有的每一吋土地都抵押求現，而債主就是希斯克利夫。希斯克利夫不僅得到了恩蕭(Earnshaw)的遺產呼嘯山莊，讓哈里頓·恩蕭的兒子身無分文，而且還得到了埃德加林頓的遺產。即使希斯克利夫的兒子林頓死了，凱瑟琳也不是繼承人。凱西小姐不願意相信希斯克利夫是個壞人。按照林頓上一代人的遺囑，畫眉山莊只能由男性後代繼承，所以聰明且心思狡猾的希斯克利夫用計讓兒子林頓與凱西小姐成親。

Part 1

Part 2

Part 3

Part 4

Part 5

影子跟讀和中譯

Part 6

❶ intention 意圖

❷ private 私人的

❸ ameliorate 更改

❹ descendant 後代

❺ utilize 利用

❻ mortgage 抵押

❼ mortgagee 受抵押人

❽ moneyless 身無分文的

❾ estate 財產，資產

❿ contemplation 意圖；期望

Resolving an inheritance issue is not as easy as it seems. Sometimes it involves several people who maliciously vie for the property in court. Margaret in *North and South* is probably the happiest person that gets the inherited money, lending it to Mr. Thornton for a loan. Mrs. Casaubon's great wisdom of not valuing the property too highly is also very admirable. It is true that more money only creates more problems. We can only pray that we will not be ending like Mr. Heathcliff, living unhappily till his death.

解決遺產繼承問題並不像看起來那樣撒水拿魚。有時候涉及到幾個人在法庭上惡意爭奪財物。《北與南》裡的瑪格麗特可能是最幸福的人，得到了繼承的錢，把它借給了桑頓先生貸款。卡索邦太太不計較財產的大智慧也令人敬佩。更多的錢只會製造更多的問題是千真萬確的。我們只能祈禱不會像希斯克利夫那樣，在死之前都過得鬱鬱寡歡。

利用此篇章中英對照觀看並另外進行跟讀練習提升聽力專注力。

Wealthy or poor, investment has been tightly linked with people's life. Poor people wish to multiply their money through numerous investment opportunities, whereas rich people set their sights on getting richer by utilizing lucrative information. As a saying goes, the purpose of a novel is a reflection of reality. Great lessons can be learned from the following three novels: *Of Human Bondage*, *North and South*, and *Vanity Fair.*

無論貧富，投資都與人們的生活息息相關。窮人希望透過大量的投資機會來增加他們的財富，而富人則希望透過利用有利可圖的信息來變得更富有。俗話說，小說的目的是反映現實。從以下三部小說中可以得到很好的訓示：《人性枷鎖》、《北與南》和《浮華世界》。

❶ tightly 堅固地

❷ multiply 使（成倍地）增加

❸ lucrative 有利可圖的

❹ reflection 反映；表達

It is understood that a poor investment can lead someone to wait in line for a free soup quicker than one might think. In *Vanity*

Part 1

Part 2

Part 3

Part 4

Part 5
影子跟讀和中譯

Part 6

Fair, an inferior judgment in investment soon makes a rich person, like Mr. Sedley, bankrupt. **"Funds had risen when he calculated they would fall." "His bills were protested, his act of bankruptcy formal. The house and furniture of Russell Square were seized and sold up, and he and his family were thrust away."**

據了解，一項糟糕的投資可能會導致人們排隊等候免費湯的速度比人們想像的要快。在《浮華世界》中，投資若缺乏判斷力很快就會讓像薩德利先生這樣的富人破產。「他以為會下跌的基金全都上漲。」「他的支票全跳票了，他正式被宣告破產。羅素廣場的宅邸和傢俱都被查封拍賣，一家人被趕了出去。」

❶ judgment 評斷

❷ funds 基金

❸ calculate 計算

❹ protest 跳票

❺ bankruptcy 破產

❻ formal 正式的

❼ furniture 傢俱

❽ seize 沒入

Similar to the situation of Mr. Sedley in *Vanity Fair*, Mr. Thornton's condition in *North and South* shares the same fate. Both start out as rich from the beginning of the novel, but eventually the vicissitude of life emerges. Mr. Thornton's problem lies in his use of capital. Using it in new machinery and expansion results in not having enough cash for emergencies during a bad economy. During the economic recession, the value of all large stocks plunges, and Mr. Thornton's shares almost halve.

　　與《浮華世界》中薩德利先生的處境相似，桑頓先生在《北與南》中的境遇也是一樣的。兩人從小說開端都是富有的，但最終都出現了人生變化無常。桑頓先生的問題在於他對資金的使用。資金運用在新機器和工廠擴張會導致在經濟不景氣時沒有足夠的現金來應對緊急情況。在經濟衰退期間，所有大型股票的價值都暴跌，桑頓先生的股票幾乎減半。

❶ vicissitude 人生變化無常　　❺ expansion 擴張

❷ emerge 浮現　　❻ emergency 緊急情況

❸ capital 資金　　❼ economy 經濟

❹ machinery 機械　　❽ plunge 下跌

　　This corresponds to a wise saying from Nelly Dean in *Wuthering Heights* that no one can guarantee one's wealth throughout the entire life. One cannot always be rich, so using one's richness or wealth as a criterion when it comes to choosing a mate is not wise. Still, being rich is an irresistible quality in the market because wealth almost equals the sense of security. Henry in *North and South* provides us with the same insight. Margaret's inherited property is just a part of her. Even though it means that Margaret's money can instantly make him succeed, that should not be the criterion for choosing a life-partner. However, both Mr. Thornton and Henry have the contemplation

Part 1

Part 2

Part 3

Part 4

Part 5

影子跟讀和中譯

Part 6

of using Margaret's fortune to assist their own business. As in the case of Mr. Thornton, he lacks enough money to keep the company going, while Henry needs enough currency to start the law business.

這與《呼嘯山莊》中耐莉·迪恩的一句至理名言相吻合,沒有人能保證一生的財富。 人不可能永遠富有,因此用富有或財富作為擇偶標準是不明智的。富有仍是擇偶市場上不可抗拒的特質,因為財富幾乎等於穩定感。在《北與南》中的亨利為我們提供了同樣的見解。瑪格麗特的財產繼承只是她的一部分 雖然這意味著瑪格麗特的錢可以讓他瞬間成功,但這不應該成為選擇終身伴侶的標準。然而,桑頓先生和亨利都打算用瑪格麗特的財富來幫助他們自己的事業。桑頓先生的情況是他缺乏足夠的資金來維持公司的運轉,而亨利則需要足夠的資金來開展法律業務。

It's true that **"those who are happy and successful themselves are too apt to make light of the misfortune of others."** Ultimately, Margaret is willing to loan eighteen thousand and fifty-seven pounds to Mr. Thornton.

「那些成功又快樂的人,通常沒辦法設身處地體會別人的不幸。」最終,瑪格麗特願意借一萬八千五十七英鎊給桑頓先生。

Reversed fate makes the story a happy ending, but not everyone is as lucky as Margaret in *North and South* and Philip in *Of Human Bondage*. Margaret inherits the money and property worth 42,000 pounds, while Philip has an inheritance enough for him to finish medical school, making his fate much better than the rest of his classmates. Philip can focus all his attention on the study. Inheritance or extra money through other means can be good or bad really depends on the use of the person. In the case of Philip, it is definitely a bad thing. However, Philip squanders some of the money on girls instead of spending it on what's necessary, and worst of all, he gambles his tuition fees and money for the daily use on the stock market. **"History was being made, and the process was so significant that it seemed absurd that it should touch the life of an obscure medical student."** Selling shares now during the market plunge would mean that he can only have 80 pounds left, making him unable to continue his medical school.

　　命運的逆轉讓故事有了圓滿的結局，但並不是每個人都像《北與南》中的瑪格麗特和《人性枷鎖》中的菲利普那樣幸運。瑪格麗特繼承了價值 42,000 英鎊的財產，而菲利普則擁有足夠他完成醫學院學業的遺產，使他的命運比其他同學要好得多。菲利普可以將所有注意力都集中在學習上。透過其他方式得到遺產或獲取額外的金錢是好是壞則真的取決於使用的人。對於菲利普來説，這絕對是一件壞事。然而，菲利普把一些錢浪費在女生身上，而不是花在必要的東西上，最糟糕的是，他把學費和日常使用的錢都賭在了股市上。「當歷史書寫著全新的篇章，過程反映了重大的宏觀意義，竟影響一位小小醫學生的人生軌跡。」現在在市場暴跌期間出售股票意謂著他只能剩下 80 磅，使他無法繼續醫學院學業。

　　It can be concluded that investment money should come

Part 1

Part 2

Part 3

Part 4

Part 5

影子跟讀和中譯

Part 6

from the sources that will not influence one's living; otherwise, there is going to be a disaster. No matter how lucky a person can be, not being able to control the spending can result in serious damage in life (like Philip). Being too speculative can also have the same fate like Mr. Sedley, losing enormous wealth and his hard-to-build enterprise. Working industriously and diligently can still end up like Mr. Thornton, lacking enough money to keep the company afloat. Predictions of one's life trajectory are too unlikely, but what we can do is do our part and not investing recklessly or dreaming of becoming a rich billionaire in a day.

可以得出的結論是，投資資金來源應來自不影響生活開銷的部分；否則就會造成災難。無論一個人多麼幸運，無法控制開支都會對生活造成嚴重損害（如菲利普）。過於投機也會和薩德利先生一樣，失去巨大的財富和好不容易建立起來的事業。工作勤奮認真，最終仍可能像桑頓先生一樣，缺乏足夠的資金來維持公司的運轉。預測一個人的人生軌跡太煎水作冰，但我們能做的就是盡自己的一份力量，而不是盲目投資或夢想一天之內成為億萬富翁。

❶ speculative 投機的　　　❷ afloat 免於負債的

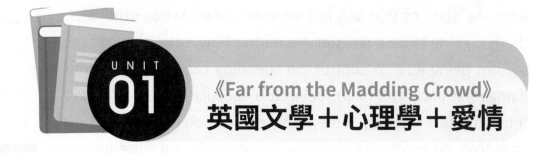

There are numerous love songs that are gripping and make people **resonate**. Among them, topics related to "love someone who truly loves you" and "choose the person you love" are the most popular. How to make the right choice and select the ideal life partner can be quite difficult. Often a lot of sayings on social media platforms and views of those celebrities in the show are misleading and are often rife with claims that don't stand up to scrutiny. Luckily, by reading British romance novels, like *Far from the Madding Crowd*, we can have a better understanding about making smarter choices.

1 The word **resonate** in the passage is closest in meaning to
(A) benefite
(B) reinvente
(C) reproduce
(D) reverberate

Part 1

Part 2

Part 3

Part 4

Part 5

Part 6

新托福全真模擬試題

Three promising guys in *Far from the Madding Crowd* can be seen as the summarized version of the real life. Three candidates are Oak, Boldwood, and Troy.

As anyone can remember from high school and college, most girls would go for the handsome and bad boy types, simply because they want to be tamed. **They** deem the guy with principles and integrity as boring and easily controlled, but that pushes them away from real happiness. That is also the main reason why Oak is not accepted by heroine, Bathsheba at the very beginning of the novel. Oak has several admirable traits that make him an ideal husband for Bathsheba. He is kind-hearted and has a real passion for Bathsheba. Oak proclaims that he will work twice as hard after marriage.

2 The word **they** in the passage refers to
(A) high school and college
(B) types
(C) girls
(D) principles

3 According to the passage, why does the author mention **"most girls would go for the handsome and bad boy types"**?

(A) to elucidate good-looking hunks and bad boys will get most of the girls.

(B) to elucidate the guy with principles and integrity will not have authentic happiness

(C) to elucidate the reason why Oak is not getting picked

(D) to explain working twice as hard after marriage is still not enough

So far, this has been about all the readers' perception of him. What about Boldwood's account about Oak? Near the very end of the novel, Boldwood has a heart-felt confession with Oak, when Boldwood has the sense that his prospect with Bathsheba is around the corner. **"You have behaved like a man, and I, as a sort of successful rival - successful partly through your goodness of heart I should like definitely to show my sense of your friendship under what must have been a great pain to you."**

As for Boldwood, he has a crazy devotion for Bathsheba that separates him apart from both Troy and Oak, and he is also the man who can wait for the girl for six years. At a much later time, a locked box that

Part 1

Part 2

Part 3

Part 4

Part 5

Part 6

新托福全真模擬試題

contains expensive silks, satins, poplins, velvets, muffs (sable and ermine), and a case of jewellery that includes four heavy gold bracelets and several lockets and rings can symbolize the importance of Bathsheba in Boldwood's heart.

4 According to the passage, why does the author mention **luxurious items** in the sixth paragraph?

(A) to show that Bathsheba is quite worth the wait

(B) to demonstrate the difficulty of getting them all

(C) to demonstrate girls will take these into considerations

(D) to demonstrate significance of Bathsheba in Boldwood's heart

In the middle part of the story, Bathsheba chooses Troy to be her husband, and Troy seems to fall into the untamed type. Troy can be good for a diversion, but not for a long-lasting relationship. However, Troy does have his charm. Troy volunteers to sweep and shake bees into the hive to impress Bathsheba. Troy further demonstrates his swordsmanship in their next appointment, creating a special moment to **imprint** a kiss on Bathsheba. The sense of novelty and surprise prevails, making her act on impulse and without reason.

5 The word **imprint** in the passage is closest in meaning to
(A) envelope
(B) implore
(C) impress
(D) induce

According to the author, Troy is good at concealment and superficiality so that ethical defects will not be perceived by women, whereas Oak stands in a sharp contrast with Troy because Oak's shortcomings can be apparently seen. Beneath the **veneer** of Troy, there are flaws most people will not notice. However, no matter how good one is at varnish, he will eventually show the true colors.

6 The word **veneer** in the passage is closest in meaning to
(A) expression
(B) facade
(C) emotion
(D) defects

Part 1

Part 2

Part 3

Part 4

Part 5

Part 6

新托福全真模擬試題

According to the author, **Troy is good at concealment and superficiality so that ethical defects will not be perceived by women, whereas Oak stands in a sharp contrast with Troy because Oak's shortcomings can be apparently seen. Beneath the veneer of Troy, there are flaws most people will not notice**. However, no matter how good one is at varnish, he will eventually show the true colors.

7 **Which of the sentences below best expresses the essential information in the highlighted sentence in the passage? Incorrect answer choices change the meaning in important ways or leave out essential information.**

(A) To make apparent defects indistinct is important because shortcomings can be apparently seen by women.

(B) Troy's flaws go unnoticeable because women choose not to discern, and Oak should learn to hide obviously seen drawbacks to get back on track.

(C) Most people judge a person based on the appearance so they are unable to discern Troy's inherent flaws and Oak's merits.

(D) Proficiency in concealment and superficiality is the key because no people want to end up like Oak without the like from most women.

(A) "Every voice in nature was **unanimous** in bespeaking change." **(B)** Unprotected ricks equal to 750 pounds of food. **(C)** The storm is coming closer, but Troy is nowhere to be seen. **(D)** According to Oak, Troy is asleep in the barn, neglecting all the harm that the weather might do to the crop and the consequence that will cost their barn. **(E)** Oak's endeavor to protect the crop shows his true love for Bathsheba. **(F)** Troy; however, demonstrates his indifference, making Bathsheba realize Troy as a person.

8 The word **unanimous** in the passage is closest in meaning to
(A) animated
(B) unimpressed
(C) sensitive
(D) concurrent

9 The author's descriptions of Troy mention all the following **EXCEPT**:
(A) Troy possesses the kind of wildness that easily attracts Bathsheba.
(B) Troy showcases his skills of sword to bewilder Bathsheba.

Part 1

Part 2

Part 3

Part 4

Part 5

Part 6

新托福全真模擬試題

(C) Bathsheba's has never been a reasonable type so Troy's peculiarity can easily prevail.

(D) Troy's insouciance about the approaching storm is an indication that his love for Bathsheba is not strong.

10 Look at the four squares 〔 ■ 〕 that indicate where the following sentence could be added to the passage.

He uses his actions to validate the love.

Where would the sentence best fit?

Click on a square 〔 ■ 〕 to add the sentence to the passage.

Boldwood loves Bathsheba deeply by wanting to provide her material comfort as a way to possess a beauty. Oak, on the other hand, wants to love Bathsheba by using all his life. Troy seems to have an agenda on Bathsheba because of Bathsheba's wealth and barn. Bathsheba at first gets married with Troy by choosing the one she truly loves, and till the end she figures out it is the one who truly loves her that she should be with. As a Chinese saying goes, "people look for him thousands of Baidu. Looking back suddenly, the man was there, in a dimly lit place." Perhaps Bathsheba just comes to the realization about this a bit too late. True love is always around us, but our perception prevents us from seeing **it** clearly.

11 What can be inferred about the statement "people look for him thousands of Baidu. Looking back suddenly, the man was there, in a dimly lit place." In the last paragraph?

(A) One has to go through certain life's vicissitude to get true love.

(B) One has to be wise and choose the tamed type to find true love.

(C) One has to discern motives of others to find true love.

(D) Because of its adjacency, one does not have to find true love

12 The word **it** in the passage refers to

(A) perception

(B) love

(C) realization

(D) place

 **內容**總結題

Part 1

Part 2

Part 3

Part 4

Part 5

Part 6
新托福全真模擬試題

Directions

Directions: An introductory sentence for a brief summary of the passage is provided below. Complete the summary by selecting THREE answer choices that express the most important ideas in the passage. Some answer choices do not belong in the summary because they express ideas that are not presented in the passage or are minor ideas in the passage. This question is worth 2 points.

Statement

Validation of love used in the novel can be the proof for us to discern one's value in another's heart.

•	
•	
•	

Answer Choices

A. True love does not validation of certain actions because it is always around.

B. Oak's willingness to protect ricks during the storm, even if it is not his duty.

C. Bathsheba falls for novelty and surprises, unable to discern Troy's true motive.

D. Troy's readiness of sweeping bees and demonstration of the swordsmanship.

E. Boldwood's confession serves as a great way to prove the integrity of Oak as a person.

F. Boldwood's preparation of a list of valuable treasures to wow Bathsheba.

解析

Part 1

Part 2

Part 3

Part 4

Part 5

Part 6
新托福全真模擬試題

1 【字彙題】：resonate 指的就是 reverberate，表示無數情歌扣人心弦，所引起的共鳴，故答案要選 D。

2 【代名詞指代題】：they 指的是前面的主詞 most girls，所以要選 C。

3 【修辭目的題】：作者寫這句話其實是引入一個主題，並接續闡述女主角也是這個情況，所以 Oak 的好才未被看見，當然也會拒絕 Oak 的追求了，故答案要選 C。

4 【修辭目的題】：寫這段落主要是講述 Boldwood 的追求手法，三個男主角都各有優點，最令人感到心動的是他秘密收藏了許多女主角都可能會喜歡的物件，所以會提到這些物件的主要原因就是這個段落的最後一句，這些都都象徵著貝莎芭在包伍德的內心的地位，故要選 D。

5 【字彙題】：imprint 指的就是 impress，指的是曹伊展示劍術等的舉動，讓這個行為深深烙印在女主角身上，故要選 C。

6 【字彙題】：veneer 指的是 façade，指的是表層，也就是一個人所披上的外衣，曹伊擅長掩飾，所以 veneer 就不容易被看穿，故要選 B。

7 【句子簡化題】：所標示的句子包含了兩個主角的性格差異等，

其實就是 C 選項所描述的意思，指是以比較隱晦的方式述說，因為沒有在主詞中提到兩個主角的名字，而是去描述現象，而這個現象才會導致說察覺不出曹伊的缺點和理解到歐克的優點。

8 【字彙題】：unanimous 指的是一致的、同時發生的，等同於 concurrent，故要選 D。

9 【細節和否定資訊題】：不包含 C 選項，因為閱讀段落中僅提到曹伊使劍和協助趕蜂等這些新奇感和驚奇，讓女主角失去理性和防備，但是沒有提到女主角本身性格是如何的。

10 【插入句子題】：主詞 he 一定是代替男主角也就是名詞，He uses his actions to validate the love 中，根據句意 he 不可能代替 Troy，曹伊在穀倉裡睡著了，不可能以睡著忽略作物去 validate the love，故可以刪去 E 選項。只有可能接在 F 處，指代 Oak，且因為敘述 Oak's endeavor to protect the crop shows his true love for Bathsheba，後面接續表明「他用自己的行動來證明愛」，故答案要選 F。

11 【推論題】：可以由這句宋詞名言和段落的敘述中得知，其實真愛就在近處，我們根本就不需要去追尋愛，故答案要選 D。

12 【代名詞指代題】：it 指的是上一句的 love，而不是句子中的 perception，故答案要選 B。

• 【內容總結題】：小說中有許多 Validation of love，其實要思考

Part 1

Part 2

Part 3

Part 4

Part 5

Part 6
新托福全真模擬試題

的框架就是三個男主角各展所長且各有優點吸引女主角的部分，可以很快選出答案。**B** Oak's willingness to protect ricks during the storm, even if it is not his duty.，Oak 在暴風雨中保護 rick 這點是打動女主角的重點，女主角的丈夫甚至不太重視，還喝醉昏昏大睡。**D** Troy's readiness of sweeping bees and demonstration of the swordsmanship，即使自己不擅長，Troy 也願意替女主角趕蜂，還有展示劍術時的英彩和出其不意，是讓女主角卸去本來冷靜理性和防備的主要一點。**F** Boldwood's preparation of a list of valuable treasures to wow Bathsheba，Boldwood 愛女主角很深，從他收藏的盒子中就可以發現出琳瑯滿目的東西，都期望有天可以交到女主角手中以展示自己的用心和愛意。

《Middlemarch》、《Frankenstein》
英國文學＋心理學＋愛情

A A saying from *Frankenstein* seems to convey the message of Justine's viewpoint that men inherently possess a good heart. B While various people may hold different views on this statement, Justine's conjecture about the devil who frames her is entirely correct. C The devil has a good heart from the start, but Victor, the main character, resists **acknowledging** the devil as his creation or his own baby, resulting in a distorted mind for the devil. D **There has been some mental separation** between the two. Acceptance and refusal are two antithetical concepts, and feeling loved is essential for anyone's personal development. E The devil's atrocious behavior results from getting rejected and not being amended. F Not getting loved makes someone feel neglected, unaccepted, being excluded. All these factors **engender** serious psychological behavior that creates some of the social crimes.

Part 1

Part 2

Part 3

Part 4

Part 5

Part 6

新托福全真模擬試題

13 Look at the four squares 〔 ■ 〕 that indicate where the following sentence could be added to the passage.

"I believe that I have no enemy on earth, and none surely would have been so wicked as to destroy me wantonly."

Where would the sentence best fit?

Click on a square 〔 ■ 〕 to add the sentence to the passage

14 The word **acknowledging** in the passage is closest in meaning to

(A) disregarding

(B) accentuating

(C) recognizing

(D) empowering

15 According to the passage, why does the author mention **"Justine's conjecture about the devil"**?

(A) to show accuracy of Justine's predictions

(B) to show men naturally possess a good heart

(C) to criticize Victor's narrow-minded view about the devil

(D) to show the mental barrier between Victor and the devil

16 What can be inferred about the statement "**there has been some mental separation.**" in the first paragraph?

(A) Both Victor and the devil have mental illness.

(B) Both Victor and the devil need to cure by studying antithetical concepts.

(C) Victor should acknowledge the devil as his own creation.

(D) Both Victor and the devil cannot have a mutual understanding.

17 The word **engender** in the passage is closest in meaning to

(A) surrender

(B) surmise

(C) galvanize

(D) resist

Education seems to be the key to amending people's mind. As the story progresses, the devil demands the creation of an identity similar to him so that he can find someone to love and to be loved. Victor at first concurs another attempt to create a new one for him, then out of the blue shifting into thinking that manufacturing the spouse for him **equates** with producing a monster. He can barely handle the devil, let alone dealing with two bad-looking creatures. The novel itself conveys several important messages essential for human beings to pay serious attention so that more

Part 1

Part 2

Part 3

Part 4

Part 5

Part 6

新托福全真模擬試題

societal problems can be avoided, thus making **it** especially great and eternally valuable.

18 The word **equates** in the passage is closest in meaning to

(A) fixates

(B) corresponds

(C) perpetrates

(D) replicates

19 The word **it** in the passage refers to

(A) the novel

(B) attention

(C) the devil

(D) problem

20 The author's descriptions of the devil mention all the following **EXCEPT:**

(A) The devil makes a request for a creation.

(B) The devil needs Victor's cognizance.

(C) The devil needs a spouse to feel loved.

(D) The devil fears that Victor's creation will be not as great.

Education seems to be the key to amending people's mind. **As the story progresses, the devil demands the creation of an identity similar to him so that he can find someone to love and to be loved. Victor at first concurs another attempt to create one for him, then out of the blue shifting into thinking that manufacturing the spouse for him equates with producing a monster. He can barely handle the devil, let alone dealing with two bad-looking creatures.**

21 **Which of the sentences below best expresses the essential information in the highlighted sentence in the passage? Incorrect answer choices change the meaning in important ways or leave out essential information.**

(A) Victor really needs to learn the skills of dealing with the formidable devil so that he can manufacture monsters without any worry.

(B) Victor is so afraid of creating another creature not good-looking that so he does not want to risk ingredients and take time to create a new one.

(C) Victor's endorsement rests on wanting his creation to feel loved, but on a second thought, the consequence of bringing another can be disastrous.

(D) Victor's thinking patterns are eccentric in a sense that

Part 1

Part 2

Part 3

Part 4

Part 5

Part 6

新托福全真模擬試題

he cannot think in the devil's shoe to create a new creature to love his creation.

A lot of murder crimes relating to love can be evaded if proper education and giving others more love have seriously been paid attention to. One does not have to take rejections too seriously. As a saying goes, **"things that seem disastrous at the time usually do work out for the rest."** Sometimes it does mean that God has a better idea, wanting to give you something much better.

22 According to the passage, why does the author mention **"things that seem disastrous at the time usually do work out for the rest."**?

(A) to show the importance of a good education

(B) to show there is bound to be a good arrangement

(C) to show societal problems will become more rampant

(D) to highlight consequences relating to disasters

As can be seen in another classic, *Middlemarch*, God certainly wants James to have not just someone better, but someone more suitable for him. In towns, neighbors and farmers have the predilection for Celia over Dorothea simply because Celia is more approachable, innocent, clever, and sophisticated. Dorothea has a quality of not self-admiring, thinking Celia is more charming than she is. James, on the other hand, has a crush on Dorothea. **"He felt that he had chosen the one who was in all respects the superior; and a man naturally likes to look forward to having the best."** However, James does not even have any chance with Dorothea.

His rival Mr. Casaubon does not have to do much and wins over the heart of Dorothea in such a short time. Luckily, James does not take this as a defeat or as something that will crush him. Getting rejected does not make someone a failure as most people would think. It is one's mindset that makes a man. Some would writhe under the idea of failure and rejection and then do the harm to the rival, hurt themselves, or cause quite a damage to someone you love. The thing is you do not have to act like that.

Part 1

Part 2

Part 3

Part 4

Part 5

Part 6

新托福全真模擬試題

Other people, including Dorothea's uncle, are shocked at Dorothea's choice of a man, not choosing James as a husband. Celia has a feeling that James will be a great husband, but from her observations, they will not be a good fit. Dorothea's choice may be good for both of them. It should not be interpreted as seriously harming someone. James claims that Dorothea should wait until she is mature enough to make the decision and is mad at Dorothea's choice, but eventually he gladly accepts this news. It does mean that more **saccharine** fruits are waiting for him definitely.

23 The word **saccharine** in the passage is closest in meaning to
(A) seductive
(B) sedentary
(C) serene
(D) sugary

A As the story progresses to a much later time, his feelings of getting rejected have gone already, having been replaced by getting engaged with Celia. **B** True love deserves some time to wait. **C** Two classics *Middlemarch* and *Frankenstein*, should all be the required reading during high school, shaping those feelings so that more tragedy can be avoided. **D**

24 Look at the four squares 〔■〕 that indicate where the following sentence could be added to the passage.

"His disregarded love had not turned to bitterness; its death had made sweet odors – floating memories that clung with a consecrating effect to Dorothea."

Where would the sentence best fit?
Click on a square 〔■〕 to add the sentence to the passage

 內容總結題

Part 1
Part 2
Part 3
Part 4
Part 5
Part 6
新托福全真模擬試題

Directions

Directions: An introductory sentence for a brief summary of the passage is provided below. Complete the summary by selecting THREE answer choices that express the most important ideas in the passage. Some answer choices do not belong in the summary because they express ideas that are not presented in the passage or are minor ideas in the passage. This question is worth 2 points.

Statement

Acceptance and refusal are two antithetical concepts, and feeling loved is essential for anyone's personal development. However, one does not have to go extreme because "things that seem disastrous at the time usually do work out for the rest."

•	
•	
•	

Answer Choices

A. James' maturity for not getting furious at Dorothea's choice is the reason why he eventually gets married with Celia.

B. Victor's inability of managing another monster makes him retracted the promise.

C. The devil's atypical behavior results from not getting accepted and feeling loved, so a new creation is mandatory.

D. James feels bittered for losing, but ultimately there is a better arrangement for him.

E. The devil's proposition is a good way for him to remedy the force of refusal inside the body.

F. Victor's foresight is right all along because the devil has become so uncontrollable at the end of the novel.

Part 1

Part 2

Part 3

Part 4

Part 5

Part 6
新托福全真模擬試題

 解析

13 【插入句子題】：從 A 處後方的 a saying 可以快速判別出插入句在此之前，且後面進一步表明這是賈斯婷對此訊息的看法，故要選 A。

14 【字彙題】：acknowledging 指的是認可或認同，故要選 C recognizing。

15 【修辭目的題】：賈斯婷對於誣陷她的惡魔的臆測，不是要說明她神準猜中，是要去說明惡魔性本善的部分，故要選 B。

16 【推論題】：維克特的拒絕和惡魔的渴望被接受是矛盾的，也就是因為這樣造成惡魔和維克特兩人之間有心靈隔閡存在，也就是兩人無法有共識等，故答案要選 D。

17 【字彙題】：engender 指的是 galvanize，所有這些因素會引起某些社會犯罪的嚴重心理行為，故要選 C。

18 【字彙題】：equates 指的是 corresponds，表示等同於創造出一個猛獸，故要選 B。

19 【代名詞指代題】：it 指的是上一句的 the novel，將 novel 代入後發現也符合句意，讓這本小說特別偉大且具永恆價值，故答案要選 A。

20【細節和否定資訊題】：惡魔並沒有擔憂所創造出來的對象，只有創作者也就是 Victor 有這個顧慮，怕製造出醜陋的生物。

21【句子簡化題】：其實就是 C 選項的描述，同意創造讓惡魔感受到被愛，但細想後就深怕帶來無法承受的災難。

22【修辭目的題】：提到這句話是因為，不管結果如何，在當下都是最好的安排了，所以不用覺得自己失去了什麼，也意謂著部用因此而產生許多負面不好的部分，就是接受結果，故答案要選 B。

23【字彙題】：saccharine 指的是甜蜜的；和顏悅色的，等同於 sugary 意謂著更甜美的果實在等待著他，故要選 D。

24【插入句子題】：發現不適合插入在 A 處後，在 his feelings of getting rejected have gone already, having been replaced by getting engaged with Celia 後，插入句進一步描述出 His disregarded love had not turned to bitterness 和 sweet odors，明顯是接續陳述前面句子的意思。在描述完後後句接著寫道，所以真愛是需要時間等待的，很明顯吻合，故答案要選 B。

- 【內容總結題】：要從接受和拒絕這兩點切入 **C** The devil's atypical behavior results from not getting accepted and feeling loved, so a new creation is mandatory。**D** James feels bittered for losing, but ultimately there is a better

Part 1

Part 2

Part 3

Part 4

Part 5

Part 6

新托福全真模擬試題

arrangement for him。**E** The devil's proposition is a good way for him to remedy the force of refusal inside the body。

- **A** James' maturity for not getting furious at Dorothea's choice is the reason why he eventually gets married with Celia.，前句 James' maturity for not getting furious at Dorothea's choice 符合題目的概念 things that seem disastrous at the time usually do work out for the rest，所以根本不需要因為被拒絕而心生怨懟。但是後面的 is the reason why he eventually gets married with Celia 是不正確的，除非改成因為老天有 better arrangement。 **B** Victor's inability of managing another monster makes him retracted the promise.（維克特後來打消替惡魔創造另一個伴，但不是他本身的 inability，他是有能力再創造一個的，且這與題目敘述無關）。**F** Victor's foresight is right all along because the devil has become so uncontrollable at the end of the novel.（小說最後，惡魔最後不受控制等等和拒絕與接受等概念沒有關係，雖然維克特有這個顧慮）

《Great Expectations》
英國文學＋心理學

"It would have been cruel in Miss Havisham, horribly cruel, to practice on the **susceptibility** of a poor boy, and to torture me through all these years with a vain hope and idle pursuit, if she had reflected on the gravity of what she did."

25 The word **susceptibility** in the passage is closest in meaning to
(A) suppression
(B) vulnerability
(C) serendipity
(D) astonishment

In *Great Expectations*, Miss Havisham's enormous wealth does not give her the joy that she is in desperate need of. Miss Havisham's use of the little girl, Estella, to torture the boy that she hires, on the other hand, fulfills

Part 1

Part 2

Part 3

Part 4

Part 5

Part 6

新托福全真模擬試題

her **whim** and the sense of satisfaction. As a saying goes, pain and conflict only bring more pain and conflict. Not letting go of the past rigorously hurts or erodes Miss Havisham's body and soul.

26 The word **whim** in the passage is closest in meaning to
(A) fancy
(B) memory
(C) creation
(D) emotion

Miss Havisham's hurt can be traced back to an incident happening about twenty years ago. Pip's encounter with both Magwitch and Compeyson paves the way for a further development. Magwitch, a poor and unlucky guy, under the guidance of fortune, meets with self-pretentious, handsome, **erudite** Compeyson. The chance encounter leads Magwitch to learn the truth about Compeyson and his partner, Arthur. The deception from a rich lady, which is believed to be Miss Havisham, earns them a great deal of fortune. However, Compeyson's lavish spending habits cannot keep up with the money he earns from doing the dirty things.

27 The word **erudite** in the passage is closest in meaning to

(A) scrupulous

(B) prolific

(C) knowledgeable

(D) capricious

Magwitch, a poor and unlucky guy, under the guidance of fortune, meets with self-pretentious, handsome, erudite Compeyson. The chance encounter leads Magwitch to learn the truth about Compeyson and his partner, Arthur. The deception from a rich lady, which is believed to be Miss Havisham, earns them a great deal of fortune. However, Compeyson's lavish spending habits cannot keep up with the money he earns from doing the dirty things.

28 **Which of the sentences below best expresses the essential information in the highlighted sentence in the passage? Incorrect answer choices change the meaning in important ways or leave out essential information.**

(A) Magwitch's encounter shows the importance of possessing good countenance and knowledge; otherwise, goddesses of luck will not favor you.

(B) Compeyson's extravagant spending is the main reason

Part 1

Part 2

Part 3

Part 4

Part 5

Part 6

新托福全真模擬試題

that he stages the plot with Arthur to get the fortune from the lady.

(C) Magwitch's encounter dives deep into the core of the story, finding out Compeyson and Arthur's imposture from Miss Havisham.

(D) Magwitch is not shrew enough to learn the agenda of both Compeyson and Arthur so he remains unlucky the whole life.

Doing bad things, and not getting caught for a while seems normal, but committing a list of crimes and not getting captured will be deemed unlikely. Pretty soon, both are taken to court for a trial. **A** They both are charged with putting stolen notes in circulation. Compeyson demands that they go **separate** ways, and Compeyson smart thinking does work. **B** Magwitch can only get Mr. Jaggers as a lawyer for the defense.

29 According to the passage, why does the author mention **"doing bad things, and not getting caught for a while seems normal, but committing a list of crimes and not getting captured will be deemed unlikely."**?

(A) to indicate committing fewer crimes will do them more good

(B) to indicate the charge will entirely rest on smart thinking

(C) to indicate people committing a crime always get caught

(D) to warn them that the police has already targeted them

ⓒ The "birth" issue and one's education also weigh heavily on criminals in court, making Compeyson's sentence the half of Magwitch's. ⓓ **They** are in the same prison ship, but Magwitch cannot get closer to Compeyson. ⓔ Fleeing the prison ship leads to the encounter of Pip, the main character, and Compeyson. This time Magwitch has enough time to smash Compeyson's face to get revenge.

30 The word **separate** in the passage is closest in meaning to

(A) serendipitous

(B) sanguine

(C) different

(D) enchanted

31 The word **they** in the passage refers to

(A) birth and education

(B) criminals

(C) ways

(D) Magwitch and Compeyson

32 Look at the four squares [■] that indicate where the following sentence could be added to the passage.

Magwitch has been unfairly judged at the court and eventually gets 14 years in prison.

Where would the sentence best fit?

Click on a square [■] to add the sentence to the passage

33 According to the passage, why does the author mention **"the birth issue and one's education also weigh heavily on criminals in court"**?

(A) to show British courts value one's birth and education

(B) to sway the jury so that Compeyson will get the half of Magwitch's sentence

(C) to further explain why Compeyson wants them to go separate ways

(D) to show the penalty will be relevant to the kind of prison ship they will be staying

Part 1
Part 2
Part 3
Part 4
Part 5
Part 6
新托福全真模擬試題

Magwitch and Compeyson will try every way to bring each other down. Compeyson can report there is a refugee that flees from the prison ship. Magwitch and Pip's flee then encounters The Hamburg, the steamer, sailing swiftly towards them. People on the steamer demand the assistance to capture the person wrapping with a cloak on Pip's ship. As Magwitch goes behind the person who tries to seize him, he has the time to tear off another person with a cloak on the steamer to verify whether his identity is Compeyson. Compeyson is in shock and then waddles. Thereafter, they have a struggle, falling into the river. Other guys trying to seize Magwitch eventually cause the capsizing of the Pip's ship. Magwitch is found seriously injured, and with no traces of Compeyson. Pip has no reason to doubt Magwitch's account of what just happened because it is the same as **that** of the officer who steers the ship. At Police Court, it is revealed that Compeyson eventually falls into the river and is found dead. Compeyson and Arthur, Miss Havisham's brother, all pay the price. Arthur dies from serious illness right before the sentence of both Magwitch and Compeyson.

34 What can be inferred about Philip's reaction after Compeyson's disappearance?

(A) Philip is fully convinced that Magwitch might be concealing something.

(B) Philip's intuition tells him to trust Magwitch, but his heart does not.

(C) Deep down, Philip is still worried the consistency of the account between Magwitch and the officer can be a coincidence.

(D) The officer's account weighs heavily, so Philip believes what Magwitch has to say.

35 The author's descriptions of the incident on the ship mention all the following **EXCEPT**:

(A) Compeyson and Arthur all pay the price.

(B) Compeyson does not don a cloak.

(C) The person wrapping with a cloak on Pip's ship is Magwitch.

(D) Compeyson and Magwitch have a fight on the ship.

36 The word **that** in the passage refers to

(A) officer

(B) reason

(C) ship

(D) account

Part 1
Part 2
Part 3
Part 4
Part 5
Part 6
新托福全真模擬試題

Miss Havisham's distorted mind resulting from the harm caused by Compeyson and Arthur could totally be cured if she knew the notion of "what comes around goes around" and "unjust is doomed to destruction." Karma will eventually do the justice for her. Miss Havisham eventually comes to her senses right before her death that she has done quite a damage to another human being, Estella.

"That she had done a grievous thing in taking an impressionable child to mould into the form that her wild resentment, spurned affection, and wounded pride, found vengeance in, I knew full well."

During her chat with Pip, Miss Havisham tries to seek inner peace. Forgiveness really is a cure for all bad things. Miss Havisham would have lived a much happier life, if she had mastered the art of forgiveness.

 內容總結題

Part 1

Part 2

Part 3

Part 4

Part 5

Part 6

新托福全真模擬試題

Directions

Directions: An introductory sentence for a brief summary of the passage is provided below. Complete the summary by selecting THREE answer choices that express the most important ideas in the passage. Some answer choices do not belong in the summary because they express ideas that are not presented in the passage or are minor ideas in the passage. This question is worth 2 points.

Statement

There are several causes and effects throughout the novel. Present actions result from previous behavior. Compeyson is among them that causes further development of the story.

•	
•	
•	

Answer Choices

A. Estella is the puppet employed by Miss Havisham as a way to balance her loss from imposture.

B. Magwitch's serendipitous encounter with Compeyson and Arthur reveals what actually causes the awry mental state of Miss Havisham.

C. Miss Havisham needs to squander her fortune to fill the imagination so that she can maintain her state of happiness.

D. Compeyson's smart thinking lessens his sentence to halve so that he does not have to pay for what he did.

E. Magwitch's smashing of Compeyson results from Compeyson's previous conduct.

F. At Police Court, Pip has to believe Magwitch's account because Magwitch is the one who will give him a great deal of fortune.

解析

Part 1

Part 2

Part 3

Part 4

Part 5

Part 6
新托福全真模擬試題

25 【字彙題】：susceptibility 等同於 vulnerability，指的是 Pip 是易受攻擊玩弄的，故答案要選 B。

26 【字彙題】：哈維森小姐利用小女孩艾絲黛拉來折磨她僱用的男孩，滿足了她的幻想和滿足感，whim=fancy，故答案要選 A。

27 【字彙題】：erudite= knowledgeable，指的是貧窮倒霉的馬格韋契在命運的指引下，邂逅了自命不凡、英俊博學的康培生，故答案要選 C。

28 【句子簡化題】：很明顯 C 選項是摘要精選句，是整本小說和這個段落的核心，馬格韋契的偶遇讓他了解到哈維森小姐受到欺騙的背後經過。

29 【修辭目的題】：提到這句當作段落首句，是要引入康佩生和馬格韋契犯了一堆罪後鐘就被捕了。也就是逃不過法網，一定會被抓到的，故答案要選 C。

30 【字彙題】：separate=different，指各走各的，他們都被控將讓盜取的紙幣流通到市面上。康佩森要求他們分道揚鑣，故答案要選 C。

31 【代名詞指代題】：they 不可能指段落第一句的主詞，birth and education 不可能在船上，所以要排除 A。由前個段落和這個段落的敘述，只有可能去推斷指的是 Magwitch and Compeyson，故答案要選 D。

32 【插入句子題】：從插入句中的 14 年，對應到 D 選項前面的 the half of Magwitch's，可以知道所判的刑期。康佩森的刑期只有馬格韋契的一半→馬格韋契在法庭上受到不公平的審判，最終被判入獄 14 年。在句意上也吻合，故答案要選 D。

33 【修辭目的題】：在段落中，這句是進一步解釋出身和教育是會影響判決的，所以康佩生的刑罰只有馬格韋契的一半。但主要還是要回到上一段，康佩生耍小聰明，所以要兩人分道揚鑣，分開請律師，所以這樣看起來，他不是共犯，比較像是受人影響被帶壞或誤入歧途而導致這個行為，所以能引起法官同情等等。而表面上也是如此，因為康佩生所受的教育高且出身好，在外界的認定上，他不太可能會去犯這些罪行，更會被大家解讀成是因為誤交損友，故要選 C。

34 【推論題】：康佩生失去蹤跡後，所能推測出的主要就是後面敘述的部分，也就是馬格韋契受傷後，但是在兩人打鬥落海後，只有馬格韋契知道後來發生了什麼事，而皮普或許可能內心有所疑問，但是馬格韋契的陳述與掌舵的官員的描述是如出一轍，所以皮普更沒有理由去懷疑馬格韋契的陳述，故答案要選 D。

35 【細節和否定資訊題】：康佩生有穿斗篷。「當馬格韋契走到試圖抓住他的人身後時，他有時間在汽船上撕下另一位披著斗篷的人，以驗證他的身份是否是康培生。康佩生先是感到震驚，然後搖搖欲墜。」可以推測出另一位披著斗篷的人就是康佩生。

Part 1
Part 2
Part 3
Part 4
Part 5
Part 6
新托福全真模擬試題

36 【代名詞指代題】：從 Pip has no reason to doubt Magwitch's account of what just happened because it is the same as **that** of the officer who steers the ship. 中可以馬上找出，that 一定是指代 doubt 後的主詞，且是單數的名詞，答案要選 D。

- 【內容總結題】：關鍵在於因果關係，所以釐清後就能馬上選出選項了，而康佩生是導致很多事件發生的主要人物 **Present actions result from previous behavior**，**A** Estella is the puppet employed by Miss Havisham as a way to balance her loss from imposture，是因為 Miss Havisham 過去受到傷害所導致現在將 Estella 當成 puppet。**B** Magwitch's serendipitous encounter with Compeyson and Arthur reveals what actually causes the awry mental state of Miss Havisham，Magwitch 在命運牽引下遇到 Compeyson and Arthur，才發現導致 Miss Havisham 的心靈扭曲，**E** Magwitch's smashing of Compeyson results from Compeyson's previous conduct，康佩生受到 Magwitch 的攻擊，也是導因於受拘捕後，康佩生要求兩人分道揚鑣，進而導致 Magwitch 的刑期是康佩生的一倍。

In our daily life, we rarely take the idea or wisdom from time-enduring classics into account, so we are still struggling in several aspects of our life. The storylines of *Vanity Fair* ring alarmingly true to most readers. By taking an in-depth look into how Becky capitalizes every opportunity to get the desired outcome, we can probably have a better life.

Not having parents and being poor are two main factors that put heroine of *Vanity Fair*, Becky Sharp into a **disadvantaged** position. Since most girls have their parents' assistance to settle matters with the young man to change the fate, Becky has to do this all on her own, and one does not have to be extremely clever to know the truth that getting married with a wealthy husband will more or less make one's later life a lot smoother. The chance event comes when one of her wealthy friends, Amelia invites her to stay at her house for a week before Becky moves on to do the private tutor job.

Part 1

Part 2

Part 3

Part 4

Part 5

Part 6

新托福全真模擬試題

37 The word **disadvantaged** in the passage is closest in meaning to

(A) unfavorable

(B) reversed

(C) reserved

(D) redeveloped

Becky soon finds out a golden opportunity that Amelia's brother, Joseph is still single. Becky is ready to put the move on Joseph, but she is not yet ready. Mr. Sedley deliberately wants Becky to try some curry with cayenne pepper and a chili that Becky obviously cannot put up with, and then Mr. Sedley enjoys this show along with his son, Joseph, and also informs his son that Becky has set her sights on him. Then all things have been in Becky's favor, but George Osborne considers Becky and Joseph a **mesalliance**, frightening Joseph for a bit. Osborne's intervention ends Becky's prospect of marrying with Joseph outright.

38 According to the passage, why does the author mention **Mr. Sedley's move**?

(A) to demonstrate Mr. Sedley's disdainfulness towards Becky

(B) to demonstrate Mr. Sedley is a womanizer

(C) to get Becky familiarized with the taste of curry with cayenne pepper

(D) to observe Becky's reactions with things she does not seem to enjoy

39 The word **mesalliance** in the passage is closest in meaning to

(A) coordination

(B) annihilation

(C) mismatch

(D) legitimacy

However, this setback does not dissuade young Rebecca from reaching her goal. It does mean she has not yet mastered the art of deception. Becky embarks on her journey of being the governess of Sir Pitt's two daughters, making her much closer to a real celebrity circle. Her goal has been **constant**: to find a rich husband. Winning the heart over Sir Pitt's two daughters and being baronet's **confidence** at Queen's Crawley are the first step towards Rebecca's success, and the mastery of the hypocrisy the second, the marriage with Rawdon Crawley the third.

Part 1

Part 2

Part 3

Part 4

Part 5

Part 6

新托福全真模擬試題

40 The word **constant** in the passage is closest in meaning to

(A) recondite

(B) successful

(C) pragmatic

(D) unalterable

41 The word **confidence** in the passage is closest in meaning to

(A) scepticism

(B) intimacy

(C) phlegm

(D) retention

A Becky earns the accolade from Miss Crawley that she has more brains than half the shire, and "as her equal." **B** Sir Pitt wants Becky to be his bride by saying **"you've got more brains in your little vinger than any baronet's wife in the country."**, but Becky's true success is to tie the knot with Rawdon Crawley, who will inherit most of Miss Crawley's fortune. **C** Rawdon Crawley's viewpoints about Becky are concordant with **those** of his aunt, Miss Crawley and his father, Sir Pitt. **D** He has met multiple clippers, but has never encountered someone as witty as his wife, Becky.

E These correspond to several notions mentioned in one of the bestsellers, *The Wealth Elite*. It is not about the inheritance or Luck. One does need to have the exact DNA to keep money or acquire more wealth. In one of the British classics, *Treasure Island*, an idea relating to this has also been put forward at the very end of the chapter that it is not the amount of the money that you get. It is about one's nature.

42 Look at the four squares (■) that indicate where the following sentence could be added to the passage.

Distinguished brilliance can certainly make up for poor birth as in the case of Becky.

Where would the sentence best fit?

Click on a square (■) to add the sentence to the passage

43 The word **those** in the passage refers to
(A) viewpoints
(B) fortune
(C) clippers
(D) success

Part 1

Part 2

Part 3

Part 4

Part 5

Part 6

44 According to the passage, why does the author mention **The Wealth Elite and Treasure Island**?

(A) to contrast messages conveyed by *Vanity Fair*

(B) to delineate different aspect of successes

(C) to coincide Rawdon Crawley's viewpoints about Becky

(D) to solidify notions mentioning earlier

The following development does not let Rawdon Crawley down as Becky exhibits more of her **inborn** talent. Becky seizes the moment during the war to make a fortune by selling a horse to Joseph. Wealthy people aspiring to flee also lack the key transportation, the horse. Even Lord Bareacres is willing to pay the price for two horses under this circumstance. The sum is enormous enough to be considered a fortune to Becky. With the money and the sale of the **residue** of Rawdon's effects, and her pension as a widow, she will be financially independent, not having to worry about money for her entire life. Later, it is believed that the value of two horses equals a luxurious life in Paris a year for both Rawdon Crawley and Becky.

45 According to the passage, why does the author mention **"Even Lord Bareacres is willing to pay the price for two horses under this circumstance."**?

(A) to show wealthy people artificially inflate the price of the horse

(B) to feel pity for Joseph that he will not get the horse

(C) to show scarcity makes the value of the horse soared

(D) to show popularity of riding a horse to flee the country

46 The word **residue** in the passage is closest in meaning to

(A) balance

(B) wealth

(C) value

(D) inheritance

47 The word **inborn** in the passage is closest in meaning to

(A) instinctive

(B) acquired

(C) learned

(D) independent

The couple's reunion after war brings more joyful news, as concealment of cash, checks, watches, and other valuables in Becky's coat reveals themselves. Becky has had unprecedented success even in Paris.

Part 1

Part 2

Part 3

Part 4

Part 5

Part 6

新托福全真模擬試題

It can be concluded that despite Becky's poorness and lack of the background, she possesses an admirable quality against adversity and cruel fate, surpassing her classmates, Amelia, born into a wealthy family and with the worth of the 10,000 pounds, where she has none. "So in fetes, pleasures, and prosperity, the winter of 1815-16 passed away with Mrs. Rawdon Crawley, who accommodated herself to polite life as if her ancestors had been people of fashion for centuries past – and who from her wit, talent, and energy, indeed merited a place of honor in Vanity Fair."

It can be concluded that despite Becky's poorness and lack of the background, she possesses an admirable quality against adversity and cruel fate, surpassing her classmates, Amelia, born into a wealthy family and with the worth of the 10,000 pounds, where she has none. "So in fetes, pleasures, and prosperity, the winter of 1815-16 passed away with Mrs. Rawdon Crawley, who accommodated herself to polite life as if her ancestors had been people of fashion for centuries past – and who from her wit, talent, and energy, indeed merited a place of honor in Vanity Fair."

48 **Which of the sentences below best expresses the essential information in the highlighted sentence in the passage? Incorrect answer choices change the meaning in important ways or leave out essential information.**

(A) Mrs. Rawdon Crawley is an exemplary character that demonstrates one's inherent natures can get you there, earning an honorable place in Vanity Fair.

(B) Amelia should be so grateful for having a life with a great deal of fortune from the start, otherwise, her life will be more miserable, and cannot seem to catch up with Mrs. Rawdon Crawley.

(C) Becky's success rests on her desire to win Amelia so that she imitates other's admirable to help her eventually get there.

(D) Mrs. Rawdon Crawley's predecessors are themselves aristocrats, so she has the kind of personality to fight against tortured life and get in the celebrated circle in Paris.

Part 1

Part 2

Part 3

Part 4

Part 5

Part 6

新托福全真模擬試題

 內容總結題

Directions

Directions: An introductory sentence for a brief summary of the passage is provided below. Complete the summary by selecting THREE answer choices that express the most important ideas in the passage. Some answer choices do not belong in the summary because they express ideas that are not presented in the passage or are minor ideas in the passage. This question is worth 2 points.

Statement

Becky's demonstration that without birth, inheritance, and other factors, one can still get to the top.

•	
•	
•	

Answer Choices

A. Have a connection with a celebrated circle in Paris so that you will get a great deal of fortune sooner.

B. Initiating an invitation to stay at her rich friend Amelia's house so that she can get closer to Joseph.

C. Making a fortune when grasping the right moment, and that multiplies the money that one can earn.

D. Making Osborne change his mind so that she can still have a chance with Joseph.

E. Selecting the right life-partner that will inherit a great deal of fortune.

F. Impress key people and get their recognition so that your place will be firm.

解析

Part 1

Part 2

Part 3

Part 4

Part 5

Part 6
新托福全真模擬試題

37 【字彙題】：disadvantaged=unfavorable 指夏普處於不利的處境，故答案要選 A。

38 【修辭目的題】：薩德利先生算是刁難，他有點看出蓓琪對自己兒子有意思，而儘管 Joseph 外在條件等不太好，蓓琪渴望自己能藉由嫁到富人家翻轉貧窮的命運，但她的掌握還不夠純熟，就被看穿了，薩德利先生故意要蓓琪試下她顯然無法承受的一些辣咖哩和辣椒，在小說中還特地向她提到並不是什麼都是適合自己的。薩德利先生的這個舉動可以理解成是他看不起蓓琪窮，故要選 A。而後面奧斯朋認為蓓琪和喬瑟夫門不當戶不對。在小說中，奧斯朋覺得這樣他娶 Amelia 的話，就要跟蓓琪這樣的窮女子當親家，他頗感到不滿，就開始干涉事情的發展，讓蓓琪大失所望的離開薩德利先生家，轉而前去別處當家庭教師。

39 【字彙題】：mesalliance 指的是喬治·奧斯朋認為蓓琪和喬瑟夫門不當戶不對，故要選 C mismatch。

40 【字彙題】：constant 指的是雷貝卡對自己的目標**堅定不移**或**恆定不變**的，故答案要選 D unalterable。

41 【字彙題】：confidence 雖然常見的意思是信心，但在這裡指的是在皇后克勞利成為準男爵的心腹，所以要選 intimacy。

42 【插入句子題】：從段落第一句和第二句可以看到有 Miss

Crawley 和 Sir Pitt。且在 C 後面可以看到 Rawdon Crawley，且後面有 are concordant with those of his aunt, Miss Crawley and his father, Sir Pitt.這樣的敘述，代表分別是對 Becky 能力的贊同和認可，插入句不可能插入在這之間的段落中，所以可以排出 B 和 C。在重回來看插入句 Distinguished brilliance can certainly make up for poor birth as in the case of Becky.並閱讀句意，可以發現這只可能是整個段落的主題句且至於首句，至於首句後閱讀發現句意也吻合，故答案要選 A。

43 【代名詞指代題】：those 很明顯指的是指代前面的主詞 viewpoints，故答案要選 A。

44 【修辭目的題】：提到這點的原因是接續闡述前面提到的論點，也就是蓓琪本身的天賦補足了出身的不足，所以能討好這三位貴族人家，且能力都受到他們三個認可。而這兩本提的書籍，也是述說著重點還是在 DNA/NATURES，而不是其他因素影響一個人能否往上爬並獲取成功，故答案要選 D。

45 【修辭目的題】：巴雷克雷斯大人也願意以這樣的價格購買兩匹馬，代表馬在這個時候因為稀有而使得價值飆升，物以稀為貴，故答案要選 C。

46 【字彙題】：residue 指（償債、納稅、遺贈等後的）剩餘財產，在小說裡指的是洛頓所遺留下來的剩餘財產（這是當下蓓琪在丈夫參戰後的推論，如果洛頓真的因為上戰場而死的話，事後洛頓平安歸來），而 balance 指剩餘的部分或餘額正好符合，故要選 A balance。

Part 1
Part 2
Part 3
Part 4
Part 5
Part 6
新托福全真模擬試題

47 【字彙題】：inborn 指的是蓓琪展示了更多她與生俱來的才能，故要選 A instinctive。

48 【句子簡化題】：要選 A，Becky 根本堪稱是模範，整個段落的濃縮意思就是，Becky 憑藉著天賦而在浮華世界中有一席之地。

• 【內容總結題】：關鍵在於選出所有段落中有敘述到 Becky 使用上的手段且這些手段讓她往上爬升。C Making a fortune when grasping the right moment, and that multiplies the money that one can earn，蓓琪在文中有好幾次都抓準時機，像是在缺馬的時候高價賣馬等等，讓她快速致富。E Selecting the right life-partner that will inherit a great deal of fortune，蓓琪選擇 Rawdon Crawley 當夫君，因為他能繼承克勞利夫人的龐大財產。F Impress key people and get their recognition so that your place will be firm，蓓琪討好重要的人物像是 Miss Crawley 和 Sir Pitt，並且得到這兩人的高度認可。

253

People are so focusing on "birth" that they forget it is a series of choices that eventually make or break someone. Bad decisions in every key life moment can drag someone down the path, leading to an **inferior** outcome. The term "birth" will be just glamorous from the start and disastrous in the end.

49 The word **inferior** in the passage is closest in meaning to
(A) obliterated
(B) subordinate
(C) inconclusive
(D) confined

Part 1

Part 2

Part 3

Part 4

Part 5

Part 6

新托福全真模擬試題

A In *Of Human Bondage*, with some deliberation, Philip's first life decision is to be an intern at the office of Messers. Herbert Carter & Co. in which his uncle and friends believe that under the tenure, Philip will learn professional skills enough for him to stand on his own feet and make a living. **B** **"Every profession, and every trade, required length of time, and what was worse, money."** However, Philip is just like some of the twentysomethings, and not yet understands the **mortifying** conviction that three years at the first job are quite an important step for your next job.

50 According to the passage, why does the author mention **"Every profession, and every trade, required length of time, and what was worse, money."**?

(A) to show that Philip is bound to gain professional skills at the firm

(B) to show some of the twentysomethings are more mature than Philip

(C) to demonstrate in every profession, a certain effort is required

(D) to show Philip's uncle and friends are fully aware of the concept

51 The word **mortifying** in the passage is closest in meaning to

(A) practical

(B) annoying

(C) unnoticeable

(D) emboldening

C "I cannot imagine you sitting in an office over a ledger." "My feeling is that one should look upon life as an adventure, one should burn with the hard, gem-like flame, and one should take risks, one should expose oneself to danger." **D** His friend's belief in Philip's ability in art does not equal with how the reality views about him as a person. Despite the Vicar's disagreement for Philip's life trajectory change, Philip insists on going to Paris to learn art. **E** Still Philip has to wait for a year to get his small inheritance from his father.

52 Look at the four squares (■) that indicate where the following sentence could be added to the passage.

Bad advice from one of his friends also dissipates his valuable twentysomething years.

Part 1

Part 2

Part 3

Part 4

Part 5

Part 6

新托福全真模擬試題

Where would the sentence best fit?

Click on a square 〔 ■ 〕 to add the sentence to the passage

"I cannot imagine you sitting in an office over a ledger." "My feeling is that one should look upon life as an adventure, one should burn with the hard, gem-like flame, and one should take risks, one should expose oneself to danger." His friend's belief in Philip's ability in art does not equal with how the reality views about him as a person. Despite the Vicar's disagreement for Philip's life trajectory change, Philip insists on going to Paris to learn art.

53 **Which of the sentences below best expresses the essential information in the highlighted sentence in the passage? Incorrect answer choices change the meaning in important ways or leave out essential information.**

(A) Life is always involved with a risk, so Philip's friends are giving him encouragement he really needs.

(B) Philip's friends really do not want Philip to regret for not pursuing art during his valuable twentysomething years.

(C) Being an accountant drains one's valuable life, so that Philip should pursue art and shine like a gem in the fire.

(D) How the world actually views about someone should also be taken into considerations when one wants to embark on an adventure.

Aunt Louisa gives Philip her savings, an amount worth around a hundred pounds to pay for Philip's living expenses in Paris. **Her generosity only lasts for a short time, and soon is replaced by the young man's visions in Paris.** Eventually, the suggestion of the great artist proves that Philip's uncle is right all along. **"Take your courage in both hands and try your luck at something else"** The heart-felt, visceral advice ends Philip's two-year journey in Paris and **terminates** his dream of becoming an artist.

54 According to the passage, why does the author mention **"her generosity only lasts for a short time, and soon is replaced by the young man's visions in Paris."**?
(A) to show Philip's future prospect is more important than Louisa
(B) to show Philip is ungrateful
(C) to show insufficiency of the money for a list of activities in Paris
(D) to show Philip is able to save his inheritance for other uses

55 According to the passage, what can be inferred about the great artist?

(A) He is the spy sent by Philip's uncle to end Philip's impractical dream.

(B) He is doing this for the effects of the show to knock down attendants.

(C) His straightforward suggestion actually saves Philip from meandering.

(D) He really wants Philip to go somewhere else to polish his skills, but not in Paris.

56 The word **terminates** in the passage is closest in meaning to

(A) shortens

(B) cultivates

(C) inflames

(D) completes

Part 1

Part 2

Part 3

Part 4

Part 5

Part 6
新托福全真模擬試題

Perseverance is what Philip obviously lacks. His next step is to follow in his father's footsteps to become a doctor. **A** With the qualification of entering a medical school, he chooses St. Luke's. For people entering on the medical profession, there are all kinds, and readers have yet to know how Philip will become. **B** Philip believes that with his intelligence that he will scrape through the test, but in fact he fails at the anatomy examination, making him among the list of the **incompetent**. **C** Love affairs distract Philip too much attention, when he should be focusing on the study. His worst decision is to involve himself with the stock market. **D** He writes a letter to his uncle asking for money, but is turned down. **E** Without enough money, he has to find the job to pay daily expenses and **discontinue** his medical studies. **F** He cannot believe that he screws things up, changing his entire life trajectory.

57 The author's descriptions of Philip's uncle mention all the following **EXCEPT:**

(A) His predictions of Philip's pursuit in Art are entirely correct.

(B) His unwillingness to give Philip money

(C) His predictions of Philip's unsuccessful attempt at the

anatomy examination

(D) His effort for Philip's cultivation of professional skills

58 The word **incompetent** in the passage is closest in meaning to

(A) unqualified

(B) motionless

(C) eligible

(D) blindsided

59 Look at the four squares 〔■〕 that indicate where the following sentence could be added to the passage.

Even though at first, he does have several wins, he eventually pays a hefty price for that.

Where would the sentence best fit?

Click on a square 〔■〕 to add the sentence to the passage

60 The word **discontinue** in the passage is closest in meaning to

(A) persist

(B) determine

(C) condone

(D) intermit

Part 1

Part 2

Part 3

Part 4

Part 5

Part 6

新托福全真模擬試題

In Philip's case, the birth does not make his life wonderful. His father's small inheritance should have been a great assistance for him, but his poor decision effaces what has been given to him.

In *The History of Tom Jones, a Founding*, Tom's birth does not give him the upper hand when he is unable to live with his co-father. Good education and wealthy family from birth do not make Tom capable of standing on his own feet. Instead, he lacks professional skills needed for survival, ultimately accepting 50 pounds from Lady Bellaston.

So for those who are still jealous of your friends' rich parents, you might as well have to focus on what you can do at every key decision, making it tremendously beneficial to the next step of your life. Once you have become greater and greater, you will find that the world is a better place. You will even notice that Goddess of Fate makes a light smile at you.

 內容總結題

Part 1
Part 2
Part 3
Part 4
Part 5
Part 6
新托福全真模擬試題

Directions

Directions: An introductory sentence for a brief summary of the passage is provided below. Complete the summary by selecting THREE answer choices that express the most important ideas in the passage. Some answer choices do not belong in the summary because they express ideas that are not presented in the passage or are minor ideas in the passage. This question is worth 2 points.

Statement

Good birth, inheritance, education, and others will not favor someone if one is not able to make a right decision.

•	
•	
•	

Answer Choices

A. Philip begs his uncle for money so that his study will not cease.

B. With friends' encouragement of embarking on an

adventure, Philip insists on pursuing a study in Paris.
C. Philip wants to follow his father's footstep to become a doctor, and he happens to have the qualification of entering a medical school.
D. Philip has several wins in the stock market, so he gambles his father's inheritance on the stock market.
E. There is a diversion that distracts Philip from focusing on the study.
F. Philip's journey in Paris ends when the artist informs him that he does not have any talent in art.

Part 1

Part 2

Part 3

Part 4

Part 5

Part 6
新托福全真模擬試題

 解析

49 【字彙題】：inferior 指（品質等）次的；較差的，這裡指做錯決定而導致了較壞的結果，故答案要選 B。

50 【修辭目的題】：主要是指都是需要付出特定的努力的，雖然沒有明顯在重述需要時間和金錢，但需要特定的努力就是隱晦的改寫表達了，故要選 C。

51 【字彙題】：mortifying 這裡要理解成一個惱人的道理，所以要選 annoying 比較合適。

52 【插入句子題】：A 後方的句子 In *Of Human Bondage*, with some deliberation, Philip's first life decision is to be an intern at the office of Messers. Herbert Carter & Co…是段落主題句，所以不可能插入在此處。B 前後方的句意自立並謀生和後面的引用名言句探討的話題也是緊密相連，故也不可能插入在此處。D 後方的 His friend's belief in Philip's ability in art does not equal with how the reality views about him as a person.和 C 後方的兩個句子均表達現在職位不夠好和鼓勵辭職等意思是相關聯的。也因為朋友講的這些話語，促成下句的否定表達，所以朋友所認定的能力和菲利普本身是否有能力是不同的，所以不可能插入在 D 處。讀到這裡更可以感受到，段落目前缺乏一個主題句，而兩句引用的名言，也就是朋友所說的話其實就等於是 bad advice，重新閱讀後更可以確定插入地方要在 C。

53 【句子簡化題】：主要講的就是 D 選項的描述，從朋友給的建議到展開冒險等，其實是要衡量自己本身情況再去作決定，這些都是很大的決定且最後承擔的人是你自己，不是講得冠冕堂皇的朋友。

54 【修辭目的題】：露易莎伯母把她的積蓄給了菲利普，這是一個很不容易的舉動，因為這是伯母的養老金，且菲力普只是幻想著自己有能力當個偉大的畫家，然後伯母卻拿自己的養老金去支持菲力普的夢想，而菲力普對伯母的感謝到上了火車後就遺忘了，因為他滿腦子都是法國的那些酒光聲色和憧憬，所以要選 B。

55 【推論題】：藝術家的建言雖然終結了藝術家的大夢，但是卻也幫助了菲力普，因為菲力普不用在繞一堆彎路，畢竟都花費了兩年時光了。這時候能有個人直接給予最佳的忠告，告訴你你本身就是沒有藝術家天分，不用在花費心力在這上頭了。你可以馬上做停損然後思考自己的下一步，畢竟青春有限。所以人生當中有人能這樣提點你的話等於是省掉你很多走冤枉路的時間，所以這題要選 C。菲力普也因為這樣馬上構思自己人生下一步。

56 【字彙題】：terminates 指的是終結，這裡是述說這句發自內心深處且真誠的忠告結束了菲利普兩年的巴黎之旅，也終結了他成為藝術家的夢想，故要選 D。

57 【細節和否定資訊題】：他伯父並未預測出關於解剖學考試這點，故要選 C。

Part 1

Part 2

Part 3

Part 4

Part 5

Part 6

新托福全真模擬試題

58 【字彙題】：這裡指未能通過解剖學考試，躋身該屆學生中無能者之列，故要選 A。

59 【插入句子題】：**D 後方出現** He writes a letter to his uncle asking for money, but is turned down.，他向伯父要錢，也代表說一定是有什麼事情出錯了。**D 前方出現**他涉及股票市場的訊息，更可以由此推斷出在股票市場中 **he does have several wins, he eventually pays a hefty price for that.**，句意完全吻合在 D 選項，故要插入在此處。

60 【字彙題】：這裡指沒有足夠的錢，他不得不找工作來支付日常開銷且中斷學業，所以要選 D。

• 【內容總結題】：關鍵點在選出那些做出錯誤決定的敘述，這些決定都是讓主角儘管有遺產優勢等，卻還是將人生搞得一團糟。**B** With friends' encouragement of embarking on an adventure, Philip insists on pursuing a study in Paris，去法國留學是個錯誤的決定，最後藝術大師更表明菲力普完全沒有天賦。**D** Philip has several wins in the stock market, so he gambles his father's inheritance on the stock market，菲力普不該將父親遺產投入股市，而導致後來無法繼續讀醫學系。**E** There is a diversion that distracts Philip from focusing on the study，a diversion 指的是愛情，愛情分散掉菲力普很多時間和金錢等等，也是他做的錯誤決定之一。

The fact that no third person must directly touch on other people's love affairs is a fundamental respect for people who are in love, yet meddling, out of curiosity, protection and other factors is commonly seen in reality. Among them, parents can be said to be the most frequent disturbance to their kid's marriage or love affairs. Parents may hold different ideas when it comes to this topic. Regret has often happened after years of marriage with someone, making it reasonable for parents to interfere. Gerald in *Gone with the Wind* has chosen to inform his child, Scarlett, whereas Mr. Brooke, Dorothea's uncle has adopted a **liberal** approach. However, the outcome for both Scarlett and Dorothea has remained the same, making us wonder what should someone do when there is actually a need to make an interference.

61 The word **liberal** in the passage is closest in meaning to

(A) authoritarian

(B) tolerant

(C) pioneered

(D) diverse

62 According to the passage, why does the author mention **"however, the outcome for both Scarlett and Dorothea has remained the same"**?

(A) to show the best laid plans

(B) to show there is no need to meddle

(C) to show parents have to right to meddle

(D) to show parents are not ideal arbitrators

Part 1

Part 2

Part 3

Part 4

Part 5

Part 6

新托福全真模擬試題

A However, in *Drop Dead Diva*, Jane's coworker Owen and Kim, have decided to meddle in Jane's love affairs when they know Ian Holt, a cold-blooded killer is dating their colleague. **B** Kim, who used to have some quarrels with Jane, because at the law firm they are in direct competition with Jane, now is willing to pay US 10,000 dollars to Ian Holt for him to go away. **C** Ian Holt rejects the offer and then is met with Owen's direct opposition of his conduct. **D** It seems that Kim and Owen are doing the right things, but they are still not in the relationship with either one of them. **E** It's best if Kim and Owen just stay out of this.

63 Look at the four squares (■) that indicate where the following sentence could be added to the passage.

"It is as fatal as a murder or any other horror that divides people."

Where would the sentence best fit?

Click on a square (■) to add the sentence to the passage

Part 1

Part 2

Part 3

Part 4

Part 5

Part 6

新托福全真模擬試題

To go deeper into the story, Grayson comes closer to getting married to Jane, but unfortunately, he dies after an operation in the hospital. Grayson hits the return button, so that he gets a second chance to live. Ironically, his soul is placed in Ian Holt's body, making his identity questionable for others.

The janitor outside the cell tells Jane that a ruthless killer like Ian Holt does not have the right to get a second chance. Jane, now being Ian's lawyer, argues on Ian's behalf that there should be a stay of execution and she believes that Ian is innocent. Despite the fact that there are no new facts sustaining a stay, Ian comes up with the idea that there should be a new death warrant. Without the new death warrant, the new execution will be postponed, making Ian capable of living for another 24 hours. Having an **excogitation** of sufficient reason to get Ian acquitted in a day is insane. Owen and Jane can only surmise the idea that makes Ian stay life imprison. However, Ian demands **they** fight for a claim of actual guiltlessness because letters and other evidence makes Ian truly believe his innocence.

64 The author's descriptions of Ian Holt mention all the following **EXCEPT:**

(A) Grayson's soul has entered Ian's body and takes control.

(B) Ian's claim for true innocence can be difficult.

(C) It is Owen's clever strategy that gets Ian's execution postponed

(D) The doorkeeper thinks that Ian does not deserve a second chance

65 The word **excogitation** in the passage is closest in meaning to

(A) exhortation

(B) consideration

(C) exacerbation

(D) meditation

66 The word **they** in the passage refers to

(A) hours

(B) warrants

(C) Owen and Jane

(D) letters and other evidence

Part 1

Part 2

Part 3

Part 4

Part 5

Part 6

新托福全真模擬試題

Jane, now being Ian's lawyer, argues on Ian's behalf that there should be a stay of execution and she believes that Ian is innocent. **Despite the fact that there are no new facts sustaining a stay, Ian comes up with the idea that there should be a new death warrant. Without the new death warrant, the new execution will be postponed, making Ian capable of living for another 24 hours. Having an excogitation of sufficient reason to get Ian acquitted in a day is insane. Owen and Jane can only surmise the idea that makes Ian stay life imprison. However, Ian demands they fight for a claim of actual guiltlessness because letters and other evidence makes Ian truly believe his innocence.**

67 Which of the sentences below best expresses the essential information in the highlighted sentence in the passage? Incorrect answer choices change the meaning in important ways or leave out essential information.

(A) A new death warrant will not only get one exonerated, but also postpone the day of the death sentence.

(B) There is a need to come up with new evidence to postpone the execution, but Jane and others have enough proof to get the charge dropped.

(C) Owen, Jane and Ian are equally clever so that the new

execution will be postponed, and Ian will not get executed in the end.

(D) Ian's smart thinking earns him one more day to live, but to be immune from those accusations is still a long way to go.

During the penalty of the trial, the victim's wife Cheryl did testify on Ian's behalf that he was innocent. Cheryl **implored** the judge that Ian, a man convicted of killing her husband, should be set free. Cheryl's **testimony** does make Owen and Jane rethink about things happening during the night at the club. They eventually figure out the real killer is Breeman, resulting in a happy ending for Jane and Ian. After the release, Jane and Ian's love affair may sound like an eccentric combination. Even though Ian's name has been cleared, others might still think Ian has mistaken his gratitude for Jane as true love. Jane cannot handle her grief with the loss of Grayson, so she starts the relationship with Ian.

68 The word **implored** in the passage is closest in meaning to

(A) swayed

(B) beseeched

(C) bribed

(D) nurtured

69 According to the passage, why does the author mention **"Cheryl's testimony"**?

(A) because it can get the charge dropped

(B) because imploration to the judge will work somehow

(C) because of the infidelity

(D) because of the eccentricity

70 The word **testimony** in the passage is closest in meaning to

(A) countenance

(B) consideration

(C) statement

(D) tendency

Part 1

Part 2

Part 3

Part 4

Part 5

Part 6

新托福全真模擬試題

In *Middlemarch*, there is a great divide between Dorothea and Will if they have to be with each other. **A** There is bound to be a great hindrance for the two, even if Dorothea does not care about the money. **B** It is true that destitution will soon wear out two people's love after their marriage. **C** Like what's stated before, the best thing we can do is congratulations for any couple and let nature take **its** course. **D** After all, it is not your marriage, so mind your own business. **E** People's relationships will soon end the moment one of the parties cannot endure, and there is no need for one to act like a judge, arbitrating trivial matters happening in other people's marriage.

71 Look at the four squares (■) that indicate where the following sentence could be added to the passage.

The long-enduring unsolved problems for all generations: The rich and the poor.

Where would the sentence best fit?
Click on a square (■) to add the sentence to the passage

72 The word **its** in the passage refers to

(A) marriage

(B) couple

(C) nature

(D) thing

Part 1

Part 2

Part 3

Part 4

Part 5

Part 6

新托福全真模擬試題

 **內容**總結題

Directions: An introductory sentence for a brief summary of the passage is provided below. Complete the summary by selecting THREE answer choices that express the most important ideas in the passage. Some answer choices do not belong in the summary because they express ideas that are not presented in the passage or are minor ideas in the passage. This question is worth 2 points.

Statement

Meddling with other people's love affairs happens all the time and for different reasons.

•	
•	
•	

Answer Choices

A. Others sense that there might be some dangers.

B. Others really want one to let nature take its course.

C. Others have the worry that dividing two people in love will bring more crimes.

D. Others have the worry about inability of processing the loss.

E. Others consider that financial reasons will always be a hurdle.

F. Some sense that regrets often occur after the marriage.

Part 1

Part 2

Part 3

Part 4

Part 5

Part 6

新托福全真模擬試題

解析

61 【字彙題】：這裡指多蘿西亞的叔叔布魯克先生則採取了自由之道，也就是不是權威式教育，是更為寬容且易於傾聽等的，讓小孩自己做主的教育，故答案要選 B。

62 【修辭目的題】：兩本經典名作中《亂世佳人》中的傑拉爾德選擇了告知他的孩子思嘉麗，而多蘿西亞的叔叔布魯克先生則採取了自由之道。然而，思嘉麗和多蘿西亞的結局是如出一轍，父母選擇干涉與否最後結果居然都相同，那麼也就等於根本沒必要去干涉，因為結果會一樣，**不如像中國俗諺說的兒孫自有兒孫福，故答案要選 B。**

63 【插入句子題】：閱讀插入句後，從 A 後方的 However 和 Jane's coworker Owen and Kim, have decided to meddle with Jane's love affairs，判斷出答案就是 A。插入句是述說拆散人的負面表達，但 Jane 的同事卻仍要去做這件拆散佳偶的事情。運用承轉詞和語意等協助判斷答案也是非常重要的閱讀技能。

64 【細節和否定資訊題】：歐文沒有讓死刑的執行延後，是 Ian 自己想到方法讓執行期延後，故答案要選 C。在劇中其實歐文本身當過法官，後來轉到律師事務所工作，算是經驗超級豐富，而簡本身就是律師事務所裡能力非常好上司倚重的律師。但是在法庭上，兩個人卻突然不知道要如何應對。這時 Ian 想出了讓死刑延後的辦法，才讓歐文和簡鬆口氣。歐文甚至對於 Ian 的表現感到非常驚訝，但是歐文所不知道的是，Ian 的身體現在被 Grayson

Part 1

Part 2

Part 3

Part 4

Part 5

Part 6
新托福全真模擬試題

附身了，而 Grayson 本身是律師，所以才能在情急生智下想出這個辦法。

65 【字彙題】：excogitation 指的是構想出，這裡指要在一天內想到足夠的事證讓伊恩無罪釋放是瘋狂的，選項中只有 meditation 較符合。

66 【代名詞指代題】：they 很明顯指的是前句的主詞且只有 Owen 和 Jane 能執行後面的動作，也就是 fight for a claim of actual guiltlessness。

67 【句子簡化題】：包含了很多訊息，不過重點在成功想到辦法延後執行，以及後面要去面對的事情。而歐文和珍只能想出讓伊恩從被判處死刑改成被判終身監禁的主意。然而，伊恩要求他們須主張「真正無罪」，因為他從信件等資訊中察覺出自己不可能犯罪，要從被判處死刑爭取到無罪以情況來說太困難了，所以其實要說的是 is still a long way to go，故答案為選項 D。

68 【字彙題】：這裡指綺麗兒懇求法官釋放殺害她丈夫的男子伊恩，故要選 B，如果因為不知道 B 選項這個字而答錯，那就是字彙量不足影響答題，而非理解力不夠。

69 【修辭目的題】：除了綺麗兒的證詞確實讓歐文和珍重新考慮了在俱樂部之夜所發生的事情並找出真兇外。值得思考的一點是，綺麗兒身為受害的人妻子，但是卻願意出庭作證以證明 Ian 是清白的，儘管她當時出庭作證後，Ian 仍被判處死刑。也就是這點，讓律師覺得奇怪，而進一步去思考當初綺麗兒為何願意出庭作證，所以很有可能真兇是另有其人，而不是 Ian，故答案要選 D。（因為兩位律師後來表明僅能替 Ian 爭取到免除死刑但判處終身監禁。）

70 【字彙題】：這裡指綺麗兒的證詞，也就是陳述，她在法庭上所陳述的事件經過，故答案要選 C。

71 【插入句子題】：閱讀插入句後，可以從 a great divide，知道有很大分歧，所以後面接續貧和富這個大問題，就是讓這段感情會有 divide 的原因，故答案要選 A。

72 【代名詞指代題】：its 很明顯指的是代替前方的 nature，故答案要選 C。

• 【內容總結題】：試題有比較隱晦且不好答，但是只要在各主題和人物事件中找出干涉點的原因就能馬上判斷出答案。**A** Others sense that there might be some dangers（這裡指的是 Jane's coworker Owen and Kim 察覺 Jane 和 Ian 交往可能會有危險，因為 Ian 是曾被判處死刑的犯人）。**E** Others consider that financial reasons will always be a hurdle.（financial reasons 可以迅速對應到 there is a great divide between Dorothea and Will...，兩者之間存在的貧富差距等，促使其他人干涉兩人感情）。**F** Some sense that regrets often occur after the marriage.（regret 可以對應到 It is true that destitution will soon wear out two people's love after their marriage.，因為

Part 1

Part 2

Part 3

Part 4

Part 5

Part 6
新托福全真模擬試題

貧困磨掉兩人本來的感情而導致後悔結婚）。

- **B** Others really want one to let nature take its course.（文中要提到 to let nature take its course 完全一樣的論述，但是是作者的觀點，而非涵蓋在試題句子裡所要討論的部分，要選以不同的理由去干涉別人感情相關的部分，而通常試題中有字句完全一樣的敘述通常都是錯誤的選項，尤其是在細節和否定資訊題裡。）**C** Others have the worry that dividing two people in love will bring more crimes.（文中有跟擔憂有關的部分，所以才會有歐文等的干涉行為出現，但是文中完全沒有提到去干涉或拆散佳偶會導致社會上更多的犯罪問題。）**D** Others have the worry about inability of processing the loss.（文中沒有提到關於處理這方面的情緒或失去另一半要如何撫平傷痛的方式，僅有提到簡可能因為不知道要如何處理失去另一半而誤將 Ian 當成了傷痛過渡期的依靠，所以才跟他交往，但是他們卻是彼此相愛的，簡也知道 Ian 的身體是被 Grayson 附身的，而她本來就愛著 Grayson。）

Most people have less of outward vision, focusing their attention on how to be financially independent, but in today's world, downsizing among large, profit-driven companies is so common, lots of people are not able to secure high-paying jobs as **they** have been used to. What makes things worse is that prices of commodities are getting increasingly higher, resulting in not having enough cash to live an ideal life. Some sit in their rented apartments in **lethargic** melancholy, whereas others fix their minds on getting the inheritance from parents so that they do not have to worry about money.

73 The word **lethargic** in the passage is closest in meaning to

(A) vivacious

(B) nocturnal

(C) lackadaisical

(D) imaginative

Part 1

Part 2

Part 3

Part 4

Part 5

Part 6

新托福全真模擬試題

74 The word **they** in the passage refers to

(A) companies

(B) people

(C) prices

(D) jobs

A However, not all cases of inheritance end up with a pleasant result. **B** In *Drop Dead Diva*, Violet Harwood is an heiress with a great deal of fortune. Unluckily, Violet Harwood's parents create a trust that is regulated by her brother. Without the **approbation** of the trustee, Violet Harwood is unable to use the money freely. **C** Violet Harwood's plan of using her fortune on the shelter house has shattered because her brother controls the expenses. **D** Fortunately, Violet Harwood's lawyer comes up with the idea of the dead-hand clause. **E**

75 Look at the four squares [■] that indicate where the following sentence could be added to the passage.

In *North and South*, Margaret is lucky enough to get a large inheritance, making her an even better pick among single men.

Where would the sentence best fit?

Click on a square [■] to add the sentence to the passage

76 The word **approbation** in the passage is closest in meaning to
(A) signature
(B) discountenance
(C) disapproval
(D) permission

The definition of the dead-hand clause is to prevent dead people from exercising control from the grave beyond a single generation. The trick is Violet Harwood's parents cannot mandate her to give the antique watch to someone who did not exist when **they** died, making the whole trust **ineffective**. "What's good for the goose is good for the gander", so the inheritance shall be distributed equally between Violet Harwood and her brother.

77 The author's descriptions of Violet Harwood mention all the following **EXCEPT**:
(A) Violet Harwood eventually wins the case.
(B) Violet Harwood does not have the money for fixing a shelter house even though she is rich.
(C) Violet Harwood's brother has the total control of the money.

Part 1

Part 2

Part 3

Part 4

Part 5

Part 6

新
托
福
全
真
模
擬
試
題

(D) Violet Harwood's past indiscretion is the main reason why her parents mandate the trust.

78 The word **ineffective** in the passage is closest in meaning to
(A) efficacious
(B) unthankful
(C) fruitless
(D) palpable

79 The word **they** in the passage refers to
(A) dead people
(B) goose and the gander
(C) Violet Harwood and her brother
(D) Harwood's parents

80 According to the passage, why does the author mention **"what's good for the goose is good for the gander"**?
(A) to indicate goose and gander are always in conflict as in Harwood's case
(B) to indicate different sexes
(C) to validate the power of the antique watch
(D) to indicate equality between goose and gander

In *Middlemarch*, the idea of the dead-hand clause has also been used by Mr. Casaubon. "But well-being is not to be secured by ample, independent possession of property; on the contrary, occasions might arise in which such possession might expose her to the more danger." **A**

81 According to the passage, why does the author mention **"But well-being is not to be secured by ample, independent possession of property; on the contrary, occasions might arise in which such possession might expose her to the more danger."**?

(A) to show required shrewdness is needed to guard the assets

(B) to show the need for a woman to be financially independent

(C) to show the need to get rid of fortune to be safe

(D) to demonstrate the importance of the security to guard those assets for you

Part 1

Part 2

Part 3

Part 4

Part 5

Part 6

新托福全真模擬試題

B It might be reasonable to deduce that Mr. Casaubon has the foresight to protect his wife from men's deception, but a closer inspection can reveal his agenda. **C** Mrs. Casaubon will lose the inheritance if she is married with Will, making her unable to tie the knot with the person she truly loves. **D** Mr. Casaubon's intent can also be perceived as an insult to his own wife, who remains loyal to him while he is alive. **E** Mrs. Casaubon has never been a materialistic young lady. Eventually, she figures out true love transcends all things, including a great deal of inheritance, and has a happy ending with Will.

82 Look at the four squares (■) that indicate where the following sentence could be added to the passage.

The inheritance will be the control of his wife even after his death.

Where would the sentence best fit?

Click on a square (■) to add the sentence to the passage

In *Wuthering Heights*, Edgar Linton is aware of Mr. Heathcliff's intention of claiming his private property and Thrushcross Grange. Originally, Edgar Linton wants Miss Cathy to use the property at her disposal, but later he ameliorates the will, putting it in the trust, for Miss Cathy to use and for her descendants to utilize after Miss Cathy dies. If Linton dies, the property will not go to Mr. Heathcliff. In *Wuthering Heights*, **"Earnshaw had mortgaged every yard of land he owned for cash to supply his mania for gaming; and he, Heathcliff, was the mortgagee."** Mr. Heathcliff not only gets Earnshaw's inheritance, Wuthering Heights, making Hareton, Earnshaw's son, moneyless, but also the estate of Edgar Linton. Even if Mr. Heathcliff's son, Linton dies, Catherine will not be the heir. Miss Cathy is reluctant to believe Mr. Heathcliff is a bad guy. According to the will of the previous Linton generation, Thrushcross Grange will only be inherited by a male descendant, so Mr. Heathcliff's contemplation is **foxy** and smart enough to let his son Linton get married with Miss Cathy.

83 The word **foxy** in the passage is closest in meaning to

(A) uncanny

(B) cunning

(C) formidable

(D) scary

Part 1

Part 2

Part 3

Part 4

Part 5

Part 6

新托福全真模擬試題

In *Wuthering Heights*, Edgar Linton is aware of Mr. Heathcliff's intention of claiming his private property and Thrushcross Grange. Originally, Edgar Linton wants Miss Cathy to use the property at her disposal, but **later he ameliorates the will, putting it in the trust, for Miss Cathy to use and for her descendants to utilize after Miss Cathy dies. If Linton dies, the property will not go to Mr. Heathcliff**⋯.. Even if Mr. Heathcliff's son, Linton dies, Catherine will not be the heir. Miss Cathy is reluctant to believe Mr. Heathcliff is a bad guy. **According to the will of the previous Linton generation, Thrushcross Grange will only be inherited by a male descendant, so Mr. Heathcliff's contemplation is foxy and smart enough to let his son Linton get married with Miss Cathy.**

84 **Which of the sentences below best expresses the essential information in the highlighted sentence in the passage? Incorrect answer choices change the meaning in important ways or leave out essential information.**

(A) Edgar Linton has no idea that Linton will have a marriage with his daughter Miss Cathy, otherwise, he will come up with something better, not putting the will in the trust.

(B) Edgar Linton's foresight gets decoded by Mr. Heathcliff, so Mr. Heathcliff is the ultimate winner.

(C) Edgar Linton's amelioration of the will can protect Miss Cathy outright so that Mr. Heathcliff will not get the money from the trust.

(D) Miss Cathy has to die earlier so that Thrushcross Grange will be protected from Mr. Heathcliff, and Edgar Linton's scheme of putting the money in the trust can be considered successful.

Resolving an inheritance issue is not as easy as it seems. Sometimes it involves several people who maliciously vie for the property in court. Margaret in *North and South* is probably the happiest person that gets the inherited money, lending it to Mr. Thornton for a loan. Mrs. Casaubon's great wisdom of not valuing the property too highly is also very admirable. It is true that more money only creates more problems. We can only pray that we will not be ending like Mr. Heathcliff, living unhappily till his death.

 內容總結題

Part 1

Part 2

Part 3

Part 4

Part 5

Part 6

新托福全真模擬試題

Directions

Directions: An introductory sentence for a brief summary of the passage is provided below. Complete the summary by selecting THREE answer choices that express the most important ideas in the passage. Some answer choices do not belong in the summary because they express ideas that are not presented in the passage or are minor ideas in the passage. This question is worth 2 points.

Statement

Men's control for money and assets will never end because everyone more or less wants to live financially independent. Battles for money continues so many people employ different strategies to retain their fortune.

•	
•	
•	

Answer Choices

A. Violet Harwood's lawyer uses the dead-hand clause to

make her client get half of the money from the trust.

B. Mr. Casaubon is fully aware of his wife's vulnerability to men, so he wants Mrs. Casaubon to be financially independent.

C. Margaret hires the most unethical lawyer to guard her inheritance so that she can lend the remaining money for Mr. Thornton.

D. Earnshaw falls into the trap of Mr. Heathcliff, influencing the future prospect of his own son.

E. Mr. Heathcliff's strategy of using ancestor's legacy makes Miss Cathy unqualified for the asset of Thrushcross Grange.

F. Mr. Heathcliff's late life is so miserable because he has claimed so much fortune that is not belonged to him.

解析

Part 1

Part 2

Part 3

Part 4

Part 5

Part 6
新托福全真模擬試題

73 【字彙題】：lethargic= lackadaisical，這裡指的是毫無生氣的，故要選 C。（同義字還有 languid, listless, sluggish 等）

74 【代名詞指代題】：they 很明顯是指前面的主詞 people，故要選 B。

75 【插入句子題】：閱讀插入句後，可以從 However, not all cases of inheritance end up with a pleasant result.得知前面的敘述一定是描述正面的，剛好瑪格麗特幸運地得到了一大筆遺產吻合，故答案要選 A。

76 【字彙題】：沒有受託人的准許，維奧萊特·哈伍德無法隨意使用這筆錢，所以答案要選 D。

77 【細節和否定資訊題】：文章中沒有提到這部分，雖然在影集中有提到，故答案要選 D。

78 【字彙題】：ineffective=fruitless 故答案要選 C。

79 【代名詞指代題】：仔細區分並理解句意後可以知道是指 Violet 的父母，故要選 D。

80 【修辭目的題】：這句話是要說明均分，goose 和 gander 分別代表雌和雄。而也暗指 Violet 和他哥哥，the inheritance shall

be distributed equally between Violet Harwood and her brother = equality between goose and gander。the inheritance shall be distributed equally between Violet Harwood and her brother 是用於解釋上一句"What's good for the goose is good for the gander"，故要選 D。

81 【修辭目的題】：這句話是要説明擁有獨立的財產是件好事，但是也要具備一定的精明幹練才能守住這些財，不然就會被其他男人騙去。因為很可能有些男人接近有錢女生會是有目的的，卡索邦在立遺囑時就有想到過這點，算是很為自己妻子著想，而他確實也比自己妻子早走，所以也留下大筆遺產給自己妻子。他擔憂自己的妻子會因為有這些財產而惹上更多的危險是正確的，故答案要選 A。

82 【插入句子題】：閱讀插入句後，can reveal his agenda 後一定是要描述 agenda 為何，所以剛好接插入句的敘述，可以控制其妻子。C 後方也接著描述失去遺產等訊息，所以答案要選 C。

83 【字彙題】：foxy=cunning，這裡指希斯克利夫的心思是狡猾的，聰明到讓兒子林頓與凱西小姐成親，故答案要選 B。

84 【句子簡化題】：要理解所有發生的事件經過，最後可以得出 Edgar Linton 的招數被破解掉了，故答案要選 B。

• 【內容總結題】：關鍵在於要選出使用的保護資產的策略，釐清後就能馬上找出答案了。**A** Violet Harwood's lawyer uses the

Part 1

Part 2

Part 3

Part 4

Part 5

Part 6
新托福全真模擬試題

dead-hand clause to make her client get half of the money from the trust.（很明顯 Violet Harwood 的律師採用了 dead-hand clause 這個策略）。**D** Earnshaw falls into the trap of Mr. Heathcliff, influencing the future prospect of his own son.（乍看之下，好像不是答案，不過這是保護或留住且增加自己本來資產的一個方式，也就是讓別人成為自己的奴隸替自己工作。Earnshaw 的資產都抵押給 Mr. Heathcliff，Earnshaw 的兒子自出生後就要替其工作）。**E** Mr. Heathcliff's strategy of using ancestor's legacy makes Miss Cathy unqualified for the asset of Thrushcross Grange.（Mr. Heathcliff 採用的策略是利用 Thrushcross Grange 僅能由男性繼承這點，並讓自己兒子跟 Miss Cathy 成親，兒子因病死後，繼承人就是他自己）。

- **B** Mr. Casaubon is fully aware of his wife's vulnerability to men, so he wants Mrs. Casaubon to be financially independent.，這句僅能表明卡索邦先生的擔憂且後句的敘述不對，既然繼承遺產，卡索邦太太其實也不用為錢煩惱了，卡索邦是怕她被男人騙。要修改成包含有卡索邦採取死手條款防止其他男人像是 will 跟妻子結婚，這樣才符合試題要求。**C** Margaret hires the most unethical lawyer to guard her inheritance so that she can lend the remaining money for Mr. Thornton.，瑪格莉特並沒有這麼做且文中僅敘述她將遺產借給桑頓先生而已。**F** Mr. Heathcliff's late life is so miserable because he has claimed so much fortune that is not belonged to him.，生活狀態和試題敘述完全無關。

UNIT
08
《Of Human Bondage》、《North and South》、《Vanity Fair》
英國文學＋社會學＋商管投資

Wealthy or poor, investment has been tightly linked with people's life. Poor people wish to multiply their money through numerous investment opportunities, whereas rich people set their sights on getting richer by utilizing **lucrative** information. As a saying goes, the purpose of a novel is a reflection of reality. Great lessons can be learned from the following three novels: *Of Human Bondage*, *North and South*, and *Vanity Fair*.

85 The word **lucrative** in the passage is closest in meaning to
(A) trendy
(B) profitless
(C) propitious
(D) noticeable

Part 1

Part 2

Part 3

Part 4

Part 5

Part 6

新托福全真模擬試題

It is understood that a poor investment can lead someone to wait in line for a free soup quicker than one might think. In *Vanity Fair*, an inferior judgment in investment soon makes a rich person, like Mr. Sedley, bankrupt. **"Funds had risen when he calculated they would fall." "His bills were protested, his act of bankruptcy formal. The house and furniture of Russell Square were seized and sold up, and he and his family were thrust away."**

86 The word **they** in the passage refers to

(A) bills

(B) funds

(C) the house and furniture

(D) he and his family

In *Vanity Fair*, an inferior judgment in investment soon makes a rich person, like Mr. Sedley, bankrupt. "Funds had risen when he calculated they would fail." "His bills were protested, his act of bankruptcy formal. The house and furniture of Russell Square were seized and sold up, and he and his family were thrust away."

87 Which of the sentences below best expresses the essential information in the highlighted sentence in the passage? Incorrect answer choices change the meaning in important ways or leave out essential information.

(A) The house and furniture of Russell Square was considered quite a fortune, so selling out all would make up for Mr. Sedley's bad investment in the funds.

(B) Rich people all have a millionaire mindset, so Mr. Sedley's situation is only temporary. He can endure the loss of the house and furniture of Russell Square.

(C) There was no connection between bills getting protested and formalization of his bankruptcy, so there was still a chance to get back his assets.

(D) Funds' volatility made Mr. Sedley's investment gone awry, leading to a severe consequence that he could no longer endure.

A Similar to the situation of Mr. Sedley in *Vanity Fair*, Mr. Thornton's condition in *North and South* shares the same fate. **B** Both start out as rich from the beginning of the novel, but eventually the vicissitude of life emerges. **C** Mr. Thornton's problem lies in his use of capital. **D** During the economic recession, the value of all large stocks plunges, and Mr. Thornton's shares almost halve. **E**

Part 1

Part 2

Part 3

Part 4

Part 5

Part 6

新托福全真模擬試題

88 Look at the four squares 〔 ■ 〕 that indicate where the following sentence could be added to the passage.

Using it in new machinery and expansion results in not having enough cash for emergencies during a bad economy.

Where would the sentence best fit?

Click on a square 〔 ■ 〕 to add the sentence to the passage

A One cannot always be rich, so using one's richness or wealth as a criterion when it comes to choosing a mate is not wise. B Still, being rich is an **irresistible** quality in the market because wealth almost equals the sense of security. C Henry in *North and South* provides us with the same insight. Margaret's inherited property is just a part of her. D Even though it means that Margaret's money can instantly make him succeed, that should not be the criterion for choosing a life-partner. E However, both Mr. Thornton and Henry have the contemplation of using Margaret's fortune to assist their own business. F As in the case of Mr. Thornton, he lacks enough money to keep the company going, while Henry needs enough currency to start the law business.

89 Look at the four squares (■) that indicate where the following sentence could be added to the passage.

This corresponds to a wise saying from Nelly Dean in Wuthering Heights that no one can guarantee one's wealth throughout the entire life.

Where would the sentence best fit?

Click on a square (■) to add the sentence to the passage

90 According to paragraph 3 and 4, which of the following is **NOT TRUE**?

(A) Mr. Thornton cannot compete with his rivalry, Henry because of his inability of managing the firm.

(B) Mr. Thornton's loss in those shares will have an impact on his factory.

(C) With inheritance, Margaret's able to finance someone.

(D) Mr. Thornton does not have sufficient fortune to pour into the company.

91 The word **irresistible** in the passage is closest in meaning to

(A) incremental

(B) poignant

(C) compelling

(D) incongruous

Part 1

Part 2

Part 3

Part 4

Part 5

Part 6

新托福全真模擬試題

It's true that **"those who are happy and successful themselves are too apt to make light of the misfortune of others."** Ultimately, Margaret is willing to loan eighteen thousand and fifty-seven pounds to Mr. Thornton.

92 According to the passage, why does the author mention **"still, being rich is an irresistible quality in the market because wealth almost equals to the sense of the security."**?

(A) to indicate the importance of being wealthy

(B) to indicate Margaret is able to make her future spouse instantly succeed

(C) to caution that we cannot choose someone because of money only

(D) to show that being wealthy does make Margaret quite a catch

93 According to the passage, why does the author mention **"those who are happy and successful themselves are too apt to make light of the misfortune of others."**?

(A) to show Mr. Thornton's pessimism

(B) to show Mr. Thornton have no chance of staging a comeback

(C) to make Margaret empathic for the situation

(D) to show a reflection of Mr. Thornton's mood

Reversed fate makes the story a happy ending, but not everyone is as lucky as Margaret in *North and South* and Philip in *Of Human Bondage*. Margaret inherits the money and property worth 42,000 pounds, while Philip has an inheritance enough for him to finish medical school, making his fate much better than the rest of his classmates. Philip can focus all his attention on the study. Inheritance or extra money through other means can be good or bad really depends on the use of the person. In the case of Philip, it is definitely a bad thing. However, Philip squanders some of the money on girls instead of spending it on what's necessary, and worst of all, he gambles his tuition fees and money for the daily use on the stock market. **"History was being made, and the process was so significant that it seemed absurd that it should touch the life of an obscure medical student."** Selling shares now during the market plunge would mean that he can only have 80 pounds left, making him unable to continue his medical school.

Part 1

Part 2

Part 3

Part 4

Part 5

Part 6
新托福全真模擬試題

94 According to the passage, why does the author mention **"History was being made, and the process was so significant that it seemed absurd that it should touch the life of an obscure medical student."**?

(A) to criticize government's lack of supervision on the volatility of the stock market

(B) to satirize it can have the impact on the life trajectory of someone

(C) to make readers feel sympathetic for the situation

(D) to commemorate the day of Philip's big day and that of the history

It can be concluded that investment money should come from the sources that will not influence one's living; otherwise, there is going to be a disaster. No matter how lucky a person can be, not being able to control the spending can result in serious damage in life (like Philip). Being too **speculative** can also have the same fate like Mr. Sedley, losing enormous wealth and his hard-to-build enterprise. Working **industriously** and diligently can still end up like Mr. Thornton, lacking enough money to keep the company afloat. Predictions of one's life trajectory are too unlikely, but what we can do is do our part and not investing recklessly or dreaming of becoming a rich billionaire in a day.

95 The word **speculative** in the passage is closest in meaning to

(A) handsome

(B) chancy

(C) guarded

(D) replenished

96 The word **industriously** in the passage is closest in meaning to

(A) indolently

(B) effortlessly

(C) assiduously

(D) slothfully

 **內容總結題**

Part 1
Part 2
Part 3
Part 4
Part 5
Part 6
新托福全真模擬試題

Directions

Directions: An introductory sentence for a brief summary of the passage is provided below. Complete the summary by selecting THREE answer choices that express the most important ideas in the passage. Some answer choices do not belong in the summary because they express ideas that are not presented in the passage or are minor ideas in the passage. This question is worth 2 points.

Statement

Predictions of one's life trajectory are deemed impossible. The vicissitude of life will take away from all.

•	
•	
•	

Answer Choices

A. Nelly Dean's lament that retention of wealth is deemed unlikely.

B. Rich Mr. Sedley's investment in funds makes him bankrupt, losing a great deal of fortune.

C. Margaret inherits the money and property worthing 42,000 pounds, but she lends some to help Mr. Thornton.

D. Mr. Thornton's bad-timing during the economy results in not having enough capital for the operation of the factory.

E. Henry needs Margaret's fortune to start the law business.

F. Philip's unwise use of his father's inheritance costs him the future of becoming a doctor.

解析

Part 1

Part 2

Part 3

Part 4

Part 5

Part 6
新托福全真模擬試題

85 【字彙題】：lucrative=propitious，指富人則希望通過利用有利可圖的信息來變得更富有，故答案要選 C。

86 【代名詞指代題】：they 指的是前面的主詞 funds，故答案要選 B，把指代的名詞代回去句意也吻合。

87 【句子簡化題】：D 選項其實就是濃縮式的段落改寫，基金的不穩定性導致投資失利以及無法承受的後果，無法承受的後果是隱晦式的改寫，而不是直接說明資產不保等等。

88 【插入句子題】：閱讀插入句後，可以從 capital 和 it 找出關聯性，且將 capital 代入 D 後方的句子後發現吻合句意，故答案要選 D。

89 【插入句子題】：**從 A 後方的句子** One cannot always be rich, so using one's richness or wealth as a criterion when it comes to choosing a mate is not wise.可以看出「人不可能永遠富有」，這與插入句中的 **no one can guarantee one's wealth throughout the entire life** 訊息相關，更能代表出是接續描述插入句的論點來講述關於人生和富有的話題，故要插入在 A 這個地方。

90 【細節資訊題】：段落中沒有提到兩人是情敵且是競爭關係，更沒有說因為桑頓先生不擅經營公司這點讓他輸給亨利，指有提到桑頓先生公司所出現的經營問題。

91【字彙題】：irresistible= compelling，這裡指富有仍是擇偶市場上不可抗拒的特質，因為財富幾乎等於穩定感，故答案要選 C。

92【修辭目的題】：是要表明有了這些遺產後，瑪格麗特也變得富有了。變富有就能讓一個人在市場上更有身價，因為富有等同於讓人生活安定無慮。她在小說中所遇到的兩個主角桑頓先生和亨利，在事業上都會需要大量金錢的幫助。在感情世界中，也包含很多利益關係在才能讓一段關係維持住，例如有房有車。儘管不去設想那麼多太現實的事情，有錢也算是種極佳的條件。這個條件等同於讓瑪格麗特在同齡女子中更為與眾不同。何況這兩位男子都因為自己的事業狀況需要資金協助，讓瑪格麗特成了選擇人的那一方，而不是被選擇方，故答案要選 D。

93【修辭目的題】：是要表明桑頓先生在有這些經歷後的無奈感，或許能說有些悲觀，但是不完全是，所以更適合的答案是指桑頓先生的心境，故答案要選 D。

94【修辭目的題】：整個段落都述說著菲利普的行為種種，這些錯誤決定導致醫學院的學習中斷。而這句話最主要的部份就是諷刺，因為這居然能影響一位小小醫學生的人生軌跡，真的太荒唐了，一個有父親遺產能支付基本生活開銷和醫學院學費的學生，會淪落到這個地步，故答案要選 B。（就好比一個在台灣就讀醫學系的學生突然下學期無法繼續念書了，原因竟是錢被亂花完

Part 1

Part 2

Part 3

Part 4

Part 5

Part 6
新托福全真模擬試題

了，而不是因為興趣和其他因素無法就讀。應該很多父母會氣瘋了吧。菲力普在之後遇到自己的醫學系同學追問，怎麼好好的就不來上課了，還面有難色不知道要如何解釋。就這樣改變了他的人生軌跡，他也必須要去找其他工作支付生活開銷。）

95 【字彙題】：speculative=chancy，這裡指的是過於投機也會和薩德利先生一樣，失去巨大的財富和好不容易建立起來的事業，故答案要選 B。

96 【字彙題】：industriously= assiduously，這裡指的是工作勤奮認真，最終仍可能像桑頓先生一樣，缺乏足夠的資金來維持公司的運轉，故答案要選 C。

• 【內容總結題】：關鍵在於人生無常這點，進而找到三個重點。其實也能從最後一個段落中找到答案，因為該段落是文章所有敘述後的摘要總結，統整了之前三個主要人物（Mr. Sedley, Mr. Thornton 和 Philip）發生的事件和這些事件跟人生無常有關的特點。B Rich Mr. Sedley's investment in funds makes him bankrupt, losing a great deal of fortune.（薩利先生投資失利）。D Mr. Thornton's bad-timing during the economy results in not having enough capital for the operation of the factory.（桑頓先生沒有足夠的資金，因為資金都拿去購買昂貴設備）。F Philip's unwise use of his father's inheritance costs him the future of becoming a doctor.（菲利普並未謹慎使用父親的遺產）。

新托福閱讀 **120** 答案表

Test 1

1. D	**2.** C
3. C	**4.** D
5. C	**6.** B
7. C	**8.** D
9. C	**10.** F
11. D	**12.** B

內容總結題：答案：B, D, F

Test 2

13. A	**14.** C
15. B	**16.** D
17. C	**18.** B
19. A	**20.** D
21. C	**22.** B
23. D	**24.** B

內容總結題：答案：C, D, E

Test 3

25. B	**26.** A
27. C	**28.** C

29. C	**30.** C
31. D	**32.** D
33. C	**34.** D
35. B	**36.** D
內容總結題：答案：A, B, E	

Test 4

37. A	**38.** A
39. C	**40.** D
41. B	**42.** A
43. A	**44.** D
45. C	**46.** A
47. A	**48.** A
內容總結題：答案：C, E, F	

Test 5

49. B	**50.** C
51. B	**52.** C
53. D	**54.** B
55. C	**56.** D
57. C	**58.** A
59. D	**60.** D
內容總結題：答案：B, D, E	

Test 6

61. B	**62.** B
63. A	**64.** C
65. D	**66.** C
67. D	**68.** B
69. D	**70.** C
71. A	**72.** C

內容總結題：答案：A, E, F

Test 7

73. C	**74.** B
75. A	**76.** D
77. D	**78.** C
79. D	**80.** D
81. A	**82.** C
83. B	**84.** B

內容總結題：答案：A, D, E

Test 8

85. C	**86.** B
87. D	**88.** D
89. A	**90.** A

91. C	**92.** D
93. D	**94.** B
95. B	**96.** C

內容總結題:答案:B, D, F

TEST 1

Far from the Madding Crowd	"You have behaved like a man, and I, as a sort of successful rival -successful partly through your goodness of heart I should like definitely to show my sense of your friendship under what must have been a great pain to you."
Far from the Madding Crowd	"Every voice in nature was unanimous in bespeaking change."
宋詞	"People look for him thousands of Baidu. Looking back suddenly, the man was there, in a dimly lit place."

TEST 2

Frankenstein	"I believe that I have no enemy on earth, and none surely would have been so wicked as to destroy me wantonly."
Getting There	"things that seem disastrous at the time usually do work out for the rest."
Middlemarch	"He felt that he had chosen the one who was in all respects the superior; and a man naturally likes to look forward to having the best."

Middlemarch	"His disregarded love had not turned to bitterness; its death had made sweet odors – floating memories that clung with a consecrating effect to Dorothea."

TEST 3

Great Expectations	"It would have been cruel in Miss Havisham, horribly cruel, to practice on the susceptibility of a poor boy, and to torture me through all these years with a vain hope and idle pursuit, if she had reflected on the gravity of what she did."
左傳	"unjust is doomed to destruction."
Great Expectations	"That she had done a grievous thing in taking an impressionable child to mould into the form that her wild resentment, spurned affection, and wounded pride, found vengeance in, I knew full well."

TEST 4

Vanity Fair	"You've got more brains in your little vinger than any baronet's wife in the country."

Vanity Fair	"So in fetes, pleasures, and prosperity, the winter of 1815-16 passed away with Mrs. Rawdon Crawley, who accommodated herself to polite life as if her ancestors had been people of fashion for centuries past — and who from her wit, talent, and energy, indeed merited a place of honor in Vanity Fair."

TEST 5

The History of Tom Jones, a Founding	"Every profession, and every trade, required length of time, and what was worse, money."
Of Human Bondage	"I cannot imagine you sitting in an office over a ledger." "My feeling is that one should look upon life as an adventure, one should burn with the hard, gem-like flame, and one should take risks, one should expose oneself to danger."
Of Human Bondage	"Take your courage in both hands and try your luck at something else"

TEST 6

Middlemarch	"It is as fatal as a murder or any other horror that divides people."

TEST 7	
Drop Dead Diva	"What's good for the goose is good for the gander"
Middlemarch	"But well-being is not to be secured by ample, independent possession of property; on the contrary, occasions might arise in which such possession might expose her to the more danger."
Wuthering Heights	"Earnshaw had mortgaged every yard of land he owned for cash to supply his mania for gaming; and he, Heathcliff, was the mortgagee."
TEST 8	
Vanity Fair	"Funds had risen when he calculated they would fall." "His bills were protested, his act of bankruptcy formal. The house and furniture of Russell Square were seized and sold up, and he and his family were thrust away."
North and South	"Those who are happy and successful themselves are too apt to make light of the misfortune of others."
Of Human Bondage	"History was being made, and the process was so significant that it seemed absurd that it should touch the life of an obscure medical student."

國家圖書館出版品預行編目(CIP)資料

魔鬼特訓：新托福閱讀120/韋爾著. -- 初版.
-- 新北市：倍斯特出版事業有限公司, 2023.
09 面； 公分. -- (考用英語系列；043)
ISBN 978-626-96563-7-0(平裝)
1.CST: 托福考試

805.1894   112013564

考用英語系列 043

魔鬼特訓-新托福閱讀120(附QR code音檔)

初　　版　　2023年9月
定　　價　　新台幣620元

作　　者　　韋爾
出　　版　　倍斯特出版事業有限公司
發 行 人　　周瑞德
電　　話　　886-2-8245-6905
傳　　真　　886-2-2245-6398
地　　址　　23558 新北市中和區立業路83巷7號4樓
E - m a i l　　best.books.service@gmail.com
官　　網　　www.bestbookstw.com
總 編 輯　　齊心瑀
封面構成　　高鍾琪
內頁構成　　菩薩蠻數位文化有限公司
印　　製　　大亞彩色印刷製版股份有限公司

港澳地區總經銷　　泛華發行代理有限公司
地　　　　址　　香港新界將軍澳工業邨駿昌街7號2樓
電　　　　話　　852-2798-2323
傳　　　　真　　852-3181-3973

版權所有・翻印必究